MAIDE
a Northum

JANE ELLERINGTON

VINCA BOOKS

VINCA BOOKS
Gutteridge Hall Lane, Weeley, Essex CO16 9AS

First published in Great Britain by Vinca Books, 1995

© Jane Ellerington

Cover design by Barry Woodcock

Maidenhope is a work of fiction. Any resemblance to actual events or persons, living or dead, is entirely coincidental.

A CIP catalogue record for this book is available from the British Library.

ISBN 0-9525580-0-9

Printed in Great Britain by Antony Rowe Ltd
Chippenham, Wiltshire.

For Northumbrian friends

Maidenhope is not the work of one person, but of many. All the people mentioned here have contributed to the book and I feel privileged and grateful to have received their kindness and generosity in such full measure.

It is a great sadness that five people I particularly wish to thank are no longer with us. The first is Mrs Anna Gray of Great Ryle who, when I was beginning my research, put me on the right track by suggesting that I write to Mrs Pat Hedley. The second is Pat's husband, Harold, who lies in Alwinton churchyard, facing Upper Coquetdale, the valley he loved. Harold, with his wonderful stories of life in the Cheviots, was an inspiration to me. The third is Mrs Mary Tait, with whom Pat and I spent a pleasant afternoon in June 1989, visiting the old Barrowburn farmhouse and looking at photographs. The fourth is Mrs Bessie Corbett, whom I met at the home of Jock and Margie Hall and who told me what makes a good shepherd. The fifth is Mrs Jessie Münchow (née Gourlay) who recounted many fascinating details of her childhood in the Cheviots: in *Maidenhope*, when Rose Lillico puts her petticoat over the birdcage to protect the canaries from the driving snow, she is repeating the gesture of Jessie Münchow's mother.

In 1989 I wrote to the Northumberland Record Office. It was my good fortune that Linda Bankier, now Borough Archivist at Berwick upon Tweed, replied and put me in touch with Sandy Bankier. Sandy could not have shown me greater kindness: he allowed me to stay at Threestoneburn, he shared his rich knowledge of archaeology and ornithology and he took me to Crossmichael to meet Mrs Jessie Münchow. Through Sandy, I met Mr and Mrs George Turnbull of Wooler who also recounted their happy memories of Threestoneburn.

Pat Hedley has helped me in more ways than I can say. She took me to meet Mrs Minnie Waddell, the late Mr Jim Telfer and more recently Margie and Jon Short of Carlcroft. She has been a constant source of encouragement, help and advice. Simple thanks are not enough, but I thank her nonetheless.

I owe much to Helen Tait, Mrs Mary Tait's daughter, who lent me the photograph entitled 'Barrowburn Clippings', a detail from which appears on the cover. Helen also read the manuscript, bringing to it the unique insights of a woman born and bred in the hills and the skills of a natural literary critic. As a result of her efforts *Maidenhope* is a better book.

Through Eve Humphreys and Jimmy Walton, I met Mr Jock Hall and his wife Margie. I have spent many happy hours at Hepple, talking to Jock about his life as a shepherd. He has always shown me the greatest kindness, answering my often ignorant questions with endless patience. If, as I hope, there is something of the true flavour of life in the Cheviot hills within the pages of this book, then thanks are due in large part to him.

I would like to thank Mrs Mina Turnbull of Rothbury who gave me an old photograph of Makendon which I treasure and Mr Chris Foggon who allowed me to look at his wonderful collection of photographs.

I also wish to thank Bente Connellan who was kind enough to ask her friend, Ruth Rendell, to read the manuscript. Ruth gave me confidence and without her it is doubtful whether the book would have been published. Val Morgan was one of the first people to read *Maidenhope* and she has edited the text with painstaking care and sensitivity.

I am grateful to Jim Lawson, Photographic Archivist at Beamish Musuem, and to the staff of the British Library, the Colinton Newspaper Library, the Northumberland Record Office, Newcastle Central Library, Morpeth Records Centre and Rothbury Library.

Finally I wish to thank my husband, David, ever generous in his love and support.

Andro Man was summoned to appear at the Tolbooth at Aberdeen on the 20th January 1598, where he was accused of the treasonable crime of witchcraft. It was asserted that he was a manifest and notorious witch and sorcerer and that his master, the devil, had come to his mother's house in the likeness and shape of a woman whom Andro called the Queen of Elphen, that Andro had conversed bodily and had carnal dealings with her with the result that she was delivered of a bairn.

1

Tom Pagon looked up from his task and saw in the distance a strange silhouette. The person, it was a man, was carrying a large oval object on his head and he seemed to be making his way up the storm-swept valley towards where Tom was working.

The place had once been an illicit still, one of many tucked into the secret declivities of the hills. In the early years of the century a hundred gallons of whisky a week had flowed down into the valleys where it warmed the hearts of lowland farmers, drovers and cattle dealers as they met to conduct their business at the great fairs, such as the one held every July at Stagshaw Bank.

But now, so people said, the stills were all abandoned though Tom could still provide his guest with a dram. He could remember when the turf roof over the long low malting barn and adjoining distillery was in good repair. The roof followed the line of the hill into which it was set so that the building seemed as much a part of the landscape as the liquor it produced. The roof had been fired years before and now the ruined building served as a refuge from the inhospitable hill where Tom and his sheep were usually to be found.

Turning his attention to the dead lamb lying at his feet, Tom picked it up and slit the skin up the back legs, then pulled it back as far as the chest. Laying the animal on the cobbled floor, he set his foot on its slender thighs and pulled hard until he had worked the skin free from the front legs. The lamb's head was now encased in its own skin which was completely inside out. Tom picked up his knife and cut around the neck, finally parting the skin from the body.

He turned again to look out over the ruined gable-end. There was no sign of the stranger. Probably he was in the dip trying to cross the ford which lay downstream of where the Eidon Burn joined Heron Water. In that case he would be taking the track

1

that went up Eidonhope, a wide valley, from which the only way out was north, up over the shoulder of Maidenhope, across Cheviot and thence into Scotland.

The ford had long been a crossroads. In the 1550s it was guarded day and night against incursions from the north. Moss-troopers mounted on nimble, sturdy ponies would come to rob, rape and pillage. They slipped stealthily over the borderline through the quaking bogs and treacherous mosses, avoiding the well-trodden tracks such as the drove road that went up Heron Water along the line of the ancient Roman road, the via Geta.

The ford was still a meeting place. Once a fortnight Bill Havagal, the carrier from Willove, came with his pony and two-wheeled flat cart to bring groceries to the shepherding families who came on foot to the meeting place carrying baskets of eggs, a little butter and perhaps a few rabbits to exchange for provisions from the town.

The burns, always quick to rise, were swollen by the torrential rains of the previous days. Heron Water was a brawling torrent. The man would have a hard time of it getting across, if indeed he did.

Tom, whose every movement had been observed by Meg, his border collie, picked up the skin and turned it the right way out. It was now a black garment.

At one end of the rectangular building, near the fire hole for the kiln, stood a black-faced ewe and her twin lambs. He picked up the weaker lamb, a female, and set about working the black lambskin over her head. He was sitting with his back against the wall with the lamb in his arms when Felix Lee came into view.

Felix was drenched from the waist down as a result of his struggle to cross the burn. The object he had earlier been carrying on his head was now in his arms. It was a wicker fish basket covered with a piece of oiled canvas which was tied to the handles to stop it blowing away. He came nearer and set the basket down in the shelter of the wall.

"Good day to you!" he said pulling off his broad-brimmed, peaked cap.

"Aye, that's what I'm needing right enough," Tom replied grimly. "What with the wind and these terrible storms, the ewes are dropping their lambs too early!"

Felix watched Tom clothe the lamb, wondering what his purpose was. Tom stood up and carried the lamb over to a corner of the building where a second ewe was tethered. He set the lamb down near her head. After a few seconds she turned and ran her nose over the moist black pelt. Then after a moment's hesitation, she began to lick the lamb.

"Aye, I knew it! She'll take her!" said Tom with modest satisfaction. "She's a good mother that, not flighty like some."

Felix sat down against the wall to rest. Soon a noise was heard coming from the basket. The baby, no longer lulled by the rhythm of Felix's stride, was beginning to cry.

Though he did not show it, Tom was curious. He had noted Felix's reefer-jacket and blue pilot cloth trousers which suggested that he was a sea-faring man, not a local anyhow. Tom's fingers involuntarily ran over the rough cord of his breeches. All the same, the fellow did have a familiar look about him.

"You'll be on your way to Glittering Shiel," said Tom, knowing that a man could have no other destination this side of Cheviot.

"Aye, how much further is it?" asked Felix, too tired to wonder how Tom knew where he was going.

"About a half hour's walk from here. Just follow that track along the burn. With a bit of luck, you'll be there before the next downpour."

Tom's weather eye was as skilled as Felix's, but differently. Years of observation enabled him to predict the speed of the rain clouds as they were driven inland from the east coast. Felix picked up his burden, swinging it up onto his head in a single movement, and went down the slope to rejoin the track.

The way was long. The wind was bitter. Felix was unused to walking great distances and his legs were leaden with the cold and wet, numb from the brief rest at the still.

It was just after dawn that he had left Seamouth to set off on the thirty mile journey. A salted herring, a hunk of bread and a lemonade bottle filled with draught ale had been his only sustenance. The baby had taken almost none of the milk from the bottle prepared by Felix's mother and which he had carried tucked into the inside pocket of his jacket in an attempt to keep it warm.

The journey would have been quicker and easier had he taken the train from Morpeth to Alnwick. There he would have had to get off since the Cornhill line was not yet open. But he was penniless and so he had come the entire distance on foot except for the first few miles which he had ridden on Jimmy Robson's cart. Jimmy was a cadger who made his living selling the fish that Felix and the other fishermen caught. No fresh fish had been landed for days because of the storms so Jimmy was taking half a barrel of salted herrings to sell at Morpeth market.

Most of Felix's twenty-four years had been spent by the waters of the river Tyne where he had worked as a peedee in a keelboat. Later, when the shallow-draughted vessels were no longer needed to top up the collier brigs lying beyond the bar at Tynemouth, the family had been forced to leave the river and move up the coast in search of a living.

The Lee family set up house on the sand dunes at Seamouth. First they stripped the keelboat of its mast and grimy, square sail, then they turned it upside down and fitted it up with a window, some rudimentary partitions and a door.

Felix and his father became fishermen. Often, when they were out fishing, Felix would look westwards towards the hills and the greatest of them all, Cheviot, with its long whaleback. It was then that he would think of his dear, twin sister Lizzie and wonder what sort of life she led.

The wild and desolate moors were a foreign land to Felix. He turned a stranger's gaze upon them. Dense and shifting cloud blanketed the hilltops, but, looking ahead up the valley, he could see the soft line of the slopes as they curved down towards the burn like the interlocking fingers of some great, gentle giant.

Felix's only companion was a peewit which ran and flitted in front of him. There was no habitation in sight. The only marks of human hand on the landscape were the stone walls and the occasional circular sheep stell built on a haugh, a piece of flat ground, near the burn.

It was certainly no garden of Eden. He wondered what future lay before the child in this austere place, whose monotonous hills seemed like nothing so much as the billows of a stormy sea. Lizzie would surely take her. Three years married and no baby. But what of Andro? Felix knew nothing of the man his sister had married. Would he accept a baby, a girl, who was not his own flesh and blood? There was no alternative. Felix could not keep her. He could hardly keep himself. The meagre earnings from the fishing were not enough to feed Felix's parents and his remaining brothers and sisters. Many a time the family was so hard up they were forced to catch starlings for food. It was either that or the soup kitchen.

Lizzie had taken a liking to the hills after a trip to Rothbury with the other girls from the herring curing yard. The following winter, when the owner of the yard came offering the womenfolk ten shillings arle money if they would promise to work for him the next season, Lizzie had surprised everyone by refusing his offer. The truth was that she had never taken to the work of splitting the herrings, tentering them, and packing them in barrels ready for their journey to the Baltic ports. Instead she set her sights on the hills and after a time she managed to find work at Glittering Shiel.

By the time Felix reached the top of the dale, the day was sinking fast. A wild, wide expanse of moorland opened out before him and the thought came to him that perhaps the ocean floor might resemble these desolate wastes if, like a fish, he could see it. In the distance he could just make out several tall trees. They were wych elms, three of them planted by the hand of man, unlike the hawthorns with their corkscrew trunks or the rowan, birch and alder along the banks of the burn. The farmhouse and its buildings, he decided, were probably hidden from sight, set down in a sheltered dip near the burn.

Felix wanted to stop before he got to the house and take the baby in his arms. It would be his last chance. Once he got there, he would no longer have her to himself and, what was more, the moment of parting, something he both wished for and regretted, would be that much closer. But then he thought how cold and hungry she would be. The day would have been a far greater trial for her than for him. And yet, he did set the basket down and looked into her blue-grey eyes which gazed unblinking into his. Then, taking a deep breath, he hoisted the basket back onto his head and strode resolutely on.

The last few hundred yards were easy. The track, which had left the burnside when the valley opened out into the vast expanse of moorland, was running across open country. As he got closer to the three trees, it began to drop gently. Signs of habitation became more numerous; a gate, two small fields and then the track followed a stone wall until, rounding a bend, Felix suddenly found himself in a muddy farmyard.

The farmhouse and its outbuildings had been built on a haugh beside the Eidon Burn, which even at this early stage in its journey to the sea, had carved meandering loops. The water flowed down the west side and then to the south of the small enclave. The burn, usually a burbling stream, had burst its banks at the bend and begun to flood the farmyard. A rise of another inch or two and it would reach the scant remains of a round haystack and might even threaten the doors of the two buildings.

A long, low, stone bothy thatched with heather stood on the north side of the yard. It had a single door, which was closed, and one small window. On the opposite side of the yard, with its back towards him, stood the farmhouse, four-square and solid with a single-storeyed, windowless building attached to its east end. The house with its grey slate roof was built of the same intractable granite as the other buildings. It was from the crystals of quartz found in the stone that the farm, Glittering Shiel, had been given its name. The crystals were most dramatically exposed in the ancient circle of standing stones which stood some four hundred yards to the west of the house. Sometimes the children found smooth quartz pebbles in the sandy bed of the Eidon Burn. They thought they were diamonds.

Smoke was issuing from the massive chimney set square into the apex of the roof. The only openings to the north were a small window on the first floor and the back door which was painted dark green and had a shrivelled fox's mask nailed to it. On one side of the door stood a brimming water-butt and on the other a large block of stone, a disused cheese press. Felix went up to the door and set the basket down on the cheese press. He was about to knock on the door when it opened.

Lizzie stood on the threshold. She was little changed. Felix recognised the long, blue flannel skirt with the rows of tucks around the hem which she had bought second-hand from a fishwife at Cullercoats. She had been wearing it the early autumn day she had left the upturned keel and gone off to the hills. In her arms she was holding an orphan lamb which she had been trying to revive by the fire.

"What's this! Felix! Can it be you?" she cried, delighted yet disbelieving.

He held out his arms and embraced both her and the lamb.

He smelt of home, wet wool and the salt seashore. Tangled memories of their childhood together flooded into Lizzie's mind. But quickly the moment passed and she was filled with anxiety as to why he had come. Suddenly realising that he was soaked to the skin and would be weary, she stepped aside to let him enter. It was then that she noticed the fish basket.

Before a question could form on her lips, Felix drew back the oilskin to reveal the contents of the basket.

"See, I've brought another orphan for you to look after!"

Lizzie bent forward, looking from the baby's eyes to Felix's, seeking some connection, an explanation.

Felix went in first, carrying the basket through the narrow passage, past the scullery and into the kitchen beyond.

7

A peat fire was glowing, blown incandescent by the air roaring up the chimney. A large, square table made of ash and white from weekly scourings with fine sand, stood in the middle of the room. On the long wall opposite the fire there was an oak dresser with an ornamental cornice of fretwork. Blue and white Delft plates, wild rose dishes, willow pattern cups with blue transfer printing, bowls of tortoiseshell ware, speckled black on the outside and cream on the inside, were displayed upon its racks. In the corner by the window was a table on which stood a fine, old eight-day clock embellished with filigree work with three brass balls on top. Suspended from a beam hung two salt-sparkling sides of bacon.

The fireside with its inglenook was hung about with the impedimenta of daily life: cooking pots, utensils and clothes put to dry. On one side of the grate there was a set pot filled with seething, susurrating water and, on the other, a bread oven. A yetling, an iron pot with three stumpy legs, hung from a hook above the fire. Inside it potato peelings for the pigs were boiling vigorously, filling the room with a moist, earthy smell.

Felix took it all in and was impressed. "Why, if our Mam could see all this! Our little Lizzie set up in her very own palace!"

Lizzie shook her head. "It's not my palace no more than it's Andro's, not really. Everything here, all the nice things anyway, those plates and the books and pictures in the parlour belonged to Will and Mary Hetherton - God rest their souls."

The Hethertons were an old border family whose origins were in Coverdale over on the Scottish side. Not that the notion of being Scottish had meant much to them. In the turbulent times before the union of the Scottish and English crowns, the crosses of Saint George and Saint Andrew were no more than flags of convenience. Over the centuries, branches of the Hetherton clan had settled all over the borderland. Their roots were dug as deep and tenaciously into the Cheviot rock as the sinewy thorn trees that grew in the wild ravines.

The Hethertons were a sept or name. The law by which they lived was simple. The authority of the chief was absolute. He was the blood representative of the original father from whom all the members of the clan were descended. His most sacred duty was, in all circumstances, legal and illegal, to protect and defend his own folk. Members of the clan might steal sheep and cattle, plunder farmhouse and village, commit rape and murder, but such actions were not considered transgressions. Clan law transcended the mere laws of nations which were embodied in the Warden courts, held from time to time in an attempt to settle disputes by peaceful means. Most often, however, grievances were settled by deadly feud, a bloody and private war between the opposing parties.

Will Hetherton had died before Lizzie came to Glittering Shiel. Nobody knew the precise circumstances of his death. It had happened in March during a fresh, a thaw, when the burns were treacherous, swollen with melted snow and ice. At that time Andro had been working for Will as a shepherd. One day the two men had gone out to see to their separate hirsels, but that night only Andro had come home. Will was found two days later, his body hooked over a rowan tree several miles down Heron Water.

After Will's death Andro had moved quickly, too quickly some said. Early one May morning, he and Mary, Will's widow, had slipped across the border into Scotland where a marriage could be made without the delay of calling the banns. In the garden of the Bridge End Inn at Coldstream, a mole-catcher by the name of Willie Armstrong, had conducted the brief ceremony and immediately afterwards handed the couple their marriage lines.

Lizzie hastily put the lamb into a box near the fire and turned her attention to the baby. She started to undo the cover.

"Mam used some of the eiderdown she had put by to make a cover to keep her warm," Felix explained.

Sure enough, the baby, though needing a change of clothes, was no colder than the lamb by the fire.

"Sit yourself down while I see to the poor little thing. And tell me all about it."

Felix was hesitant, hardly knowing how to tell the tale.

"Well, you know these terrible gales we've been having?"

Lizzie nodded.

"So you'll understand a lot of ships has come to grief these last days? Well, the *Freya* was one of them!"

"The *Freya*?"

"Aye, a Norwegian barque bound for Blyth from Breunbuttel with a cargo of pit-props. There were mountainous seas running before a terrible south-easter and she got caught in them. The gale must've been driving her dead inland, straight onto the Black Middens!"

Lizzie shook her head in horror at the images Felix's words conjured up.

"You can't have forgotten the Middens and the lives they've taken! Dad and me reckon the crew must've cut her masts away and let her anchors go to try to keep her from rushing ashore. But there was nothing they could do. The anchor cables must've snapped like thread."

Lizzie could see it all; the thunderous seas beating against the shore, the cobles pulled right up the beach, the Life Brigade volunteers mustering at their station. How often she had lain curled up in her berth listening to a raging storm with galeforce winds that whipped up the sand and made the links outside the door as smooth and pristine as on the first day of creation.

"There was that many ships in distress that night, we didn't get to know about the *Freya* till first light. What a bitter-cold, grey-black dawn it was! The storm had eased, so me and dad went out along the cliffs. And there she was! The *Freya*! By some miracle she'd escaped the rocks and fetched up on the beach. We got to the crew first. There was eight of them, laid out on the sand. There was nothing we could do except wipe the sand from their dead eyes. Dad went back to get help and I went on board. Well, you wouldn't have credited it! Of course everything was smashed to smithereens on deck. The masts and rigging was in a terrible tangle but inside the cabin everything was in perfect order. The log was written up, a bucket of coal was stood by the fire with the ship's cat sound asleep beside it. That's when I saw the baby. She was in a bunk tucked in tight with blankets. They must've reckoned she had a better chance that way. Well that's about it. I just picked her up and took her home. Late that night a woman's body was washed ashore. Mam said she must have been the baby's mother, she was the right sort of age."

Felix, unused to speaking at such length, paused to collect his thoughts before going on to the most difficult part.

"Lizzie, you know how it is at home. Taking her in means another mouth to feed and it's not as if things have got any easier since you left. Mam's still out from dawn till dusk with a creel on her back bartering fish for a few vegetables and a scrap of meat. And I couldn't take her to the workhouse. Once I'd seen those beautiful eyes, that was it! I couldn't have done it! I didn't have the heart."

At this point Felix got up from the chair, went over to Lizzie who was attending to the baby which was lying on the table. He put his hands on her shoulders and drew her round so that she was looking at him full in the face.

"Lizzie, I've come to ask you, will you take her in? Will you give her a home? Bring her up like she was your own bairn. Please, will you do it, will you?"

Felix's intense grip almost hurt her. How little he knew! There was no need for him to plead. She would have done it anyway, for herself as much as for him. But she made no reply, turning back to the baby which she wrapped in a piece of soft flannel. Cradled in her arms, the baby at last began to accept nourishment. Lizzie's eyes were fixed on the child.

"Aye, Felix," she sighed softly. "I'll tell you something. I've been fair desperate for a bairn. You see, I'm afraid there's something wrong with me. I'm barren, that's what Andro says. And you know what a woman is that cannot have a child? She's useless!"

There was nothing Felix could say.

11

Lizzie continued, though she seemed to be speaking to herself rather than to Felix. "But what will I say to him? There's no hunger here, right enough. Oh, but times is hard. The price of wool has dropped and the lambing's a disaster. So many lost, there'll be nothing like the usual to sell. Money's tight, very tight. A guinea a lamb. That's all we got at the Willove sale last autumn," she said, addressing the last remark to Felix.

"I haven't a brass farthing to my name just at the minute, but me and the other men will get salvage money for the *Freya*. I promise I'll send you my share, every last penny."

Lizzie gazed into the fire. How many times had she imagined what it would be like to sit by the fire with a baby in her arms! Surely Andro would not turn the child away. He did still care for her, she had to believe that, even if recently he had been lost in dark moods that condemned her to a life of near silence.

"What's her name, Felix? Do you know?"

"No. It's up to us. We'll have to give her a name. I thought of calling her Freya after the ship what brought her!"

"Freya," said Lizzie quietly. "Aye, Freya. I've never known a lassie with that name, but it sounds good. Aye, all right then, that's settled. Freya it is!"

By this time it was dark outside. The sky was clearing from the east and it was bitterly cold. Lizzie was expecting Andro and Sam to come back at any minute. She had not seen them since midday when they had come in for dinner and Sam had brought her the cold lamb.

Sam was Will and Mary's ten year-old son. During the winter months the lad normally lodged with Mrs Matheson down at the Home Farm which was within easy walking distance of Herontop school. Recently, however, Andro had kept him at home to help with the lambing, since apart from Andro himself, there was only George to herd the thousand acres of Glittering Shiel.

For more than thirty years George and his wife, Hannah, had lived in the bothy across the yard. George had worked for Will Hetherton and for his father before him. He was not so contented now, but he stayed on because he loved the place and because he felt a loyalty to young Sam who would one day take over the farm.

Lizzie was behind with her chores. There was the cow to milk and the pigs to feed and after that the supper to see to. Reluctantly, she put Freya down and asked Felix to tie the basket under the table with a piece of cord so it could be pushed gently from time to time and rock the baby to sleep. She took a paisley shawl from the back of the chair and put it round her shoulders and, with the heavy pot of potatoes in one hand and a byrelamp in the other, she left the homely kitchen.

Half an hour later she was back in the scullery preparing the supper. Suddenly the back door burst open and a blast of cold air rushed along the passage. She knew from the powerful way the door was slammed shut that it was Andro.

Now it was Lizzie's turn to explain and her stomach was churning. It was hardly the best moment. Doubtless Andro was cold and hungry and he would be in a bad fettle on account of the miles he had tramped and his foot which would be aching.

Andro saw the light in the scullery and seconds later he appeared in the doorway. Feral frontiersman that he was, he would have struck fear into the hearts of gentle, lowland folk. On his head he wore a hat made out of a fox skin. The fox's mask with its pointed muzzle formed a grizzly peak at the front while the brush hung down his back. He was wrapped in a thick tweed plaid the colour of peat which had belonged to Will. Andro had taken it over just as he had taken possession of all Will's goods and chattels, including his wife, Mary.

The only items that rightfully belonged to Andro were his hat, boots and stick. He had a deformity of the right foot, three toes were fused and knotted together like a cluster of cobnuts and so he had his boots specially made in Aberdeenshire. Each spring a brown paper parcel would arrive which contained a new pair identical to the ones sent the previous year.

As for the stick, he had made it himself. It was a stout piece of hazel onto which he had rivetted in crude but sturdy fashion a large curving ram's horn. He never went anywhere without it.

Seeing the unpeeled onion in Lizzie's hands, he said sharply, "What's going on, woman? Is my supper not ready?"

"Something's happened!" Lizzie began. "Felix is here!"

Andro looked blank.

"Felix! My brother, my twin brother! He's in the kitchen!" Then, her voice quivering with hope and fear, she said, "And Andro, he's brought us a bairn!"

Andro's face darkened. "A bairn! What bairn? Whose bairn?"

"She can be ours!"

"What's this? A bairn! She! It's not some feeble lassie I need round here, it's lambs, strong, ewe lambs to pay the bills."

Lizzie saw her chance. "Andro! Wait! There's money in it! Felix has given his word. He'll pay you to take her."

"Aye, well, I'll see. Mind you, I'm making no promises," said Andro in a gentler tone of voice. He turned and went back into the passageway to hang up his hat and plaid.

Lizzie sighed with relief, she sensed that the tide had turned.

"Come away into the kitchen!" Andro ordered. "I want you to pull my boots off!"

Obediently she followed him into the kitchen.

Divested of his outer garments, the man beneath was revealed. He was handsome in an unconventional way, olive-skinned with jet black hair. His colouring had led some folk to surmise that he had the blood of the dark-skinned branch of the Yetholm gypsies in his veins. Broad-shouldered and thickset, there was no doubting the physical strength and stamina for which he was renowned. Nobody had ever established where he came from. Some said he was from Holy Island on account of his superstitious aversion to pigs. Others said that Man was without doubt a Scottish name. Andro himself refused to throw any light on the matter and so the conjecture continued, fed on snippets of information such as the postmark on the parcel containing the

14

boots or a chance remark made in the snug of the Three Half Moons at Willove.

He had appeared in that part of the borders some five years earlier. He was what was called a loose man, a migrant worker, who would turn up when extra labour was needed and who could turn his hand to most tasks on a farm. It was said he could sow with both hands, which was a dying art requiring both strength and dexterity. His musical skill and ready wit made him a welcome guest at social gatherings such as harvest suppers. On such occasions he would play the Jew's harp and sometimes the fiddle.

It was harvest time when he first turned up at Heron Rigg. The steward was already supplied with Irish labourers who came over from Donegal and Connaught at that time of year. At first the steward had turned him away. But then he had changed his mind: the weather was looking less settled and it seemed wise to make haste. Andro surprised the steward by asking for the wages of two women. However, the steward accepted saying that if Andro sheared twice as much corn as the women, he would pay what he asked.

Andro had gone to work with a speed and efficiency that became the talk of the countryside. He even found time from his reaping to twist a band of corn for the bindster, the woman who came along the rig behind him binding the corn into sheaves. He turned up again the following year and went to work for Will Hetherton, clipping sheep and making hay. He must have liked the wild acres of Glittering Shiel because when Will asked him if he would stay on, he said yes.

Andro had spied the basket under the table the moment he entered the room, but he said nothing. Instead, to Lizzie's relief, he greeted Felix warmly.

"So you're Lizzie's twin brother!" Then looking from sister to brother, he noted the same sandy hair, pale eyelashes and regular features. "Peas out of the same pod and no mistake!" he commented. "Now, Lizzie, away you go and fetch a dram. We'll show your brother what border hospitality is!"

Lizzie fetched a thick, green glass bottle and Andro poured a generous measure of whisky for himself and Felix.

"So you've brought Lizzie a bairn, eh?" he said to Felix.

"Aye, that's right, if you'll have her."

"Well then, you'd better show me the goods!"

With trembling fingers Lizzie untied the cord and lifted the basket onto the table. Andro picked Freya up in his coarse hands, unwrapped the cloth and laid her naked on the bare board. He gazed at her for a time, then he ran his index finger very slowly down her forehead, over her nose and chin, down her chest and belly, stopping finally at the fold of her sex.

Lizzie felt embarrassed and confused, but she did not dare say anything. Both she and Felix watched and waited to see what Andro would do next.

"Aye, she'll do," said Andro without enthusiasm.

Lizzie's heart was singing, but she hid her joy, fearing that if Andro saw it, he might change his mind.

The brightness of the lamp and the hardness of the table had upset Freya. Soon she was clenching her tiny fists and her arms and legs began to flail up and down in protest. Andro ignored the outburst and resumed his seat by the fire, leaving Lizzie to mend the hurt.

The rest of the evening was uneventful. Sam came into the room after they had had supper. He took his plate of food into a corner away from the fire and the company.

That night Felix slept in the big bedroom above the parlour. Lizzie was the last person to go up the narrow stairs. She cleared away the supper things, fed the lamb, then fed and changed Freya. She sat quietly by the fire with the baby in her arms until she was sound asleep. When Lizzie was satisfied that Freya would not disturb Andro's sleep, she tucked her into the fish basket and took her upstairs.

16

2

Freya had lived at Glittering Shiel for five years. She was a quiet child without playmates. Her days were spent trotting after Lizzie as she went about her tasks. Sometimes she would go across the yard to seek out Hannah who always had time to talk and sometimes tell her stories of the countryside while she churned the butter or did the weekly baking. One day they walked together up the track and through the gate where there was a huge oval boulder where they could sit and look at the hills to the south.

"Can you see him?" Hannah asked. "The warrior? Look, there he is lying on his back with his knees pulled up. He's fast asleep!"

Hannah was pointing towards Warrior Crag. Her finger traced the profile of the warrior's body, the fretted line of his nose, his bearded chin, then his chest, which was a fell called Cockslack and finally his legs, the hill known as Maidenhope.

Freya gazed at the wild landscape until at last she saw him.

"He's so big and he must be very old! How old is he, Hannah?"

"As old as the hills of course," Hannah replied with a chuckle.

"And is he a good man?" asked Freya, remembering how Hannah, whenever she was telling Freya about someone, would say whether or not they were a good person.

"Maybe he is and maybe he isn't, but I'll tell you one thing. Good men have always been hard to find."

"Is he going to wake up soon?"

"Ah, lassie, that I cannot say," replied Hannah with a shake of the head.

Andro rarely talked to Freya. He spoke to Lizzie about her as if she was not there. So Freya never spoke to him, never asked him the questions a child normally asked its father. It was as if Freya was almost invisible. She had no choice but to accept this situation, just as she had to accept all other manifestations of his authority. Whenever she came into the house, without thinking about it, she would look to see if his ram's horn stick was hanging on the peg in the passageway. If it was, she knew what to expect.

The minute Andro crossed the threshold, Lizzie gave him her undivided attention, for like her mother, Lizzie believed that the Lord intended women for the comfort and convenience of men.

Although Andro was not handsome in a conventional way, women were invariably attracted to him. Men, on the other hand, saw nothing remarkable in his dark eyes and aquiline features. They were only aware of his glamour second-hand; they read it in the faces of the women. Before he was married many a bondager had shed bitter tears to see him move on at the end of hay or harvest. Lizzie was no exception, having fallen under his spell very soon after arriving at Glittering Shiel.

The first year of their marriage had been a happy time. Lizzie saw herself and Andro as custodians of the farm with a duty to care for Sam until he came into his inheritance. By that time she hoped that she and Andro would have saved enough money to rent a farm of their own. However, the memory of those early days had faded, carried away on the wind of harsh winters and their bitter harvest of dead lambs. Andro had become more and more morose and restless. He took every opportunity to spend time away from the farm, driving cattle down from Scotland to Newcastle market or going off to Willove to buy and sell his own stock.

On the rare occasions when a visitor knocked at the door of Glittering Shiel, Andro would change swiftly into a different man. He became good company, hospitable, with a ready wit. Felix had greatly enjoyed the evening he had spent with him. Indeed, he had carried a highly favourable report of Andro back to his mother and father at Seamouth.

A day or two after Felix's visit, Andro had made it clear to Lizzie that he did not for one moment believe Felix's story about the shipwreck. He was convinced that Freya was Felix's bastard.

Lizzie had totally abandoned hope of bearing a child. One night Andro had called her a cold ewe and, thinking of the fate of such sheep, Lizzie had shuddered. She suddenly realised how thin the line was that separated her barrenness from that of a ewe. She knew that it was her fault. Andro's fertility, though doomed, was beyond doubt. Mary Hetherton had died bearing his child less than twelve months after their hasty wedding.

Lizzie sometimes wondered whether, if Freya had been a boy, Andro would have treated her differently, accepted her as his own child. But as it was, Lizzie felt insecure both for herself and for Freya.

Will Hetherton had been dead seven years. Sam was now fourteen and was working full-time on the farm. Andro paid him nothing. He told the lad that the farm would be his one day and therefore, since he was working for himself, he had no need of wages. Kind words were few, though in recent weeks Andro's attitude had changed. He was kinder to the lad, almost indulgent.

The autumn tasks were well advanced. Throughout the summer and early autumn, up on the boggy hilltops, the peat had been cut into domino-shaped slabs and left to dry before being led down to the farm. A long, low stack, slated with peats and thatched with reeds, stood against the north wall of the byre close to the back door ready for the winter cold. The potatoes had long since been harvested and were stored in tattie pits in the field where they had grown. Supplies of dried peas, pearl barley, oat, wheat and barleymeal to keep man and beast alive through the months of winter isolation had been ordered from Willove.

Salmon, taken illegally from Heron Water, were a further source of winter food. Autumn was the close season for salmon and trout fishing with the lower reaches of the rivers being patrolled by bailiffs. But, as with so many other things, the law was a dead letter in the upper reaches of the burns. The bailiffs knew better than to trespass into the desolate valleys where the intervention of the local constabulary was neither needed nor wanted. It was not that the affairs of the hill folk were any less ordered than in the lowlands, it was simply that they were ordered differently, without written statute and officers to enforce it.

So the inhabitants of Herondale and nearby would keep an eye on the burns and when the salmon began to run the word would go out and they would gather at darkening at the entrance to the valley. They came with ponies, carts and tar lights and, like a tribe of terrestrial Neptunes, they carried liesters, large barbed forks mounted on stout poles with which they speared the fish.

In the past, Will Hetherton and George had been invited to share in the communal harvest. However, after Will's death Andro did not receive word of when the liestering was to take place. At first he was not surprised, putting it down to his being a relative newcomer. However, as the years went by, and the exclusion continued, he became increasingly rancorous. He was convinced that George continued to go because he had seen strings of gutted fish, too large and too plentiful to have been taken out of the Eidon Burn, discreetly set out to dry in the autumn sun against the end wall of the bothy.

It never occurred to Andro that his habit of driving his sheep over the marches onto other shepherds' territory had not gone unnoticed, nor his slowness in offering a helping hand with a neighbour's hay or clipping. These were grievous faults in a community where helping one another was the cornerstone of survival.

In mid November the rams would be put to the ewes and the annual cycle of fertility would begin again. The six year-old ewes had been culled. Their life on the hills was at an end. Andro sold them to one of the in-bye farms closer to Willove where the grass was more plentiful and they would thrive sufficiently to produce one more crop of lambs before going to market.

One day in mid September Andro drove the ewes to their new owner, then took the opportunity to spend some time in one of Willove's numerous inns, the Three Half Moons, which was frequented by itinerant folk: drovers, tinkers and muggers who travelled around the country selling earthenware. There he happened to meet up with some old acquaintances, Dan Og, Thom Reid and one or two others. They drank copious quantities of ale chased down with nips of whisky and swapped news and gossip of the countryside.

On the morning of the day before Halloween as they were setting off to go round the sheep, Andro spoke to Sam. He told him to be ready to leave Glittering Shiel after darkening the following night. Sam did not ask where they would be going, he just nodded his head in assent. All he wanted was to win Andro's approval and he was only too pleased to be included in whatever Andro was planning.

They set off just before eleven o'clock. Andro wore his fox skin hat and a cloak of wild goatskin, darkest brown with splashes of white. Sam followed on behind, as trusting as Isaac with Abraham, leading Polly, the sturdy pony, which was laden with panniers.

Later the previous evening Sam had seen Andro heating up some tar and earlier that day he had noticed that the liesters and cleeks had been taken down from their place in the barn. He therefore deduced that a fishing foray was in prospect, though he was somewhat perplexed since George had made no mention of it.

Sam was surprised when Andro did not take the track down the valley. Instead they crossed the ford to the west of the farmhouse, leaving behind them the circle of stones which stood black against the wind-blanched bent-grass. They struck off to the southeast, soon coming upon the deep-rutted path of the ancient British trackway which skirted the foot of Warrior Crag. They followed it across the fell before dropping down into Herondale.

An hour later, sure-footed as wild mountain goats, they were picking their way down the narrow declivity of Corby Cleugh following the course of Corby Linn which joined Heron Water close by the meeting place.

It was a dark night with clouds scudding across a shard of moon. Not far from the entrance to the valley Heron Water flowed deep and fast in a loop known as the Devil's Elbow. There on a rocky promontory stood the grim grey walls of Beaver Tower, a border pele, built by Guillaume de Beauvoir four hundred years before, to stand guard over this gateway to the fertile valleys of Northumberland.

The tower, which was almost intact, had once been surrounded by an enclosure six yards high. Now it was breached, some of its stones having been used to make dry-stone walls. Andro led Polly through the outer door of grated iron which still hung on massive hinges, although the inner door, made of oak and clenched with nails, had long since been removed to make fast some other place.

It was pitch-black in the barrel-vaulted chamber. The others had not yet arrived. Andro told Sam to tie Polly up and sit quiet while he made ready.

He drew a sort of headdress out of one of the panniers which he handed to Sam and told him to put on. It was the skin of a black ram into which Andro had set a pair of horns. Then he got out a candle, lit it and set it on a stone. The flame barely flickered in the rank stillness of the vault. They sat and waited, Sam sitting on a stone with his back to the entrance and Andro a few feet away near the wall. Andro took a flask of whisky from his jerkin, took only enough to wet his lips, then he got up and handed it to Sam. "Here lad, take a slug of this. You'll be needing it before the night's out!"

Sam had never tasted the fiery liquor before. It burnt a track down his throat which was dry with excitement and nervousness.

Neither of them spoke. The silence was broken from time to time by Polly as she blew softly through her nostrils or gently stamped her unshod hooves on the soft earth floor. A short time later, the even sound of flowing water was broken by splashing and muffled voices. Then they heard the high-pitched voice of Dan Og who appeared in the doorway.

"Well! If it's not the devil himself!" he trilled.

The words were uttered half in horror, half in jest. From where Dan was standing, it looked as if a candle was set between the horns of a hairy black beast and for a split second Dan had taken the apparition to be none other than Satan himself in grand array.

Dan took a step in the direction of the grim figure which he quickly decided must be Andro in disguise. But, uncannily, Andro's voice came to him from a different quarter.

"Aye, you're right enough Dan! Tonight, the laddie here is standing in for the Prince of Darkness!"

Two more men appeared. Tam, normally copper-faced, had painted his face white and put on a battered and beribboned straw bonnet. Little older than Sam, he was accompanied by Phem, his wiry-haired dog. The dog, too, was horror-struck at the sight of Sam. With eyes glaring and hackles bristling, he began to growl and then bark.

"Whisht Phem! Come away boy!" said Tam.

Thom Reid, his face blackened and a long felt hat pulled down over his ears, rubbed his hands together with glee.

"There'll be sport a plenty tonight lads! It's a rare crew of boggyboes and clabbernappers we are, ready for to drive nosey folk back into their houses where they belong!"

Andro had deliberately chosen Halloween, night of ancient ritual and sacrifice marking the opening of the breeding season for pastoral peoples, for his trespass into Herondale, for while the bailiffs presented no threat to him and his companions, the inhabitants of Herondale did.

They were a deeply superstitious race whose ancient beliefs were woven into the texture of everyday life. Why else was an adder stone to be seen hanging on the back of every byre door? Why was a pig never killed when the moon was on the wane? Not so very many years before, when the cattle were struck with disease, the people would extinguish all ordinary fires and kindle a mystic needfire by rubbing a wooden axle in the hub of a wheel. Then they would drive the stricken animals through the cleansing smoke.

Andro too had a profound belief in the old religion, more profound than anybody, and yet he was not averse to turning it to his advantage. He knew that folk would have their doors shut tight that night. The young lassies and lads would be busy throwing hazelnuts into the fire in order to divine who they would marry and, if lights were seen moving up the river, he knew that nobody would dare to venture forth to see who it was.

A bottle of whisky was uncorked and handed round while each man was given his task. Andro got out some thick plaits of rush, which he had soaked in the tar that was used to mark the sheep. He took two poles and bound the rushes to them to make the tar lights that would dazzle and confuse the fish. Three men were to proceed together up the bed of the stream. Two would carry liesters or cleeks, large barbed fish hooks mounted on poles. The third man would wade between them carrying the blue-flamed light. As they speared the fish they would hurl them onto the bank and Andro would collect them into piles ready to be put into a poke on the way back down.

Andro turned to Sam as they were leaving. "Here lad!" he said. "Take this light! You must lead the way until we get past Hoarstones. After that, you must put the light out and bring up at the rear in case there's anybody minded to sneak up on us from behind. And here, take this cleek so you can snatch the odd fish!"

Liesters poised, they waded fully clothed into the cold water, picking their way up the slippery bed of the burn. Whenever they came to a deep pool where the water was more than chest-deep, they climbed out and made their way along the bank until it was shallow enough to start fishing again.

An hour later the shuttered lights of Hoarstones farmhouse could be seen in the distance. They gathered together to fortify themselves with more whisky, then they extinguished the lights before skirting the house and buildings, creeping stealthily along behind the stone walls that surrounded the small settlement.

Sam did as Andro had told him and took his place at the rear, casting anxious glances over his shoulder every few minutes. He was all alone. The others were a hundred yards or more ahead of him, hidden by a bend in the stream at a place where the water was forced through a deep, narrow chasm between the rocks. Sam knew it well, it was called Ruffie's Loup. Many a summer day he and his friends had whiled away the hours, daring one another to make the jump from one side of the chasm to the other.

Disappointed because he had not caught a single fish, he began to wonder how Andro thought he could, since it was as much as he could do to carry the two poles. What made matters worse was the headdress; it covered his ears so that he could not hear properly, it got in the way when he wanted to turn his head and look behind and the bar of wood that supported the horns was making his head throb.

He was approaching the black outline of the rocks which rose up on either side of the Loup. Once he got to them he would have to climb up one side before he could carry on further. He put both poles in one hand in order to have one hand free to help him climb. He was half way up the rock, head bent forward searching for a secure foothold, when he was felled with a single blow to the back of his head. His body crumpled and tumbled slowly down towards the deep dark water.

It was three in the morning before Andro and the others finished fishing. Only when they began to retrace their steps did they realise that Sam was nowhere to be seen.

"Wherever can the lad be?" asked Dan.

"He'll maybe have taken a tumble and be sitting waiting for us lower down," suggested Tam. "Unless of course the devil's taken the hindmost!" he added jokingly.

"The lad's not used to drink," said Andro. "He took a good few nips from my flask. Sure as life the liquor'll have gone to his legs and he'll have gone and got himself well and truly soused in the burn!"

They all laughed at this and, well contented with the night's work, they collected up their booty and set off on the long walk back down the valley.

25

It was Phem who found Sam. Tam, following the excited dog, came upon him lying at the foot of the rock. Without the ram's skin, which had come off in the fall and was hanging unnoticed on the branch of a rowan growing out of a crevice in the rock, Sam looked like the vulnerable and innocent boy he was. His head was lying on one side an inch or two above the water. Tam bent to pick him up and, as he lifted the inert body, he saw the side of Sam's head that had been hidden. There was a deep gash from temple to jaw. Sam's lifeblood was fast ebbing away down Heron Water.

"Andro! Come quick! It's Sam!" Tam shouted.

By the time Andro arrived, Dan and Thom knew that Sam was beyond help.

"It's all up with the lad, Andro. He must've taken a fall on his way up the rock and that cleek did for him! Oh geez, what a mess he's in!"

"Aye that he is!" said Andro readily accepting Dan's explanation of the tragedy, though there were others. Someone could have followed them and thought to give Sam a lesson he would never forget.

Dan hoisted Sam onto his shoulders and carried him down the track. They came at last to Beaver Tower where they had left Polly. After they had unbuckled the panniers Dan laid Sam across Polly's back.

Subdued, the four men threaded their way out of Herondale. They parted company at the ford with Andro leading Polly off up Eidonhope. By the time they reached Glittering Shiel the last drops of Sam's blood had been shed upon his native earth.

26

3

Everything was still as Andro led Polly into the farmyard. He tied her up by the back door and went indoors to wake Lizzie.

"Lizzie!" he shouted as he went up the stairs. "Get up!"

He went into the bedroom and put his hand on her shoulder to rouse her.

"Help me with Sam! He's at the door. He'll have to be brought in," he said urgently.

Andro's words seemed to belong to the realm of dreams and it was a minute before Lizzie came to her senses.

"What's the matter? Is he hurt? What's been going on ?"

"Never mind that now! Just do as I say!"

Lizzie got up from the warm hollow of the feather bed, wrapped herself in a shawl and picked up her wooden clogs. She would put them on after she got downstairs so as not to wake Freya.

They went outside. Andro told her to carry Sam into the kitchen. Farm work had made Lizzie strong, but carrying Sam's body was almost beyond her strength.

"Please, will you not give me a hand?" she implored him.

There was no reply. Andro had already vanished into the darkness. Somehow she managed to heave Sam off Polly and across her shoulders. Then, almost buckling under the weight, she tottered along the passageway into the kitchen and laid him down on the kitchen table.

The room was in darkness, the fire damped down. She lifted the tall glass chimney off the paraffin lamp and lit the black tongue of wick. As soon as the flame steadied she replaced the chimney and turned her attention to Sam.

Of course she knew that they had gone out and, from Andro's preparations, which he had made no attempt to hide, she had guessed that they had gone fishing. But how could such a dreadful thing have happened? Sam was such a careful lad, not accident-prone. And what would the Hethertons say when they learned that Will and Mary's son had died, and in this way?

She knew instinctively that he was dead. Nevertheless, she picked up his wrist to feel his pulse. His face was the colour of whey, his features pinched, his skin drawn. The extent of the gash was concealed beneath a wine-dark crust of blood that half-covered his face. It was not long before Lizzie realised that he had not had a chance. Like a lamb at the slaughter, his jugular had been severed, though she could not tell by what instrument. She touched his temple and shuddered. The blood was still viscous. As a woman she was no stranger to blood, but this was different. It was neither the bleeding of the monthly cycle nor the blood of childbirth. No, it was an unnatural blood-letting.

The water in the set pot was still warm. She lifted the lid and filled a bowl. It was to be filled several times more before the blood was all washed from his face. She fetched the clipping shears and, using both hands to manipulate the great scissors, she snipped Sam's blood-stained jersey down the chest and arms so that she could take it off. Only a rough flannel shirt remained, unbuttoned over the boy's smooth, hairless chest. She was busy undoing his hobnailed boots when Andro came into the room.

"Take his clothes off, Lizzie! All of them! And give them to me!"

Andro's gaze did not rest for an instant on the boy. His voice was firm and Lizzie knew there could be no dissent.

Andro sat in front of the dormant fire, still wearing his outdoor clothes, waiting until she had accomplished the task. She dared ask none of the questions that were forming in her confused and troubled mind, no more than she dared utter a word of reproach for Sam's untimely death.

When she had done, Andro got up from the chair, ordered her back to bed, picked up the bundle of clothes and went out.

But Lizzie did not go back upstairs. She went and sat on the chair usually occupied by Sam. Her mind needed time to catch up with events. The reality was almost beyond belief and yet there was Sam lying dead on the very board where, since earliest childhood, he had eaten his daily bread.

Lizzie had an imperfect knowledge of the rituals of death. Among the sea-faring folk at the coast, a man or boy was all too often lost at sea and then he would be mourned in the absence of his body. And when Lizzie was no more than ten, with the menfolk away at the fishing, her mother had given birth to a sickly baby which had lived only till morning light. Her mother had used a shoe box for a coffin. She had handed Lizzie a sixpence and told her to take the box to the church on the links where she knew the baby would be buried in consecrated ground. There was no money for a proper funeral and anyway dead babies were all too common.

Lizzie felt unable to leave Sam, she could not abandon him, so she lit a candle and set it on the table. Then she put out the lamp. Only the ticking of the clock broke the silence. The regular, remorseless sound was an annoyance. It seemed somehow inappropriate, wrong. She hesitated for a moment before laying a finger on the glass door of the clock. When Will Hetherton had been alive no one, not even Mary, had been allowed to touch it and after his death control of the timepiece had passed to Andro. But Lizzie managed to overcome her misgivings and, extending a trembling finger, she gently stayed the slender hand. It was four thirty-seven when she began her lonely vigil.

Lizzie did not see Andro until nearly eight o'clock next morning. He had gone straight back to Ruffie's Loup, anxious to find the black ram's skin. He had spent an hour or more feverishly scouring the burn downstream of the Loup, but it was nowhere to be found.

Lizzie did not rekindle the fire. Andro ate some bread and cold mutton before setting off to Hyldetron, a village on the turnpike road. There he would visit Jasper Long, the carpenter and undertaker, to see about a coffin.

"The Hethertons will have to be told!" said Lizzie as Andro was about to leave. "Are you not going to send word over to

Coverdale?" She had felt duty-bound to speak, fearing that Andro was planning to bury Sam without his family around him.

A shadow of annoyance passed over Andro's face. He wanted the whole business done with, forgotten as quickly as possible.

"What's the good? It makes no odds, Sam's gone and a whole tribe of Hethertons cannot bring him back!" he said fiercely.

"That's true, but they've a right to know. They'll surely want to come and see him buried," she argued obstinately.

"Aye, well, I'll think on it," he said reluctantly.

It was left to Lizzie to break the news to Hannah and George. Freya was still asleep, so Lizzie took the opportunity to go across the yard and knock on their door. She hardly knew what she would say, Andro had told her so little.

George had already left to go round the sheep, but Hannah was in the kitchen cutting slices off a side of bacon for the breakfast.

Hannah had rarely seen Lizzie so pale and distraught.

"Why, Lizzie! Whatever's wrong?"

"It's Sam! Oh Hannah! It's terrible!"

"Calm yourself! Now then, what is it?"

"He's dead!"

"Dead? No! How can this be? He was hale and hearty last night. I never saw him in better spirits! He's not been ailing, has he?"

"No! No, it's not that! He went out with Andro last night. They didn't say where they were going, but they took tar lights and liesters so they must have been after fish. Andro brought him back in the small hours. He was in such a sorry state! And his face! I could hardly bear to look at it. I think it was a liester or more likely a cleek made a gash right down the side."

"Where is he now?"

"Laid out on the kitchen table. I didn't know where else to put him. I washed him and closed his eyes and put a sheet over his bare body."

"His bare body? What are you on about, lassie? For heaven's sake where's his clothes?"

"Andro took them!"

"Aha! So that's what George was on about. The minute he stepped out of the door this morning he said he could smell burning. That man must have taken the laddie's things and burnt them."

"Burnt them? Why? What for? Why would he do such a thing?"

"Well, didn't I always say that that man was an Ee-gip-shun!"

"A what?"

"A gypsy man with gypsy ways! I never liked him nor his slickit tongue. I spoke my mind to George and he said I was a stupid old woman to say such things. He told me to hold my tongue if I knew what was good for me. Well, now look what's come of it!"

"Hannah! Remember that's my husband you're speaking of! How can you speak ill of him in front of me? He's a good man, good to me and Freya,"

"A good man? No! Never! I've held my tongue long enough! That man's evil and if you've got any sense you'll take young Freya and leave."

Lizzie was astounded at this outburst, so violent, so unexpected. Her mind went blank, numbed by the force of the attack. Then she thought of Freya. She would be waking soon. What was she going to say to her?

"I'll be over after breakfast to give you a hand," said Hannah.
"I cannot come till I've seen George and told him what's happened. He'll know what's to be done."

Lizzie turned away and retraced her steps.

She found Freya standing in the kitchen beside the table. Freya had woken a few minutes before and, finding no one in the big bed, she had come downstairs to look for Lizzie.

"Why is Sam on the table, Mam? What's happened to his face? Why is he cold? He's cold all over. Where's his clothes? Why has he not got his clothes on?"

"Sam won't need his clothes any more. He's ... he's gone away." The words were stupid and Lizzie regretted them as soon as they were uttered.

"No he hasn't! He's here!" Freya's brow puckered in puzzlement. "And he's not asleep. If he was asleep, his knees would be pulled up. He always sleeps like that, like the warrior!"

Lizzie had no idea what Freya was talking about. She went up and put her hands on the points of Freya's shoulders. She could feel the small bony angles, the cornerstones of her tiny frame, vulnerable yet resilient, warm and alive. Lizzie's hands tightened around the child, drawing strength and comfort from the small body.

"Come away upstairs Freya, and get dressed! You'll have to help Hannah today."

It was afternoon before Andro returned with the coffin, a simple box, which they carried into the parlour.

The room, little used since Will's death, had been a source of great pride to Mary. The walls were covered with a richly patterned wallpaper of large pink cabbage roses. On the wall opposite the window hung an oil-painting of David depicted as a simple shepherd lad, fair-haired and ruddy, with his sling lying on a rock. In an alcove there was a bookshelf made of simple wooden boards. The works of Strabo, Herodian and Tacitus had once been read out loud in this lonely place. There was Wallis's *Northumbria*, *Paradise Lost* and *Paradise Regained*. *The Pilgrim's Progress* had been acquired in parts and bound together in a single volume. There were books of folklore, stories of ghosts and apparitions, *The Astrologer's Magazine* and a colonial edition of *In The Back of The Black Man's Mind*. The almost total absence of novels was due to Will's father who mistrusted all such works which, he asserted, were full of made-up things and, since he repeatedly reminded all the members of his family that they must always tell the truth, a prohibition had fallen on the work of the novelist.

Will Hetherton's father had been a man of erudition. Along with the other shepherds' children from round about, he had been taught to read, to write in elegant copperplate and to calculate. It had been the custom in such isolated places as Glittering Shiel to find a teacher who would come and lodge in the house for a few weeks. Each family paid a few pence a week towards the modest salary of the dominie who would return on a regular basis to resume the children's education.

The coffin was set down on a pair of three-legged stools. Hannah came over and Freya was sent out with some corn in a wooden bowl. Hannah told her to feed the hens and after that to make a thorough search for eggs.

Before they put Sam into the coffin, Hannah told Lizzie to go to the press and look out the best linen in the house. Then she proceeded to shroud the mirror above the fireplace, explaining that Sam no longer needed to see his earthly image and that the folk who would be coming to the wake must be spared the dread sight of a corpse looking over their shoulders.

Hannah fetched the great, iron-bound Hetherton family Bible and laid it on a table beside a glass dome containing a peregrine falcon that had once stooped over Cheviot. Now, thanks to taxidermist's art, it was forever frozen at the moment of alighting, its talons clasped around a piece of Cheviot rock.

Together the women laid Sam in the coffin. Without a word Hannah fetched a small, brown-glazed dish from the dresser. She put a little salt in it and laid it on Sam's breast. Then gently but firmly she doubled his thumbs within his hands.

"It has to be done, lassie," she said, seeing Lizzie's troubled face. "We have to do everything we can to protect the lad till he finds his rest." Then she began to murmur. "To everything there is a season, a time to be born and a time to die." She shook her head sadly. "That's just it. It wasn't his right time. He should have taken after his namesake in the good book and lived a long life."

"Shall we put the lid on the coffin?" asked Lizzie.

"No! Not until he leaves the house. Folk will expect to see him and bid him farewell."

It was a relief to let Hannah take charge. Lizzie willingly became once more the servant girl meekly obeying the older woman's instructions.

"You'd better fetch some of that braxie ewe that was butchered and salted down the other week. There'll be a fair crowd here tonight and they'll be wanting food to see them through the night."

As evening fell Lizzie went outside. She took Freya by the hand and together they walked beside the Eidon Burn up to the small field where the cow was waiting to be brought in for milking. In the summer they milked her there at the dyke-back and carried the milk back to the house. Andro was nowhere to be seen. He must have shut the collie dogs in the byre that morning because when she went into the byre they were hungry and eager to get out. She had not seen George all day and Hannah had said nothing of his whereabouts. The only sign of activity outside was the smouldering remains of the fire on which Andro had burnt Sam's clothes. Fortunately Freya did not notice the thin curl of smoke rising from the pyre and Lizzie chose not to take the path which would have led them past it.

As they made their way to the field Lizzie looked westward to Maidenhope. The long back of Cheviot was momentarily hidden in a bank of clouds. Lizzie looked hard at the hills. Beyond the familiar lines of Cheviot there lay an unknown country. Coverdale, the dwelling place of the Hethertons, lay sequestered in the folds of the smooth green hills that stretched away northwards into Scotland. They would surely take the direct route over the hills. For a few seconds she fancied she saw a horse and some figures in the far distance, but then they seemed to vanish and she decided it must have been her imagination. A boulder or the reflection of the clouds on the fell could create the strangest effects, especially in someone as troubled as Lizzie.

Night, when it fell, was pitch-black. The curtains in the parlour had been closed all day. Now Lizzie drew the ones in the kitchen as well. Everything seemed so reassuring and normal in the kitchen with food ready in the pot and a bright fire in the grate. But Lizzie was on edge, nervous. Hannah had filled her with a great sense of expectancy, yet she hardly knew who or what she was waiting for. If only Andro would come back so she would not have to face the visitors alone. Only he could explain the circumstances of Sam's death.

Nevertheless the sharp rap at the door came as a surprise. At first Lizzie was confused because the knocking came not from the back door but from the front. Only strangers or the minister ever troubled to walk round to the front of the house before making their presence known.

Nervously Lizzie fumbled with the two large bolts on the front door. Being little used, they were stiff and she could hardly see what she was doing. In her haste, she had left the lamp on the table and only a little light came through from the kitchen. At last the bolts were pulled back and she opened the door.

A tall man wearing a bowler hat, with a leather riding crop in one hand stood before her. Behind him there was a woman and a child, but Lizzie could not make out who they were. She guessed that the man was Hob Hetherton, Will Hetherton's younger brother. Once, when cleaning in the parlour, she had found a photograph of Will tucked in the back of the painting of David. Now she saw a family resemblance. Both men had the same determined jaw line and Sam would have had it too had he lived to manhood.

Hob scarcely glanced at Lizzie before raising the crop to motion her aside and enter the house. The words of greeting she had practised froze on her lips as she stood with her back flattened against the wall of the porch. A moment of hesitation followed while Hob decided whether to go into the parlour, the door of which was closed, or the kitchen. He chose the latter and, turning to Lizzie, he said curtly, "The old lady's out the back on her cuddy. Away with you and help her!"

Lizzie needed no second bidding. With eyes downcast, she slipped out the front door past Hob's companions and round the west end of the house to the yard at the back.

A byre lantern had been set on the stone wall and close by stood a pair of horses. Janet Hetherton, despite her years and the long journey across the borderland, was sitting ramrod-straight in the saddle. Lizzie went up to her.

"Good Evening. I'm Lizzie Man," she said politely.

"I know fine who you are, young woman!" the old lady replied. "Now then, help me down off this nag!"

Lizzie led the animal to the cheese press so the old lady could dismount. She was wearing a black beaver hat tied down over her ears with a shawl. Her vast, woollen skirts were spread over the horse's hindquarters and her legs, encased in tightly buttoned boots, were thrust firmly into the stirrups. Lizzie stood by ready to help her lift her leg over the saddle, but Janet, taking her time, dismounted unaided. Then she straightened her skirts and turned to look at the house.

"It's many a long year since I came to this house and I never thought to come here again. It's sad circumstances that have brought me back. Lead the way, lassie, the gear can be brought in later on."

The Hethertons had come prepared. Lizzie saw the neck of a grey hen, no doubt filled with whisky, protruding from one of the panniers on the second horse, a rugged dun pony.

Lizzie went back inside and found the Hethertons in the parlour, gathered round the coffin. The old lady approached stiffly and gazed long and hard at Sam.

"The devil's had a hand in this!" she said. "My son gone before his time and now my grandson!"

She put her hand into the folds of her coat of grey Melton cloth and drew out a small bundle of ivy, laurel and rosemary which she laid in the coffin.

"But, Mother!" said Hob. "How can you know? Will you not wait till Andro's had his say. We must not be over quick to judge!"

36

"Away with you, Hob Hetherton! The Lord himself will be quick to judge! Aye, vengeance is mine, I will repay! Those are the Lord's very own words!" the old woman riposted with the fire of the righteous. Then she looked around the room and her eyes lit on the Bible. She walked over and undid the iron clasp. "I mind well the day twice seven years since that your father wrote the lad's name in here," she said to Hob as the long, horny nail of her index finger traced the flowing lines of script. "And now it's to be struck out before its time." Then she let the heavy, leather-bound cover fall shut with a soft thud. Suddenly overcome with weariness, she turned away and sank into a chair.

4

By eleven o'clock that night the parlour was full of people gathered for the lyke-wake. Hannah and George came into the house at about nine o'clock with Jenny Robson, Mary Hetherton's mother.

The news of her grandson's death had reached the workhouse in West Street, Willove, by mid afternoon. News, especially bad news, travelled the country at lightning speed. Jenny had gone straight to the keeper to ask his permission to leave her tasks in the kitchen and had set off immediately to walk the ten miles to Glittering Shiel.

She stopped off to call on her old friend, Lilian Matheson, at the Home Farm on the Heron estate. It was as if she was expected, for the table was laid ready for tea with scones and spice cake. After she had eaten and rested a while, the two women, accompanied by Will, Lilian's husband, went on to Glittering Shiel.

Jenny and Lilian were walking together several paces behind Will.

"D'you believe in second sight?" asked Jenny hesitantly.

"That all depends."

"On what?"

"On the circumstances. Come on, Jenny! Out with it! What's on your mind?"

"Well, the strangest thing happened to me last night. It was late and I was sitting quietly by the fire when I heard at tap at the window. I went over and pulled back the curtain to see who it was and whose face did I see? Sam's! So of course I let the curtain drop and went to let him in. But when I opened the door, there was nobody there, not a soul!"

"Maybe you imagined it?"

"No! I could swear it was Sam," said Jenny firmly.

"Well then, it was Halloween last night. It could have been some young lad having a bit of fun. You know what nonsense the young ones can get up to."

"I thought of that, but I'm sure it was Sam. I was in such a state I didn't get a wink of sleep all night. I had this terrible feeling that something was amiss and then today, when Tom Pagon's lad came knocking, I knew before he opened his mouth what he'd come for."

"The only other thing I can think of," said Lilian reflectively, "is that it was an apparition."

"An apparition?"

"Yes, my granny used to talk about them. She used to say that sometimes an apparition would appear at the time the real person died."

"That's spooky and no mistake! Oh dear, I cannot make sense of it and I've still got this terrible feeling in the pit of my stomach. I know it's to do with Sam and to tell you the honest truth, I'm dreading the moment I see his face again!"

They walked on in silence for a few minutes.

"There's no doubt about it, it's a terrible business!" said Lilian. "You never liked Andro Man, did you?"

"No, I did not! I saw how he wheedled his way into Will Hetherton's good books. I warned our Mary, but she would have none of it. The fact is she was besotted with the man."

"Bewitched more like!"

"What d'you mean, bewitched?"

"Well, maybe I should hold my tongue, but since you've no more kin at Glittering Shiel, what difference does it make? It was a year or two back. I never whispered a word about it to anybody, not even Will."

"What?"

"It was Hannah. One night she happened to let drop she had this notion that Andro Man was in the service of Satan!"

"In the service of Satan! Whatever made her think that?"

"It was the signs."

"What signs?"

39

"The marks of the devil!"

"What marks?"

"That foot of his for one thing."

"That's just a natural deformity."

"A cloven foot more like!"

"Oh, my goodness! What else?"

"That garter. He only ever wears the one. Ask yourself why that should be."

Jenny shook her head. "I don't know, I really don't! All this is beyond my understanding. All I know is that for the past seven years the angel of death's been a regular visitor to Glittering Shiel. First Will, then Mary and her baby, and now Sam."

By this time they were approaching the ford below the old still. There they came upon Agnes and Bartholemew Dunne from Hoarstones and together the small band wound their way up Eidonhope's desolate track.

Every chair, bench and stool in the house had been carried into the parlour. The lid had been put on the coffin so that it could be used as a table. The grey hen had been brought in and there was a keg of ale tapped ready on a side table. Rough barley bread, a boiled ham and a cheese lay unbroached upon the coffin board.

Andro's absence created an air of tense expectancy. His name had been on everyone's lips as they walked up Eidonhope, but the second they entered the farmhouse he had not been mentioned. However, the question of his whereabouts, the necessity for him to give an account of himself, was at the forefront of everyone's mind.

While they waited they ate, drank and reminisced about past times, happier times. Lizzie was kept busy running to and fro, fetching glasses and attending to everyone's needs. Once she thought she heard the back door close quietly and a footstep on the stairs, but when she went to look, there was no one.

Andro appeared just before midnight. Gaunt and ashen, he had taken some care over his appearance. He had washed and shaved and put on a white collarless shirt and a pair of velveteen breeches, the colour of moleskin. The garter of plaited leather he usually wore around his right calf had been exchanged for a more elaborate one of red and blue wool which was knotted in a sort of cockade. He moved from the doorway of the dimly lit room into the circle of light cast by the candles on the coffin.

Hob rose to his feet. "So, Andro Man, you've decided to show your face at long last!"

"I know well enough what you're all thinking," Andro began. "You're saying to yourselves that responsibility for Sam's death lies with me. Well, I'll not gainsay that! He was with me last night, right enough! I dare say I should've kept him close, kept an eye on him like, but he was dead set on getting some fish without any help from me, so I left him to get on with it and made my way up the water ahead of him. Just ask yourselves, would I harm the lad? After all, his father, Will Hetherton, was good to me!" Then before going on, Andro turned and looked at Lizzie. "Lizzie here will tell you. We took it for our bounden duty to treat the lad like he was our own son. You may not know it, but the sad fact is that my Lizzie cannot have a bairn and, as you all know my bairn by Mary died with her. So there it is! Young Sam was the closest to a son that I was like to get!"

Andro's words won him a measure of sympathy, for if the hill folk were slow to accept a stranger, they were equally slow to condemn a man.

Then Janet Hetherton rose to her feet. "Harm him? Who more like to harm him than you? You shiftied all about the countryside for your living before you got yourself fastened on here!"

"I was good at my work as anybody will tell you! If I wasn't, Will would never have asked me to stay on," replied Andro defensively. Then, suddenly realising that there was nothing he could say to make the old lady change her mind, he added, "If you are minded to think the worst of me, Mrs Hetherton, then there's no more to be said! But if it's some sort of tod you think I am, then answer me this, does the tod not keep his own hole clean?"

41

"His own hole clean?" said the old lady, eyes ablaze. "So that's how you've got it figured out, is it? This is the tod's very own hole, is it? This house and hill and sheep what have belonged to me and mine for over three hundred years! Well my wee manny, it's my opinion that you've been getting too big for your boots!"

"According to the law this place belongs to me," said Andro angrily. "The Lord himself knows the sweat I've put into it. Mary and me tied the knot good and tight at Coldstream Bridge End and I have the marriage lines to prove it. As the Lord is my witness, I never wanted harm to come to Sam, but what's done is done and since he's gone, by rights this place must come to me."

"By rights!" hissed Janet. "What's all this talk of rights? The law's no more to us than it is to the likes of you - handy at times and useless at others! Never mind, I'll tell you one thing, Andro Man, we'll be taking what's ours, if not now, then tomorrow, or tomorrow's tomorrow!"

Her energy spent, Janet Hetherton proudly walked from the room. Alison, Hob's wife accompanied her upstairs to the bedroom above the parlour where her son, Robert, a lad of nine, lay asleep. Alison had pleaded with Hob to leave him in Coverdale, but Hob and his mother had insisted that he come, saying that one day it might fall to Robert to right the wrong done to the family and that he must therefore be present at the arvel dinner.

If anybody felt sorry for Andro or doubted the justice of Janet's accusations, they held their tongue. Respect for the Hethertons went too deep for public dissent.

Andro neither ate nor drank and, after a short time he went and sat beside Bartholemew Dunne.

"Bart, I've been wanting a word with you. I'm needing some fresh blood in the flock. Have you a ram I could have?"

Bart got out his pipe, then he began to delve in his pocket for his tobacco and knife. As he was paring some tobacco off the plug he said, "Well now, I might. What sort of ram would you be after?" At this point he stopped rubbing the tobacco in the palm

42

of his hand and looked Andro straight in the eye. "A black one maybe?"

Andro hesitated for a second or two, not knowing what to make of this remark. "Well, I haven't really made up my mind. Have you got a black one I could have?"

"Oh aye, I've got one all right," said Bart tamping tobacco into the bowl of his pipe, "but I've got plans for him." Then he struck a match on the sole of his boot and lit the pipe. "No, Andro Man, it seems I cannot help you."

Andro stayed in the room only a short time after that. He knew his presence was a blight on the gathering. He had no wish to be there, but he stayed a few minutes more, for the sake of form. He had no intention of letting the Hethertons chase him from his own parlour.

As Andro made to leave, Hob spoke up. "It's all settled then! There's to be an arvel dinner at noon tomorrow before Sam goes down to the church. Mind you come!"

Andro made no reply. He knew he must attend. If he did not stand the test, he might as well leave Glittering Shiel that very instant. There was nothing more to be said and so he left.

With Andro gone, the tension eased and the assembled company settled down to see the night through. Lizzie was questioned at length about Andro and Sam. She told them what she knew about the events of the previous night, taking care to speak of Andro's recent acts of kindness to the lad. They listened carefully to what she said. Her affection for Sam was clear to all and her deep distress at what had befallen him. Her wifely loyalty earned respect even though the best they could do was suspend judgment for the time being and wait on events.

As they drank, the conversation became more animated until eventually they fell to telling stories to while away the hours. Every story brought forth another, stranger than the one before, and in that space between darkening and daylight where time hangs suspended, skeins of words came spinning forth and were once more woven into the patterns of a shared history. Together they drank the delicate, northern nectar, pale gold distillation of the very hills over which daily they tramped. As its fire, redolent of peat and crystalline streams, rose on the tongue the collective imagination was rekindled. The parlour, no more a humdrum homely place, became instead the chamber of death where the invisible world trenched on the visible. Events long buried, memories laid down in some forgotten past, were made present and presents made of them from one to all. Familiar places were rendered strange and all the countryside became a land of legend. Safe within the hallowed circle of candlelight, tales were told with Border humour and courage about Satan and evil done and undone.

George was the first to speak. "This one was told by Will Hetherton himself. There was a minister up on Tweedside and he was going home very late one dark night when his horse stumbled and the good man was flung to the ground. Then he heard a loud laugh, so full of wickedness and scorn that he had no doubt who it was. But the minister had a stout heart and so he cried out, 'Aye, Satan, you may laugh! But when I fall, I can get up again. When you fell, you never rose!'"

"That's a grand tale, George," said Jenny Robson.

"Aye, it most certainly is!" echoed Hannah. "We need plenty more folk like the minister to send the devil and his minions into the fires of hell where they belong!"

Many a guttering candle had been taken to light another as the hours passed. The sight of Hannah's leathery, work-hardened fingers as she held the flickering flame prompted Jenny Robson to tell the well-known tale of the 'Hand of Glory', a murderer's hand with the power to send the inhabitants of a house to sleep while they were robbed. When Jenny had finished her story they all sat quiet for a few minutes.

Hob was gazing thoughtfully at his own strong hands. After a time he raised his right arm in the air. "A hand can be raised for good or ill," he said. "I know the Lord's commandment well enough! Thou shalt not kill! But it's long been the custom with us Hethertons and with plenty more besides, at the christening of a boy child to leave the bairn's right hand out of the ceremony.

That leaves him free in times of deadly feud to strike unhallowed blows on the enemies of his kinfolk. So it was with me and with young Robert asleep upstairs. At noon this day before this coffin lid is nailed down, every man and woman present here, aye and Andro Man as well, will take their turn and lay their hand on my dead nephew. Them what's innocent need have no fear, for in doing this their dreams will ever be sweet and untroubled. But if guilty party there be, in deed or thought, his hand will surely bring forth blood from this bloodless corpse."

As the pale light of day chased night's dark imaginings, Alison Hetherton closed the small sash window in the parlour. Sam's soul, free at last, would have taken flight and gone to a better place. If Alison had looked out of the window, she would have seen Andro Man, wrapped up tight in his plaid with his back against the wall beneath the window. Though driven from the room, he had listened to everything that had been said.

No one showed any sign of tiredness as they shared the morning tasks. They were a people used to sleepless nights spent caring for animals or dancing reels to the strains of the fiddle.

When Freya woke, she found the house full of stangers. Already distressed about Sam, she was further confused and overcome by the presence of so many people. Lizzie took her into the bedroom to meet Robert, explaining that he was Sam's cousin from over the hills.

"Is he going to stay here instead of Sam?"

"No, lassie. He has to go back to Coverdale with his mother and father and granny. Now then, I want you to be a good lassie and show him round the place. You can have your breakfast and then maybe the two of you could take a walk up the burn to see the stones."

Hob disappeared for most of the morning. Lizzie saw him cross the yard after breakfast and knock on George and Hannah's door. Andro too had vanished. Since the collies were no longer in the byre, Lizzie assumed he had gone to look the sheep.

As noon approached, Lizzie looked down the valley and saw a tall figure clothed in black like a huge corbie crow making his way towards Glittering Shiel. It was Mr Dogberry, the minister from Herontop. At one time he had been a regular visitor to the farm where it was his custom to hold a meeting in the parlour once a month. Everybody from the farms round about would attend the simple service and enjoy a communal supper afterwards. However, since Will Hetherton's death, the minister's visits had stopped because Andro had given him no encouragement.

The parlour had been cleared of chairs. The coffin stood open in the middle of the room.

Janet Hetherton was the first to bid Sam farewell. Her anger of the previous night seemed to have gone. Sorrowing, she bent and kissed his forehead and ran her fingers over his boyish curls. With the exception of Robert and Freya, who nevertheless were witnesses to the ritual, everyone complied with the ancient injunction and touched the corpse. Then they stood in a circle around the coffin to wait for Andro.

He came in, dressed as he had been the night before.

"You know what's expected," said Hob.

Andro nodded and then, like a wooden-limbed automaton, he advanced three or four paces to the coffin. Bending at the waist, he inclined the upper part of his body until his face was immediately above Sam's head. There he remained, poised and motionless.

Suddenly, he looked up and his eyes travelled round the room from one person to the next. He knew what was going through their minds. They thought he was hesitating, they were convinced of his guilt.

There was a slight movement of the lips, then he nodded his head imperceptibly as if he had come to some decision. Glancing at Hob, he raised his right hand high and pressed his fingers to his lips. Then he turned to Sam and laid his fingers on the boy's lips as if swearing him to silence.

46

Though silence ensued, the room was turbulent. Andro's gesture, though it answered Hob's demand, seemed to betoken other things besides. It was as if there was some sort of bond, a pact between Andro and Sam, as if, in some way, the boy was his. Those present dimly perceived in Andro a power that exceeded the ties of family, a power that had its origins in primeval belief, a belief that on occasion required the sacrifice of a boy.

The silence was finally broken by Mr Dogberry who came into the room, flushed and rosy pink, from his long walk. With Bible and prayer-book clasped to his breast, he brought with him into the turbid room the reassuring certainties of the cloth.

5

More than two years had passed since Sam was carried down to the churchyard at Herontop. Hannah and George, with all their goods and chattels, had walked down the same track only a few days later. Lizzie did not know what had passed between Andro and George, but they had had words, harsh words, with no going back.

At one time George had thought to end his days at Glittering Shiel. He belonged to that special breed of Cheviot shepherds who were as thoroughly hefted onto the heather-black hills as the sheep they tended. While the hinds and byremen of the lowlands accepted the annual hiring system, which could mean packing up family and belongings and moving to a different farm, the shepherds tended to stay in one place. It took much more than a year for a shepherd to really know his sheep and the hills over which they raked. Apart from that, a shepherd's livelihood was enmeshed with that of his boss since his wages were paid not in cash but in kind.

With Sam's death the long-standing association between George and the Hethertons had come to an end. George and Hannah were the last link with the old days when the hills and stock of Glittering Shiel were as carefully maintained and husbanded as the chattels and plenishings in the house. Cheviot lambs from Glittering Shiel habitually fetched the highest prices at the autumn sales at Willove and thus George had shared both pride and profit with Will Hetherton. But those golden days were past and the number of Cheviot sheep had declined to be replaced by the sturdier blackfaces who were better able to take care of themselves.

So in early November Bill Havagal came up from Willove with his flat cart to flit George and Hannah, except it was not a proper flitting since such an event occurred only on the twelfth of

48

May when all work on the farms would cease and the roads were thronged with carts carrying the possessions of those families who were going to a new home.

Lizzie had not dared question Hannah about their plans. Hannah was a proud woman who would not have shared her anxieties with Lizzie. The couple were getting on in years and it was unlikely that they had managed to save much money for their old age. Lizzie was afraid that they would have to face the shame of applying for parish relief which was a rare occurrence among the proud hill folk who usually managed to hold fast to their independence even if it meant finding a home with their children. Lizzie thought, however, that if they could get through the winter months, there was a good chance that George would find employment at the hirings the following March. He was a good shepherd, quick to spot the early signs of the diseases sheep were prone to and renowned for his sure eye when a new ram was to be bought at the annual sale over the border at Kelso.

Lizzie had never been a stranger to hard work, but the two years that followed George and Hannah's departure were unremitting in their drudgery. Often Lizzie and Freya were left alone at Glittering Shiel while Andro went out into the world. Sometimes he would go away for days on end to work as a drover or at harvest time he would earn extra cash as a hired hand on one of the big arable farms in the fertile lowland plain bordering the North Sea.

When Andro was away, Lizzie would be up before dawn and away out onto the hills with the collie dogs. As soon as her legs were long enough Freya would battle her way through the heather, following Lizzie wherever she went.

Freya had her own special tasks. Twice a day she carried water from the spring in the little field. The pail was heavy but she found she could manage if she only filled it half-full. She fed the hens and shut them up in the evening so that the foxes that lived up on Warrior Crag would not snatch them away in the night.

Then there were the pigs to feed and clean out. There were usually two in the sties built onto the end of the byre. One of the sows had recently farrowed and had so many piglets that she did not have a teat for each, so Freya was allowed to creep inside the sty with a bottle of milk for the unlucky piglet. She liked the sweetish smell, the warmth of the dark, enclosed space. She would squat down quietly on her haunches and wait until the sow made a special grunt which was the signal that milk would soon flood down into her teats. As soon as they heard it, the piglets would rush, squealing and clambering over one another, to fasten their mouths around a teat and suck the milk till it overflowed the corners of their mouths.

One morning Freya was ready with the bottle of milk only to find that every piglet had a teat. She searched the sty, but the piglet was nowhere to be found so she hurried off to tell Lizzie.

"Like as not the little one got squashed and your dad took it away," said Lizzie, reluctant to tell Freya that a sow sometimes ate flesh, even one of her own piglets.

Observing the piglets was Freya's only contact with the hurly-burly of family life, of play and rivalry between brothers and sisters. She knew no family. Although she called Andro, dad, and Lizzie, mam, she had no sense of herself as part of a family. Of course, when she was very small, Sam had been there, but they had never been children together and she had never thought of him as a child like herself.

Freya's playground was the Eidon Burn. The stream emerged from a narrow defile about half a mile to the west of the farmhouse before spreading itself in generous loops through several small fields enclosed and protected by dry-stone walls. She gradually got to know all the stones in the burn that were of any consequence to her. She knew the best ones for sitting on when she wanted to dip her toes into the water and those that were solidly anchored for when she wanted to use them as stepping stones. At first this child's knowledge was limited to the farmyard, the small garden in front of the house and the bank of the burn, but as she grew older, she extended her territory, crossing the burn at points of her own choosing, and thus gaining access to the fields and Dancing Maidens beyond.

The standing stones, which were known as the Dancing Maidens, stood on the fell outside the boundary of the fields. They, like the stone walls, were the work of man and yet their purpose had become enigmatic. Great unhewn boulders of porphyry, their pitted surfaces were a rich canvas of colour and texture composed of shaggy lichens, palest sage, dark brown spatterings, common grey and vibrant ochre. The stones, several of which now lay on their sides, formed an oval from the centre of which the eye could look fifteen miles east to the sea, while behind them rose the perfect symmetry of Maidenhope. It was a prehistoric belvedere, a high, open place without wall or roof, where once the priests of the ancient Britons had worshipped and made their sacrifices.

Upstream from the house the burn, like a majestic river meandering through the lushest lowland meadow, had cut a serpentine course. There were several short stretches of sandy shore each with a shallow cliff behind, which had been made by the flood waters that had washed away the sandy soil and left hollowed-out bays with grassy, root-matted roofs. The sheep would seek out these sheltered recesses and their fleeces would get caught on the tough, twisted roots. Freya would go there to collect wool to put in the sack that Lizzie kept on the back of the scullery door and when she had collected as much as she could, she would go to her favourite spot.

With twoscore pairs of curious yet indifferent eyes fastened upon her, she would hooch herself under the grassy cliff, draw her knees up under her chin and gaze at the water as it slipped downstream. It rippled smoothly down the sides of the slippery stones, yet remained curiously still where it encountered a stone head-on. She noticed how the water, unlike a twig or leaf that chance might beach forever, always found its way downstream even if it was delayed for a time in some foamy backwater.

Since Sam's death, Andro had taken more notice of Freya. Often he would tell her to come and sit on his knee after supper.

She would sit motionless, sometimes staring into the fire or perhaps looking at his hand as it rested on the smooth skin of her knee. She noticed how the short black hairs on the back of his fingers rose clear of the skin, then curved down like the fine claws of a kitten; the curvature of his powerful hands as they lay at rest made her think of the grape, the fork with curved tines, that hung in the byre. And he had a particular smell - a blend of homemade soap made from rendered sheep fat and eek, the oil in sheep's wool, with which the front of his leather-bound waistcoat was shinily impregnated.

Lizzie smiled to see Freya on Andro's lap. The two of them sitting there by the fire was the very picture of a happy hearth and home, though it did occur to her sometimes that Freya sat strangely still for such a young child. She never seemed to wriggle or fidget and Lizzie wondered sometimes whether she did not slip away the moment she got the chance.

Freya was pleased that Andro took more notice of her. This was not so much for herself as for Lizzie. She saw the contentment on Lizzie's face as she sat in the chair on the other side of the fire, her head bent over her knitting.

Often when they were alone together Lizzie would start a sentence with "Your dad'll be wanting ..." or if she had forgotten Freya was there, she might say quietly to herself, "Now then, he'll be expecting me to ..." so that Freya soon understood that all things were measured by the yardstick of Andro's desire, that his pleasure came before everything else. How or why that should be were questions Freya was too young either to ask or to answer, but in her way she understood that it was so.

Early one afternoon she was walking along the cobbled path in front of the byre. The door was open and as she passed she glimpsed a figure inside. It was Andro. He had his back to her and she could hear a splashing noise. Sensing that there was someone there, he turned to look.

Once he had seen her, escape seemed impossible so she stood rooted to the spot, confused, not knowing what to do. Andro turned to face her and she saw that his breeches were unbuttoned.

"Come over here!" he said. "I've something to show you!"

Freya stepped into the doorway.

"Aye, that's it! Come in and shut the door! Come on, now, there's no need to look so worried. I'll not harm you. No more will this fellow," he added, looking down. "Now then, Lizzie's been on at me saying it's high time you began your education. Well, how about this? This fellow here is a man's thing and it's not just for widdling with neither! You can hold it, it'll not bite!" he added with a laugh.

Freya lifted her hand and placed it lightly on the soft brown skin.

"No! No! That'll not do!" said Andro impatiently. Then he put his hand over hers and bent her fingers round. "Like this. Now then, see this, eh?" Slowly and rhythmically he began to make her hand move to and fro. "See how polite he is? He always stands up for a lady! This is what it's all about! Lizzie likes it fine when I stick this up inside her of a night! That's what he's for this fine fellow of mine!"

Andro's breathing changed and began to get shorter and shorter until at last he could contain himself no longer. Suddenly he turned away and Freya heard him moan gently.

After a minute he spoke to her brusquely. "You'd best be off! And not a word to Lizzie, d'you understand? This is just between the two of us."

Freya fled to the dark bosky safety of a grove of alders beside the burn at the bottom of the garden. One venerable tree, its huge central bole ensconced on a stony island, spread its boughs out over the water, in one place elbowing an enormous boulder. Freya liked to sit above the water on one particular moss-covered bough which she could get to without getting her feet wet. She sat and listened to the music of the burn, letting it drown out all other noise including the pounding of her heart. She looked at her hand, then sniffed it. It was a strange smell. She decided she did not like it, so she climbed down from her perch, went back to the bank, knelt down and plunged her hand into the brown water.

Later, unobserved, she emerged from the garden and crept up the stairs to her tiny room above the scullery. At supper time Lizzie came up and found her curled up, fast asleep.

"What's the matter?" asked Lizzie.

At first Freya did not reply, then without looking into Lizzie's eyes, she said softly, "Nothing."

Lizzie left her in bed, clutching her special scrap of faded blue flannel. It had not been washed more than three or four times because she would never part with it, saying that it did not smell right after it had been washed.

Andro was in a good mood at supper time. He complimented Lizzie on the food. Freya ate almost nothing though Andro did not notice.

"Did you know, Lizzie, Freya's been giving me a hand this afternoon?"

"Oh! I was wondering where she'd got to! What were the pair of you up to?"

Andro had not anticipated the question. "Doing some jobs in the byre!" he replied, smiling at Freya. "She's coming on grand! She'll be even better in a year or two when she's a bit bigger."

Lizzie saw her opportunity and took it. "Andro, I want her to start school in September. She'll be eight by then. I want her to have some education, she mustn't be like me, only able to read a few words. She's a bright lassie, always looking at the books in the parlour, asking me what they say and it pains me that I cannot answer her questions."

"What about the cost? It might be just a penny or two a week but it's to find! Money's tight, you know that well enough."

"Felix said he'd send what he could for her schooling. If you would write a letter, he'd do his best, I'm sure."

"Aye, all right then! We've got to see to your education, have we not, Freya?"

Freya had remained silent throughout the conversation. The idea of going to school both excited and frightened her. Lizzie often talked to her about it, though Lizzie's idea of what went on in school was pieced together second-hand. She had never had

54

the good fortune to cross the threshold of the National School at Seamouth.

"Anyway, she might have a bit company going down to the school," said Andro.

"What do you mean, company?"

"Well, I've half a mind to see about hiring a shepherd after the turn of the year. That bothy's been empty for far too long and this place is too much for just the two of us."

"But what about wages?"

"I might get a man cheap if he's got a wife tied up with babies. What with the drop in corn prices and one thing and another, it's hard for a man to get hired without he's got a woman ready to work on the farm as well."

This was news indeed. The possibility of a family coming to Glittering Shiel, another woman, children, company for herself and Freya. It was something Lizzie had dreamt of, but had hardly dared hope for.

"Mind, I'm not making any promises. I'll have to see."

Lizzie was more than content at this. Happier than she had been for many a month, she set about clearing away the supper dishes. Then she realised that Freya, who had neither eaten nor spoken, showed no sign of moving from the table. Concerned, Lizzie went and lifted her into her arms and gave her a hug.

"Come on, Freya! Can it be my turn now? Will you give me a hand? And after we've finished the dishes, we'll go and shut the hens up so they'll be safe from the fox."

Andro smiled as they left the room. He was feeling good, believing that he had more than compensated for what he had done that afternoon.

6

Freya was sitting on the big boulder by the gate, looking down the valley of Eidonhope watching for the first glimpse of the newcomers. On an escarpment above the burn stood a stell. It was a perfect circle of dry-stone wall topped with a row of stones cushioned on turves. It had been built to give the sheep protection from the savage, winter winds which had on occasion been known to sweep the hapless animals away and deposit them on some foreign hill.

The cow was grazing close to the stell along with a few Cheviot ewes and their lambs. It was cold and the lambs' backs were arched against the northeast wind. The warrior lay to the south, his stony features motionless as ever.

Freya remembered, as she had many a time before, the day she had sat on the boulder and Hannah had told her about the warrior. She often went there to look at him, to marvel at his great size and to dream about who he was and what deeds he had done. At first she had thought she would be able to see him from any point along the northern side of the valley, but for some strange reason, all she could see from other places was a crag, a wide fell and a smooth hill and so she always returned to the boulder.

She had decided that despite Hannah's doubts the warrior was a good man. She clung tenaciously to this idea. Lizzie often told her that Andro too was a good man, providing for them the way he did. She seemed to believe that if she kept on saying that Andro was a good man, he would somehow become one, though this neither convinced nor comforted Freya.

Freya's knowledge of the intimate relations between Andro and Lizzie came from Andro, from what he said to her. She began to imagine what went on between the two of them at night in the big, iron bed with its loops and curlicues. Fearful for Lizzie, Freya would lie in her narrow bed listening to the noises coming from across the landing. Andro often told her how much Lizzie enjoyed what he did to her with his man's thing, but Freya was not convinced because Andro told her she would like what he did to her, but she did not. Not that she would have dared say so. Just as Lizzie locked certain things away in a distant recess of her mind, so too Freya learnt that some things had to remain unspoken. Thus, as far as their relations with Andro were concerned, a wall of silence separated the woman from the girl so that, although they were continually in each other's company, in this respect, they remained divided and alone.

Andro's encounters with Freya always took place beyond the walls of the farmhouse, in the buildings or, more often, out on the hills.

One hot day the previous summer Lizzie had handed Freya a basket containing bread, cheese and a bottle of homemade ginger cordial.

"Take that up to your dad!" she said. "You know where to find him, don't you?"

"Yes. He's cutting peat on Cockslack."

Freya soon found Andro. He was in a deep trench, stripped to the waist, slicing a winged spade down through a thick layer of fibrous peat.

He smiled as she approached. "I'm right glad to see you! What have you got in that basket for a hungry man?"

She brought the basket to him and set it down on the damp mossy ground. He climbed out of the smooth trench with its dark, chocolate-cake walls and undid the stopper from the glass bottle. He took several long draughts, then picked up his shirt to wipe his mouth.

"That's a whole sight better. Come over here and sit beside me!"

He lay down on his back with his knees pulled up. His face and neck were tanned and weather-beaten and Freya noticed a line around his neck where his shirt ended, below which his chest was waxy white.

After a while he sat up and reached for his jacket. It was draped over his stick which he had plunged into the ground before starting work. He drew a flask from the pocket and took a mouthful or two of whisky. Then he rolled over onto his front which brought him close to Freya who was sitting quietly nearby waiting for him to eat the food. He smiled at her as if he were about to indulge her, perhaps play a child's game. He slipped her wooden clogs off and ran his fingers over her feet.

"You've got the most lovely little feet, Freya! Did I ever tell you that?"

She made no reply. She was nervous, afraid of what he would do next.

Without looking at her he got up, took hold of her ankles and pulled her so that she was lying flat on her back. Sensing her resistance, he said, "You've nothing to fear, Freya! You know all about me and my man's thing and now it's time you learnt a bit about yourself! After all, you're getting to be a big lassie."

He pushed her skirt up and ran his hand up her legs. His powerful fingers soon found the cloth-covered button that fastened her drawers. It was easy, like undressing a rag doll.

"Dad! What're you doing? Stop! Please!" she begged

His face was directly above hers and she could smell whisky on his breath. She recognised the detached, velvety tones he sometimes used with the animals.

"Never fear, lassie!", he coaxed. "You'll like this. I'll take it nice and easy, never fear!"

She must have fainted soon after that and when she came to, Andro was nowhere to be seen. Her body felt broken and, fearful of what hurt she might discover if she moved, she lay still, staring up into the sky.

High in the blue there was a meadow pipit. She heard the descending notes of its song as it pirouetted down through the air towards her. Then its wings began to beat again, carrying it upwards once more. After she had watched it rise and fall several times, she came to anticipate its movements, so that the distance separating her from the bird was abolished and she herself took wing and was borne up into the clear sky.

She did not hear him coming, but, black against the blue, his mass eclipsed the bird.

"It's time you made a move. Here have a drop of this," he said gruffly, as he handed her his hip flask. "The first time is always the worst, but that's behind you now. Best if your dad does it, eh?"

She could not speak. After a minute or two she started to get up and, having struggled to her feet, she swayed, unable to keep her balance. Andro came up and put his hands on her slender shoulders to steady her. His voice reached her, compelling.

"Now, see here Freya! This has to be our secret, you understand?" he said, almost shaking her. "Lizzie wouldn't take kindly to it, sharing me like. And I wouldn't like for you to be sent away. You do see what I'm saying, don't you?"

He was demanding a response, he was waiting for it. A tiny nod and he was satisfied. Then he quickly unwrapped the bread and cheese and handed her the empty basket.

"Away with you, then! You'd best be getting back, or else Lizzie'll be asking questions!"

Though free at last, she had to will herself to move and as soon as she was out of sight, she stopped and dropped to her knees. She put her head down. First a wave of nausea welled up inside her, followed by a twisting in the pit of her stomach which grew and grew until at last her body vomited forth her pain.

Hannah had been quite definite about one thing. Jesus was a good man and when Freya had asked Lizzie about Jesus, she got the same reply, "Aye Freya, you've got a friend in Jesus, we all have!" Then Lizzie suggested they go into the parlour to look for a picture of Jesus. They found one in a black leather-bound prayer-book which they took back into the kitchen and opened on the table.

Freya put her elbows on the table so she could examine the picture closely. Being unable to read, the main fascination of books lay in the illustrations. She gazed at the picture and saw a kind, gentle face. Jesus seemed to be looking staight at her. His cheeks were smooth and he had long brown hair which fell in soft curls on top of a rich magenta cloak. Behind him was a dazzling sapphire sky and above his head there was a bird with a twig in its beak. One of his hands was raised and she saw a brownish-red mark in the middle of the palm. Then she looked at the other hand. Jesus was holding a crook, the top of which, although more slender and elegant than Andro's ram's horn stick, had the same unmistakable, convoluted shape.

"But mam," she said to Lizzie, "he's got a stick like dad's!"

"That's because Jesus was a shepherd just like your dad," said Lizzie, pleased with the similarity.

It was as if a door had slammed shut. Freya closed the book and slotted the black leather tongue into its keeper. Without another word she climbed down from the chair and took the book back to its place in the parlour.

She consoled herself by lifting down another book, one she already knew. It was a large volume bound in green leather with swirling, marbled endpapers of pink, mauve and purple and it fell open immediately at her favourite picture.

There, alone in a dark wood was a beautiful woman with fearless eyes. Her hair, unbound beneath a hood of black lambskin lined with white catskin, was fair and flowing. Her black cloak was clasped with precious stones and around her neck she wore a string of glass beads. A loose girdle of puffballs hung around her waist, and in her hand she held a staff with a knob, mounted with brass and set with stones. Her shoes were of animal skin and bound with thongs and there was a bird sitting on either side of her. Freya had decided that one was a corbie crow and the other a pigeon.

Freya had waited and waited for the twelfth of May and now at last it had come. The twisted hawthorns that grew beside the track leading up to the gate were heavy with richly scented blossom and a drift of white petals had collected in the rutted track. She bent down to pick up a handful, then opened her hand and watched the wind blow them away.

Now she was sitting on her boulder, waiting, hoping to catch a glimpse of the pony and cart bringing the new folk to Glittering Shiel. As soon as she saw them coming, she intended to rush back down to the house to tell Lizzie.

Since it was the responsibility of the new employer to transport the family to their new home, Andro had harnessed Polly and set off down the valley before dawn. His destination was Roselaw, an arable farm about five miles to the east of Hyldetron, a distance of some ten miles from Glittering Shiel. He had to be there well before midday, so that the cottage could be emptied ready to receive its new occupants who would be arriving in the course of the afternoon.

Freya had had a long wait. The morning had dawned bright and clear, but by late afternoon the wind had got up and it was getting colder by the minute. Squally rain would be falling on the lower ground, but in the hills there was driving snow and sleet. Freya wrapped the woollen shawl tighter around her shoulders and crouched down behind the boulder to shelter. From time to time she bobbed up to see if they were coming.

At last her patience was rewarded. Far away in the distance she spied the cart. It was piled high and behind it she could see two figures, a woman with billowing skirts who was carrying something. Then there was a cow being led by a man. They were making slow progress, bodies bent, shoulders turned against the sleet and snow coming at them from the northeast.

Long before it was necessary, Freya ran back down the track, leaving the gate open for the weary travellers.

She found Lizzie in the bothy.

"They're coming, mam! I saw them!"

"Poor things. They'll be frozen. The bairns'll be all in."

Lizzie fetched some more peat and asked Freya to bring the bellows from the house so they could breathe some life into the sluggish fire.

She looked around the bothy. It was little more than a stable with roughly plastered walls, one window and a single door. The ceiling was made of matting attached to a series of poles, nailed across from one side of the roof to the other, just above where the roof began to slope. If Lizzie had had some calico, or better still some flowery chintz, she would have covered the matting to make the room look more welcoming. As it was, she had done her best. The earth floor was clean and swept and she had whitewashed the walls and cleaned the pane of glass in the window.

The only object in the room was a piece of yellowing cardboard hanging on a nail beside the fireplace. It was a quotation from Proverbs: 'As the whirlwind passeth, so is the wicked no more: but the righteous is an everlasting foundation.' Hannah had left it behind and though Lizzie could not read it, she guessed from the little border of crosses around the edge that it was from the Bible so she had carefully taken it down before whitewashing the wall and returned it to its place afterwards. She had also found, lying neatly folded on the window-ledge, an old newspaper with yellowed pages. The narrow columns of print were a mystery to her, but she could tell that it was a copy of the *Newcastle Weekly Chronicle* dated March 1873. She had taken it home, thinking she might ask Andro to read it to her one evening.

The overladen cart, its great iron-bound wheels turning slowly in the ruts, creaked and lurched down the final slope into the farmyard. Lizzie was standing in front of the bothy ready to greet the new folk with Freya standing a little behind her.

Rose Lillico, carefully setting down a large bell-shaped object draped in a petticoat, came forward to shake hands. Seeing Lizzie's eyes on the sodden undergarment with its limp frills, Rose coloured slightly. "It's the birds, the canaries!" she said. "The snow was blowing that hard, it was drifting into the cage! It's all I could think to do!"

Rose was a short woman with even features and the delicate skin of Northumbrian women. She had always been proud of her complexion. In the days when she worked in the fields before she married Billy, she had taken great care of her skin. Beneath her bondager's bonnet she used to wear a large handkerchief which came down over her cheeks and knotted under her chin. Like most of the other young women she was in the habit of chewing raw rice. She always took a handful when she went off to work, believing that it would make her skin whiter.

Like a hen blackbird on a frosty morning, she looked much plumper than she really was because she was carrying almost her entire wardrobe on her back. A few wisps of fine brown hair had escaped from her black straw bonnet and there was an uneven tidemark around the hem of her grey striped dress below which everything, including her sturdy hobnailed boots, was wet and muddy.

"This is Billy, my husband!" said Rose.

Despite his equally bedraggled state, Billy Lillico stepped forward with a smile on his cheery face. Lizzie felt a twinge of longing. Something about him reminded her of Felix.

"I'm pleased to meet you, ma'am," said Billy pulling off his sodden cap.

Lizzie hardly knew how to respond to this courtesy. For the Lillicos, such formality, respect for the owner's wife, was normal. It formed part of the strict hierarchy of life at Roselaw where Billy Lillico had been just one of an army of workers living with their families in a dreary quadrangle of stone cottages. The steward's cottage was at the other side of a vast range of stackyards, granaries and other farm buildings close to the big house where the owner, Mr Pestol, and his family lived.

"Come away in out of the cold! The kettle's on the boil. I'll make you some tea," said Lizzie.

"Thank you kindly, Mrs Man, but I'll just see to the little ones," said Rose.

In the excitement and confusion of the meeting, Lizzie had completely forgotten the Lillico children.

Rose went round to one side of the cart where two small children were peeping out between the rails. Stiff with cold, they were patiently waiting to be released from the tiny space between the legs of a large, square table, which had been loaded upside down, and the planks from two dismantled box beds. In addition there were a pair of benches, a stout wooden box, a meal chest containing the Lillicos' few treasured possessions, a tin bath full of plates, dishes and cooking utensils, a pelargonium in a pot and the roots of several plants. Rose had dug them up from the tiny flower-bed in front of the cottage at Roselaw. She knew nothing about their new dwelling, but had brought the plants in the hope that they might have a garden big enough to grow both vegetables and flowers.

At last Freya got a look at her new playmates. There was young William Lillico, who had received not only his father's name but also his looks. He remembered to take off his cap as he had been told and, with his eyes resolutely fixed on his muddy toecaps, he managed a mumbled "Good-day" to the assembled company. His sister, Violet, remained in her mother's arms, her legs locked around Rose's waist, her face buried in the coarse wool of her coat. Only three years old, she was overcome with shyness.

Freya, realising that the Lillico children's timidity was even greater than her own, felt brave enough to emerge from behind Lizzie's skirts.

"Freya, you can show the little ones where to get water and where the netty is!" said Lizzie. Then she turned to Rose and Billy. "We'll have a cup of tea and then Andro and me can help you with your things."

That evening they did little more than unload the cart and set the table the right way up. The children fed the fire with the bunches of straw that had been used as packing round the furniture. Rose unpacked the food she had brought for their first meal at Glittering Shiel. Her neighbour at Roselaw had given her a farewell present of a piece of boiled bacon. Now it lay on the simple board beside the flat loaf made with pea and barley flour that Rose had cooked on the griddle the day before.

Andro was well pleased that night. He had succeeded in engaging a man and the only money that had changed hands, or indeed ever would, was the arling money, a single silver shilling, pressed into Billy's grateful palm in the market square at Willove.

Like all those who came to the annual hirings, Billy Lillico had made his bargain as best he could. Mr Pestol, the boss at Roselaw, had not 'spoken to him' in the early part of the year, which meant that, come the May, Billy would be without a roof and employment. He had feared that such a thing might happen. Labour was scarce, or rather female labour was scarce. When Jack Lamb, Mr Pestol's steward had seen Rose's belly begin to swell yet again, he had conveyed the news to his master who rightly concluded that Rose would not be returning to the fields for some time. Billy could have chosen to employ a woman to take Rose's place, but he would have had to pay her wages and she would have had to lodge with them in the tiny cottage. Rose and he had decided that it would be better if he tried his luck at the hirings.

He had gone to the hirings at Alnwick, where he had stood all day with an ear of corn in his cap to show he was looking for work as a hind. Several bowler-hatted farmers had come up, but as soon as they learned of Billy's circumstances, they lost interest and moved on.

The Willove hirings had been Billy's last chance. Forced to consider any employment at all, he had taken the ear of corn from his cap. He had always worked with horses, but now he knew he would have to think of working as a spademan or a byreman. He had often heard it said that a man who could not make his own bargain was not a man, so when Andro approached him, he had done the best he could for Rose and the children.

Andro had quickly realised that he could drive a hard bargain. They agreed that there would be no upstanding wage with Billy receiving all his payment in kind. He would have the keep of ten ewes, hay and grazing for the cow which he would bring with him from Roselaw. Andro would provide him with oats, barley, beans, wheat, a thousand yards of potatoes and paraffin for his lamps. There would be no coals brought for the fire. Billy would have to cut his own peat up on the hill. The only cash the Lillicos would have to buy clothes and other necessities would come from the sale of lambs born to their ewes and the fleeces from their sheep. As a concession, Andro agreed that Billy should be allowed to have the clarts, the dirty matted wool which was cut from the rear end of the sheep before clipping and which had to be soaked, washed and bagged up ready for the man who came round every year to collect it.

It did not matter to Andro that Billy knew next to nothing about sheep. What was important was that he was strong and willing and would do as he was told. Andro was determined to purge the memory of George with his superior knowledge of the sheep and the hills and his repeated references to the Hethertons and the way things had been done in the past.

7

Images of the long night of Midsummer's Eve remained as sharp and vivid as a dream story in Freya's mind.

All through the afternoon they came: courting couples with eyes only for each other, young people, larking and carefree, and older folk in companionable groups, progressing more slowly.

By many routes they came to the summit of Maidenhope. Those from Herontop and Hyldetron came by way of Glittering Shiel. There they rested, refreshing themselves with cool water from the stone trough. Lizzie, Andro and Freya along with Billy and young Billy joined them for the final stage to the top of the hill. Rose stayed at home with Violet because her baby was expected soon and she was tired, her body too heavy and cumbersome for the long climb.

As they wound their way up the valleys, the people collected sticks and twigs. Some of the lads, proud of their strength, carried branches on their broad shoulders, flotsam, bone-dry and sun-bleached, which had been thrown up onto the velvet sheepsward by the springtime floods.

Thus they made their way to the high place to celebrate the summer solstice. By late evening, when the rim of the sun's golden disc touched at last on the purple line of the western hills, the bonfire stood ready.

As the flames sprang up into the darkening sky, some of the people felt in their pockets for the bent pin they had brought. Then they went to a place close by called the bloody trough, so named on account of the ferruginous lichens and red-tipped devil's matchsticks, which grew around its edge. Each in turn, they dropped their pin into the still water and made a wish. Then they joined the others to feast and make merry to the sharp clear notes of the fiddler's tune.

Mary Black from Herontop was the maiden. As yet unmarried, she was dressed as a bride. The linchpin of a wheel symbolising the sun, she stood with eight dancers weaving an intricate pattern around her. Intoxicated with the clear night air and the rhythmic cadences of the dance, the dancers called out for answers to their questions, for they believed she possessed, that night, the power to tell future things.

Freya sat down on a springy bed of heather, bilberry and cloudberry threaded through with wavy hair-grass. For a long time she gazed at the tongues of fire licking up into the dome of the night sky. Then her attention was drawn to the dancers. Entranced, she watched Mary, so beautiful in a white muslin dress, a circlet of plaited clover flowers lying low on her brow.

Freya felt a hand on her shoulder. Andro, having noticed she was alone, had skirted around in the darkness behind the revellers to approach from the rear.

He saw the enchantment in her eyes and leant close.

"Maybe it can be your turn one day, Freya. You're a bonny lassie! I know I've never told you that before, but it's true all the same!" And, as if to confirm what he had said, Andro ran his fingers over her pale flaxen hair. Then he too turned his gaze on Mary.

Every now and then someone would throw a dry branch onto the fire which crackled and blazed up, giving out a burst of intense light which momentarily revealed the lissom lines of Mary's body beneath the gossamer fabric of her dress.

"What a brazen hussy!" said Andro half to himself. "If it's not the devil himself has got into her!" Then he muttered wryly, "Aye, that's maybe what she's needing! And just look at those lads over there, falling about her like puppies, tongues hanging out! She could do what she likes with them, the little temptress!"

Freya saw nothing of this. To her, Mary was an angel or a summer fairy.

Andro turned his attention back to Freya and, speaking in soft persuasive tones, he whispered, "But see, your dad here knows all about these things. You can have the power as well, just like Mary over there! I can give it to you."

From the moment she had realised that it was Andro's hand on her shoulder, Freya's eyes had remained fixed on Mary. She turned her head only when she saw Lizzie moving towards them around the fringes of the dancers.

"What a fine night," said Lizzie, "a magic night, is it not, Freya?"

Lizzie put her arm round Freya and together they looked up at the pale crescent moon.

"There's no little man with his bundle of sticks up there tonight," said Lizzie laughing. "I dare say he's down here with us and his sticks are on the fire!"

Freya smiled. Then she and Lizzie settled down with their backs against a tussock of bent-grass to watch the dancing. Andro had slipped back into the darkness from which he had come. Safe beside Lizzie, a fitful sleep overcame Freya and in the days that followed she could not have said whether what followed was dream or reality.

Andro appeared in the middle of the circle. He planted his stick down into the soft, mossy ground and squatting on his haunches, he began to play the fiddle. As he played, he sang a lilting croon in a familiar yet foreign tongue. The couples responded, dancing round in a circle, moving widdershins, against the course of the absent sun. After a time the rhythm changed, it quickened and became more lively and insistent. Back to back, the dancers locked arms, the men lifting the women off their feet and whirling them round. Over and over again they separated before coming together once more, buttock to buttock, in a hot and hasty jig.

Much later Freya stirred again. She thought to see Mary's sylphlike form, but she had vanished and instead there was a different figure, a dark and capering silhouette. It was a man clad in a hairy cape of darkest brown splashed with white, his face hidden beneath a black-horned hood. He was leading the dancers in a sinuous dance over the dying embers of the fire, then out of sight behind the cairn which marked Maidenhope's summit. Now there were only women following his snaking path. With their arms raised behind them, they thrust their bellies forward and lifted their feet high in obeisance to their leader.

In that hour before dawn when nature holds its breath and all is still and silent, Lizzie stepped over to the spent fire and picked up a handful of the sacred dust. Then she took hold of Freya's hand and led her down from the green hill and, just as the first light of midsummer day was dawning, they set foot once more in the valley of Eidonhope.

Freya lifted Violet up onto the top of the stone wall so that she could watch the sheep being washed.

The one year-old hogs were the first to have the eek washed out of their thick-matted fleeces. About two weeks later, when the oil began to return, shepherds from the farms from round about would come to help with the clipping. After the hogs were washed, it would be the turn of the ewes. Having given birth and then suckled their lambs, they needed time to thrive before the new wool began to rise. For the time being they enjoyed the freedom of the hills. Parts of their fleeces had become detached and white necks, smooth and pristine, could be seen emerging from ragged *décolletés*.

The same pool was always used because it was the best suited to the purpose, being some twenty yards long and three feet deep. Every year it was dammed up to make the water even deeper. Violet's contribution had been to trot to and fro carrying tiny quantities of sandy mud in her plump, little fists which she carefully piled on top of the big stones that Andro and Billy had heaved into the burn.

Andro had explained to Billy where to make a series of buchts, or pens, out of hurdles. Other hurdles were arranged in a funnel shape leading into the upper end of the pool and into which the sheep were to be driven.

There were ten score sheep gathered ready in the little field below the Dancing Maidens and the air was filled with

70

cacophonous bleating, deep-throated complaint and tremulous quaverings.

From their vantage point on the top of the stone wall, Freya and Violet looked over a sea of jostling, woolly backs and spiralling horns. Billy was standing waist-deep in the brown water. With one hand clasping a horn and the other grasping a handful of wool in the middle of the sheep's back, he caught hold of each frightened animal and plunged it down into the water, swaying it to and fro until its baptism was complete. Then he turned the sheep round so that it was facing downstream and gave it a powerful push. At first the sheep swam well, glad to be released from Billy's powerful grip, but as the water soaked into the wool, the animal became heavier and in desperation it began to make for the bank.

"Come over here, Freya!" Billy shouted. "Take that stick and stand on the bank to stop the hogs climbing out! And Violet, you can stand on the other side!"

Young Billy already had his task. When he wasn't pushing and prodding the reluctant sheep into the water, he was whooping with glee and waving a hazel stick in the air.

Andro had the easiest task. Since he was the only one who knew how to work the collies, he was sorting the sheep and making sure they entered the funnel of hurdles. One collie was crouching on the ground, muzzle flat on the grass, eyes watchful and knowing. A sharp shrill whistle or a "Come by!" and the dog would spring up. Often the collie knew what was expected even before the signal came. Off it streaked to head off a wayward sheep which had broken ranks and was hurtling off to freedom, clarts swinging and clacking like castanets.

The last six or seven weeks had been the hardest that Billy Lillico had ever known. At the age of fourteen he had progressed from odd jobs on the farm, such as herding crows off potatoes or thinning turnips, to doing small carting work. Horses had been Billy's first love and it was with a heavy heart that he had said farewell to the pair of carthorses that had been his working companions at Roselaw. He had had no choice but to accept

Andro's offer, though he was perplexed as to why Andro had chosen someone with as little knowledge of sheep and the hills as himself.

Andro had divided the acres of Glittering Shiel into two hirsels, separate areas of hill and fell. He kept the one closest to the house and gave Billy the one that went right up onto the marches, on the top of Maidenhope. Billy was not used to walking fifteen miles or more each day. Unlike the rolling rigs and pasture land of Roselaw, the moorland with its hidden holes and bogs was as treacherous for him as it was for the solitary walkers from the city who could be seen on the fells in the summertime.

The sheep washing went on till early evening when Billy and Andro went to drive the sheep back up onto the hills before they set about sorting those that were to be washed next day.

Violet and Freya were released from their tasks so they began to wander towards the farmyard, stopping a while by the trough. Then they crossed the bridge over the burn and came round the corner into the farmyard.

Rose was sitting on the bench Billy had carried outside and set against the wall of the bothy. The hot weather was a sore trial to her and there was no respite from her tasks. The cow was still to milk, the vegetable garden and tattie patch to tend and Billy and the children to wash for and feed.

Lizzie's life had been transformed since Rose's arrival. Rose knew so much about life on a farm. She showed Lizzie how to use a special hook to twist dry bent-grass into a rope, which she proceeded to wrap round and round her legs, saying, "All us lassies did this when we used to shaw baigies! It keeps the wet out and keeps your stockings clean!"

Rose was planning to make candles the next time a sheep was killed and there was some fat she could render down. The only thing Lizzie ever did with sheep fat was mix it with soda to make soap. "At Roselaw we hardly dared make our own candles for fear of the gaugers," Rose had explained. "The one time we did have a grand pile ready for the winter, of course the bloody gauger heaved into sight! We couldn't keep them in the houses so I went round and collected them all up in my pinny and hid them in the muck heap."

"So what happened? Did he find them?" asked Lizzie.

"No, he never found them, but we didn't get the use of them either! When we went to fetch them the heat of the midden had melted them clean away and only the wicks were left!"

The two women shared many tasks: the butter making, the weekly wash. On Mondays, whatever the weather, they stoked up the fires. From one set pot they drew buckets of steaming water which they carried to the poss tub which was put outside the back door if it was fine, or in the passageway if it was not. The other set pot was reserved for boiling the whites.

Freya often had to look after Violet. Never having had a playmate, she was happy to play whatever games Violet liked, no matter how babyish. And because Violet did not understand many of the things Freya said and better still she never interrupted, Freya felt free to talk and talk, more than she had ever done before. Violet always gave Freya her undivided attention and never asked awkward questions, so Freya told her all about Sam and then about Hannah. Although she had been tempted once or twice, she never mentioned the warrior, nor did she take Violet to the special secret places to which she retreated when she needed to be alone.

Rose worried constantly that Violet might fall into the burn so the girls usually played in the farmyard. Their toys were either the remains of discarded things or commonplace objects of no value: the hoops they rolled down the slope had once done service as spinning wheels and their chucks were pieces of blanched sheep bone. Sometimes they would watch the antics of the collie puppy Andro had got for Billy. Its favourite game was to pretend that the hens were sheep. It would eye one particular hen, then bound off to the far side of it while the hen, totally unconcerned, continued on its way scratching and clucking.

Rose had dozed off in the sun, her head tipped forward onto her chest. Freya and Violet approached quietly. It was only when Freya gently sat down beside her on the bench that she stirred.

"My goodness! That's a fine mess you're in, young lady!" said Rose when she saw Violet's grubby face.

Although they had stopped by the trough on the way back and Freya had done her best to wash her, Violet still had a fine film of soil on her skin which gave her face, arms and legs a dusky bloom. Bare-footed and wearing only her liberty bodice and calico drawers, Violet stood grinning in front of her mother.

"And where's your dress?" asked Rose, realising that Violet was hiding something behind her back.

"Faya got it!" said Violet who had not yet mastered the Northumbrian burr.

Freya laid the neatly folded dress on the bench. "It's nice and clean," she said quietly. "I took it off her as soon as she started to play in the water."

"You're a good lassie, Freya. Thoughtful. Your mam must be really proud of you!" said Rose, remarking to herself that Freya's face remained curiously expressionless.

"Look mam! Look!" squeaked Violet excitedly, holding up her hands.

"Oh, lovely!" exclaimed Rose, seeing the foxglove flowers on Violet's finger ends. "And what are those flowers called?"

"Faiwy bells!"

"That's right! They're gloves for fairy folk! And where did you find them?"

"By the trough. Faya put them on."

"And what about you Freya, didn't you put some on as well?"

"Faya's is in the water," explained Violet before Freya could reply. "Faya's is fairy boats!"

"Ah!" said Rose.

Violet began to pull the flowers off her fingers and pile them on Rose's stomach. Then she took hold of one of Rose's hands and began to push the delicate trumpets onto her fingers, which, apart from her little finger, were too thick.

Rose held up her hand with a single flower, bruised and split, on the end of her little finger. She sighed in mock resignation. "Oh dear me! The gloves don't fit, so I cannot be a fairy and do magic things!"

Three days later all the sheep were washed and it was time for Andro and Billy to sharpen the long, triangular blades of their shears in readiness for the clipping. At first light they were to set off over Skirlmoor, the fell that lay to the north of Glittering Shiel. Their destination was Hevensgate, a farm similar to Glittering Shiel, which lay at the head of the narrow valley of Hevenhope. There they would join other shepherds who had come to help with the clipping.

After they had finished at Hevensgate they would move on somewhere else and ten days later they were due to return to Glittering Shiel to clip Andro's sheep. For the first time Andro was intending to put his own mark on the sheep. He had had the blacksmith make a new bust, an M enclosed in a circle.

Billy was reluctant to leave home, knowing that the baby would come soon. Only the previous day Rose had told him she could breathe a bit easier because the baby's head had dropped.

"Don't look so worried!" she'd said to him. "It's not as if this is my first. I know what to expect and anyway Lizzie's just across the yard."

But Billy remained anxious. He drew little comfort from Rose's words. After all, Lizzie had little experience of childbirth. But there was nothing he could do about it, he had to go.

The first days passed without incident. Lizzie was out on the moors for two or more hours at the beginning and end of each day, looking the sheep. Rose did as much as she could to help. She could ease herself down comfortably enough onto the three-legged milking stool, but when she leant forward to grasp the teats with the side of her head against the cow's brown flank, she could hardly get her breath.

As the days passed, Lizzie began to prepare for the return of the menfolk. There would be at least eight hungry men to feed. The wool merchant had already sent the sheets for wrapping up the fleeces. Before they were used for that purpose, they would serve as blankets for the men who slept in the stable.

After the outside tasks were done, Lizzie would build up the fire to heat the oven, roll up her sleeves and begin to bake. She made singing hinnies, plump, round loaves full of currants, great slabs of treacly, moist ginger cake, scones and spice cakes which she stored in huge crocks with wooden lids in the cool scullery.

Rose was sorry she could not give Lizzie more help. Despite her own difficulties, she could see how tired Lizzie was. Lizzie was doing a woman's work and a man's as well, though Rose never heard her utter a word of complaint.

It was past nine o'clock one evening when Rose felt the warm trickle that told her that her waters had broken. There was only Violet in the bothy and she was already sound asleep. Young Billy had gone with his father to try to earn a few pennies doing odd jobs such as kemping, twisting some of the wool into a rope to tie around the fleece once it was rolled up. Lizzie had told Rose to tell her the minute the baby started, but Rose put off crossing the yard to the farmhouse. Lizzie was in desperate need of what little rest she got between night-time baking sessions and getting up at dawn.

There were, however, other reasons for Rose's reluctance to involve Lizzie. She thought sometimes she saw a look of regret, a certain sadness on Lizzie's face when they spoke of the baby. Rose had not wished to pry and so she did not know why Lizzie had only the one child. And anyway, there seemed to be some doubt even about that.

Rose's mother was a staunch Presbyterian, a regular member of the Women's Sewing Meetings at the church in Willove. It was there one afternoon while the ladies were plying their needles that Jenny Robson, Mary Hetherton's mother, had spoken up and told them how Andro Man had married the servant lassie. Later she had heard tell that they had a little girl. There was a story going about at the time that the lassie had been brought to the farm as a baby by a man from the coast. Rose's mother had thought nothing of all this. It was just a sample of the rich diet of gossip the women enjoyed when they met together. But when Rose told her mother that she and Billy were to live at Glittering Shiel, she remembered what Jenny had said and told Rose the story.

Rose and Lizzie had quickly become friends. Lizzie had never put on airs and graces, never acted the boss's wife. But despite their growing friendship Rose would never have thought of trying to find out whether what her mother had told her was true. Yet, Rose could not help wondering. Although Freya had the same fair hair and colouring as Lizzie, Rose could see little resemblance between Freya's long oval face and blue eyes and Lizzie's fuller, more rounded features. As for Andro, she could see nothing at all of him in Freya. If Freya was not Lizzie's child, the only possible conclusion was that Lizzie was barren, which would be a source of great sadness.

So Rose kept the news of the impending birth to herself and made the simple preparations on her own. She put some more peat on the fire and made sure the set pot and the big black kettle were full. Putting her back against the table, she pushed it over towards the window. Then she went and fetched the clean rags and old newspapers she had saved. After she had scrumpled the paper up, she put it on the ground in the space she had cleared between the table and the big box bed. Finally she arranged the rags on the top and made a little hollow in the middle. When the time came, she would hold on to the side of the bed and squat down on her heels until it was all over.

8

It was the first week in September and Freya was to start school. On the first morning she washed and dressed with great care and Lizzie plaited her pale blonde hair into a single tress and tied it with a new ribbon. Lizzie took great pride in the fact that all Freya's clothes were brand new, right down to the shiny brown ankle boots which buttoned down the side.

At the end of July Lizzie had sent word to Mr Tiplady, the tailor and draper in Willove, asking him to call at Glittering Shiel. Surprised at being asked to visit the farm after so many years, he came at once on his pony, bringing with him his collection of patterns and fabrics.

Lizzie ordered a long cape in slate-blue Otterburn tweed and asked him to line it with red flannel so that it would keep Freya warm on the long walk to school. She had decided on a cape because, unlike a coat, Freya would not grow out of it too quickly.

"Now then, what about yourself, Mrs Man?" asked Mr Tiplady, hoping to fill his order book still further. "Will you be wanting anything?"

"Oh, no thank you, Mr Tiplady, er, not at present," Lizzie replied, the colour rising to her cheeks because she thought he must think she looked shabby.

Finally Mr Tiplady measured Freya's feet. Mr McNatty, the boot and shoemaker, had his shop just across the street, so Mr Tiplady undertook to convey the order for the boots to him and to bring them with other items as soon as they were ready.

It was Felix's money, accumulated with great difficulty, that paid for this finery. He had sent three guineas in response to the letter Andro had written on Lizzie's behalf. Of course, Freya knew nothing of this and Andro behaved as if it was he who was footing the bill. Lizzie said nothing either; as far as she was concerned the money was there and that was all that mattered. She had calculated the expenditure on clothing with great care so that enough money remained for a year's schooling. The coins now lay in a metal money-box, a thrifty, which was kept high up on the shelf above the fireplace in the kitchen. Andro had given it to Freya in a rare act of generosity. He called it Freya's treasure-chest and he took care to keep the key.

There was a nip in the air at half-past seven when Lizzie and Freya stepped outside. They called at the bothy to collect young Billy who was also starting school that day. Lizzie intended to walk all the way with them because she wanted to meet Miss Murray, the schoolmistress, and see them settled in.

Freya slipped her hand into the pocket of her new cotton slip, a calico overall made by Lizzie. Thinking it looked rather drab, Lizzie had sewn a red flannel pocket in the middle of the chest. Then, by chance, she had come across a hank of gold embroidery silk in Mary Hetherton's sewing box, so she had stitched Freya's initials onto the scarlet ground. Working on the elegant, intertwining letters had been an act of love.

At the bottom of the pocket lay the precious school pennies, wrapped in a piece of blue paper from a sugar bag. Freya pressed the little package against her chest just to make sure it was there. Lizzie had impressed upon her that the money must be handed to the teacher every Monday morning without fail. As for Freya's dinner, which comprised two thick slices of bread spread with salty, homemade butter and rhubarb jam and a tin bottle filled with milk, it was stowed away in a capacious pocket sewn on the inside of her cape.

The three of them strode off up to the gate with Rose standing on the doorstep, the baby in her arms and Violet by her side, waving goodbye.

Young Billy was an unwilling schoolboy. He would have much preferred to stay at home and work on the farm, but Billy had been firm.

"You remember all those moles we caught and skinned?" he'd said to young Billy. "Well, they were sent a long way away, to a place called Wisbeech, or some such place down south, for to be made into breeches and the shillings we got for them were put by so you could get yourself a bit of education. So mind you're a good lad and make the most of your chance!"

Billy's words had made a big impression on the reluctant lad for he knew how hard they had worked all through the summer, setting the traps, skinning the pink-nosed moudiwarps, then tacking their thick velvety pelts onto an old door to dry.

Freya had looked forward to this day with fear and longing. There would be older children who knew all about school. They would all know each other, have already made friends and they would play games she had never heard of. However, she consoled herself with the thought that she would be able to learn her letters and, if she worked very hard, she would be able to discover the secrets contained within the books in the parlour.

After about half an hour, Lizzie pointed out the old still, then they passed the place where the Eidon Burn joined Heron Water and soon they were joining a wider track leading down to Herontop.

The subtle shades of Eidonhope, heather faded palest mauve, bracken turning from gold to copper, grey boulders ringed with emerald mosses, gave way to a different landscape. They entered on an ocean of gently rolling hills, apparently without enclosure, punctuated by clumps of tall chestnut and sycamore trees. Cheviot sheep, rounder and plumper than the hardy blackfaces, stood out white against the smooth unbroken green.

At last the track turned and ran along the side of a stone wall, higher than any at Glittering Shiel and built of larger, more regular stones. They came to a white-painted gate fastened with an iron lever with a little knob on top. Someone mounted on horseback could open it easily, but Lizzie had to stand on tiptoe before she could pull it back. They went through and the gate clicked shut behind them.

The road stretched straight before them through an orderly wood. There were oaks and elms and tall Scots pines and along the edge of the road, huge rhododendron bushes, their exotic blooms long over. Something about the wood made them fall silent and instinctively they quickened their pace. Then, quite suddenly, the road dropped down a slope and on their right they came to a high wall.

"Now, this is the Home Farm where Mrs Matheson lives!" said Lizzie. "You remember, Freya? It's where Sam used to stay in the winter time."

In recent years the wall had been crenellated to give the farm the appearance of a fortified place. As they passed a wide archway, they looked through into a cobbled yard. A black labrador was tied to a wall with a long chain. The dog began to bark as soon as Lizzie and the children appeared and seconds later Lilian Matheson emerged from the back door to see what was going on.

"My! My! What have we here? Why, if it's not Lizzie Man with two bairns!" she exclaimed. "This must be young Billy Lillico if I'm not mistaken."

"Good morning to you, Mrs Matheson. Aye, that's right and this here is Freya. I'm going down to the school with them. It's their first day," Lizzie explained. "Please can you tell us the time for we must be there by nine."

Lilian disappeared inside to consult the clock and emerged a minute or two later. "The clock's just struck the half hour. You've plenty of time. It'll not take you more than twenty minutes."

Lilian came up to the children. "Now here's a piece of my treacle toffee for you to suck on your way down the road!" Then she turned to Lizzie. "It's a long walk for the bairns when they're just little."

Lizzie nodded.

"And what about yourself, Mrs Man?" continued Lilian. "Will you not stop for a cup of tea and a bit crack on your way back?"

Politeness demanded that Lizzie accept the invitation. In the country, where visitors were few and social contact precious, people took it amiss if anyone were to pass a neighbour's door or road-end without taking the trouble to call. Normally Lizzie would have liked nothing better than to have a rest and exchange news with Lilian, but she was afraid that Andro and she might still be regarded with some suspicion. Lilian had been at Glittering Shiel the night before Sam was buried and had witnessed Andro's strange behaviour. So, much as Lizzie liked Lilian, who had always shown her kindness, she did not relish the prospect of a cup of tea at the Home Farm. Of course Lilian would not ask direct questions, except those of a very general nature, but her perceptive eye would more than compensate for her discretion.

The road joined a wider one at the foot of the slope. On the corner there was another imposing building, also crenellated. It too had a grand arch with an escutcheon on it, bearing the arms of the de Gilderoy family. Inside was a cobbled courtyard and down one side a succession of double doors were standing open to reveal a variety of horse-drawn vehicles: carts, traps, a governess cart, an elegant phaeton and a coach with a gold line along the side and a crest on the door. The two other sides of the yard were given over to stables, tackrooms and a smithy. The place was humming with activity. A man in a bowler hat was moving about giving orders, barrows of steaming manure were being pushed across the yard and a pair of powerful carthorses were being harnessed ready for the plough. Young Billy gazed at the scene, trying to take everything in, so that he could tell his father all about it when he got home.

They walked on down a road lined with lime trees. On their left, behind the avenue of trees, there was a wide expanse of parkland with single trees, majestic and solitary, each with its own protective iron railing. Soon they passed between two massive sandstone pillars hung with a pair of wrought iron gates of intricate design. A century earlier, a plain stone ball was all that had embellished the tops of the pillars, but in recent years they had been replaced by a pair of griffins, each holding a coat of arms with multiple quarterings in its scaly grasp.

They turned left down a hill with high banks on one side and parkland on the other. In the distance Lizzie could see the top of a colossal keep-tower. It stood on a knoll overlooking, to the north, a romantic dell through which Heron Water flowed on its way to the sea. During the turbulent days before the union of the crowns it had served as a place of safety for people, cattle and goods. According to tradition, it had been destroyed by Oliver Cromwell on his way to Scotland in 1650. Now, ropes of ivy held its massive walls in a tight embrace and its only visitors were small boys hunting for birds' eggs, the occasional visiting antiquarian and the spectral herons which continued to nest, as they had done for centuries, in the tops of the tall pines nearby.

On slightly lower ground to the southwest of the keep, Lizzie glimpsed the turrets and parapets of Heron Hall, seat of the de Gilderoy family, which had in recent years been extensively remodelled in the romantic style that became known as Scottish baronial, the blueprint for which was Abbotsford, the home of Sir Walter Scott.

The Herontop estate and the title, Lord of Herontop, had been granted by William the Conqueror to his liegeman, Gilles de Roy, towards the end of the eleventh century. Herontop was part of the barony of Willove, the most northerly of the baronies into which the county of Northumberland was divided after the Norman Conquest. One of Gilles' descendants, Odonel de Gilderoy, died in 1359, leaving behind three daughters who inherited the estate but not the title which, by law, could not pass through the female line. Thus the title went into abeyance and in the course of time the estate, including the outlying land at Glittering Shiel, had been divided up and had passed into the hands of a succession of owners.

Then, in the mid nineteenth century, a certain James Hetton set out to prove that he was a descendant of Odonel's second daughter, Mathilda de Gilderoy and that he therefore had the right to call himself Lord of Herontop. He engaged the best genealogist he could find, a Mr Cordelion of London. Mr Cordelion's efforts to establish common ancestry between the

Hettons, whose wealth had come from West Indian sugar plantations and the de Gilderoys, one of Northumberland's most ancient families, proved fruitless. However, his researches did produce imposing bundles of documents of enormous erudition and complexity which were handed over to a firm of London lawyers who specialised in such delicate matters. They rendered them even more obfuscatory and authoritative. Finally, James Hetton took the simple step of changing his name to Orlando de Gilderoy. He deposited the recondite documents with his bank and proceeded to let it be known that the blood of Gilles de Roy flowed in his veins and that henceforward he was to be known as the Lord of Herontop.

Apart from the immensely lavish alterations to the family seat, Orlando had also built and endowed Herontop school which stood by a bend at the bottom of the hill midway between Heron Hall and the village of Herontop.

As they walked the last few hundred yards, Lizzie and the children saw groups of people making their way towards the school from the opposite direction. Lizzie was becoming increasingly nervous, her hands even more clammy than the children's. They walked along the front of the building but could see no door, so they turned off the road and went down the side of a building Lizzie took to be the schoolhouse and into a yard at the back.

Some twenty children were shouting and running about. The schoolroom had two doors, one at each end and in front of one of them stood Miss Murray, the schoolmistress.

Grace Murray was almost thirty, with brown hair drawn back from a high forehead and knotted into a smooth chignon at the nape of her neck. She was wearing a simple dress of dove-grey wool with a white lace collar. She stepped forward to greet Lizzie. It was then that Lizzie noticed that her hand was clasped around a walking stick.

Lizzie introduced herself and then the children.

Grace smiled warmly and shook hands with each in turn, then she said, "Come Freya, take my hand and we'll go inside!" She turned to Billy. "You have to go in through that door over there, Billy," she said, pointing to an identical green door at the other end of the building. "That's the boys' entrance!" Then, feeling that some sort of explanation was called for, she said to Lizzie, "There should be a notice saying GIRLS over this door and BOYS over that one, but after the first day, everybody knows where they're supposed to go."

Billy was looking confused and doubtful. He could not see why there had to be two doors. After all, they managed all right with just one at home. But then he remembered that Rose had given him strict instructions to do exactly what the teacher said, so he turned obediently and went off towards the correct door.

After Freya had hung up her cloak, she and Lizzie followed Grace into the rectangular schoolroom. Four mullioned windows were set high along the long south wall facing the road. Light flooded through them onto three rows of six-seater wooden desks. There was no danger of the scholars being distracted from their work because they sat facing a blank wall with their backs to the windows, which were in any case too high for the average child to see out of. Halfway along the wall on a raised dais was Miss Murray's desk with a large ledger lying open upon it.

"Just one or two details, Mrs Man. I won't keep you long," said Grace, picking up a pen and dipping it into a white china inkwell. "Now, your daughter's Christian name is Freya?"

"Yes, Miss."

Grace smiled. "It's a beautiful name! And do you have a middle name, Freya?"

"No Miss, she's just got the one," said Lizzie.

"Good. Now then, what is her date of birth?"

Lizzie was aghast. It had never occurred to her that she would have to provide such information. She had no answer and was too nonplussed to invent one.

Grace was puzzled. She knew from experience that a mother might hesitate over the year that her child was born, but she almost invariably knew the month and the day.

Freya, who had immediately realised that Lizzie was in difficulty, thought she knew the answer and was now trying to overcome her timidity enough to be able to tell Miss Murray that she had been born on a Monday. She had learnt this only a few weeks earlier when Rose and Lizzie had been discussing the luck of the baby's natal day. Violet had demanded to know on which day of the week *she* had been born and this had led to Rose reciting the nursery rhyme, which had given Lizzie time to choose a day for Freya. She had chosen Monday because it seemed appropriate. Freya had been delighted and sometimes when she was alone, she would hum quietly, "Born on a Monday, fair of face".

Freya was about to speak when Grace pre-empted her. "Maybe you could write it on a piece of paper and send it with Freya tomorrow?"

"Aye, Miss. I mean, yes, Miss! I'll see she brings it. My husband can write it out." Lizzie was ashamed, angry that her ignorance had let them both down, herself and Freya.

"Thank you, that will do very well!" said Grace reassuringly. She thought it was all very odd. Lizzie looked like an intelligent woman and Freya was well turned out, far better than most of her pupils.

At last the ordeal was over. Lizzie cast an anxious glance at Freya, gave her a quick kiss and reminded her to walk straight home after school. Then, her face flushed with embarrassment and humiliation, she made her escape.

9

Grace Murray had been the schoolmistress at Herontop for two years. She was the only woman in Northumberland to have sole charge of a school. Augusta de Gilderoy was to thank for this and for much else besides.

Ruth Murray, Grace's mother, had left the pit village near Newcastle, where her father was a miner, and gone to Heron Rigg to work as a bondager. At that time there was plenty of work on the land because the price of corn was high and thousands of acres were under the plough.

Ruth was employed by a hind called Matthew Oates and she lodged with him and his family. She had almost no privacy, washing and dressing in a narrow corridor between the wall and the box bed which she shared with the Oates' children. Anne Oates had been loath to accept Ruth into the tiny single-end cottage. "That lassie gets her wages from us, and me and Mat have to meat and wash her for nothing!" she would complain, railing at the bondage system.

Two years later it became obvious that Ruth was expecting a child and this gave Anne Oates the excuse she needed to get rid of her.

By that time one of the oldest cottages on the farm, a hovel with leaning chimney and gaping thatch, had been given rent-free to two single women who also worked on the farm. The dwelling stood at the bottom of a slope. A foul miasma from the middens, pig sties and privies at the back of the cottages at the top of the hill trickled down towards it, adding a stench to the already damp building.

The cottage was known as the bondage house and its inhabitants, Meg and Betty, were scorned on account of their supposed loose morals, foul language and general lack of decency. The truth was, that despite their wretched living conditions, they were independent women with their own money. Living together without husbands, the women were regarded as an aberration and a threat to wholesome family life.

Meg and Betty took Ruth in and shared with her what little they had. It was a matter of general conjecture and acute annoyance that nobody could make the girl say who the father was. If Ruth had enjoyed a few nights of passion at summer's close, nothing anybody could say could persuade her speak of it though suspicion did fall on one of the handsome fellows in Murphy's gang of Irish labourers who had come at harvest time the previous year.

Augusta de Gilderoy, Orlando's unmarried sister, learned of Ruth's predicament. Never having found a suitable husband, she lived on the margins of Orlando's family. She was a woman of principle, committed to egalitarianism, who deeply regretted that her education had been narrow and inadequate compared to that of her brother. She made the best of a life that might easily have descended into futility by taking an interest in the lives of the army of people who worked for her brother.

Unlike those who seized on Ruth's situation as yet another example of the moral depravity of bondagers, she forbore from moral judgment and gave practical assistance instead. She spoke to Orlando, pointing out that Ruth was one of the hardest workers at Heron Rigg, too valuable to be lost to the workhouse. She persuaded her brother to speak to Mr Matheson, his chief steward, and order him to engage Ruth as a cottar. There was an empty cottage beside the mill at the bottom of Heron Dene that Ruth could have. Augusta also arranged for the miller's wife to look after the baby so Ruth could resume her work in the fields and so earn the necessary money to support herself and the baby.

All had gone well until Grace was ten. Then, early in October, she and Ruth were in the threshing yard where Ruth was feeding sheaves of corn into the hopper on the top of the threshing-machine. Since the machine had to be fed continuously, Ruth had allowed Grace take over from her while she left the yard for a few moments. As Grace stretched up to put a sheaf of corn into the hopper, her skirt became trapped in the machinery and her foot was dragged down into the drum. Ruth was wretched with guilt and distraught at the bleak, hopeless future she saw for her crippled daughter.

Help came once more from Augusta, who, almost every day, walked down the hill from the hall to visit Grace, bringing with her food and comfort. At first Augusta planned to teach the girl to sew so that she might earn a living as a seamstress. But in the course of the hours they spent together, Augusta realised the girl was clever, so she began to bring books and writing paper. In this way Grace embarked on an education that culminated in her going to the Normal Training Seminary in Glasgow, one of the most progressive teacher training establishments in Britain.

To Augusta and Ruth's intense pride and delight, Grace returned to Herontop a certificated teacher. Since she could not walk more than twenty paces and those with difficulty, Augusta gave her a donkey so that she could get about. Orlando needed no persuasion to engage Grace as governess for his two children, William and Leonora. Eventually the time came for William to leave home and go away to boarding school and a few years later Leonora set off on the European grand tour. Grace feared she would be forced to leave, but fortunately, Mr Lightbody, the schoolmaster, chose that moment to retire and Orlando appointed Grace mistress of Herontop school.

The light, airy schoolroom was Grace Murray's domain. While Mr Lightbody had maintained order with a stout hazel stick, Grace tamed the unwilling or unruly child with kind words and humour. She understood the harshness of the children's lives, because she had endured more than any of them. She did not chastise a child who arrived at school without the school pennies. The child's presence before her was testimony enough of the parents' desire that it should learn and she knew that the money would be sent as soon as possible. The farm workers received only a few pounds of their wages in cash, the rest came as coal, wheat, hay and beans. There were many demands on this precious money, boots and clothing to buy, salt and candles, and every family waited impatiently for the day when the first-born child was old enough to get a day's work in the fields and so make a contribution to the hard-pressed family purse.

Mr Dogberry, the Presbyterian minister from the church at Herontop, came into the school on Tuesdays, Thursdays and Fridays to teach the boys drawing and to give the children religious instruction. Most people, especially those who lived in the hills, were Dissenters. It was for this reason that it fell to Mr Dogberry, rather than the Anglican vicar of Hyldetron, to visit the school, a task he was more than happy to perform, not least because he found his conversations with Grace Murray such a pleasure and a stimulation.

It was the first Tuesday of term and Mr Dogberry was standing at Miss Murray's desk, gazing intently at the children. He picked up the Bible which was lying closed in front of him and held it up aloft.

"This, children, is your signpost to heaven!" he intoned. "All the hard work you do with our dear Miss Murray," he said turning to look at Grace with tender benevolence, "learning your letters, is so that you will be able to read the messages written in the Holy Book for yourselves and so find your own way to God."

Then he ceremoniously opened the book and began to read in a mesmerising semi-chant which induced either a distant dreaminess or a bout of fidgeting in his captive audience. Mr Dogberry was a logical man and so he had decided that since it was the beginning of the school year, he should begin at the beginning. He had therefore chosen the passage from the book of Genesis, describing the creation of heaven and earth.

At the beginning of each new verse he paused and took a deep breath so that all God's sayings and doings and makings would receive the emphasis they deserved.

Freya was deeply impressed. When he had finished reading, Mr Dogberry proceeded to the final part of his instruction which the children called the minister's questions.

He pointed at Tom Nesbit, a plump lad with rosy cheeks and told him to stand up. Tom heaved himself to his feet. He had grown too big for the desk and was ill at ease squeezed into the narrow space.

"Now you see Tom here?" said Mr Dogberry. "A year ago he did not know who made him, did you Tom?"

"No, sir!" said Tom going a little pinker because everybody was looking at him.

"Well go on lad, tell us who made you!"

"God, sir! God made me."

"Very good, Tom. Now tell us who will punish you if you tell a lie."

"My da, sir! With his belt!" replied Tom without a second's hesitation.

A titter ran through the ranks.

Mr Dogberry frowned. "That may be, my lad, but it's God to whom we each of us must answer for our sins. You see it's a father's burdensome task to do God's work here on earth. He has to show his children what is right and what is wrong. So Tom, your father is, so to speak, doing no more than taking the place of your heavenly father when he punishes you for your sins."

Satisfied that he had upheld paternal authority both on earth and in heaven, Mr Dogberry brought the questions to a close. He gave a nod to Miss Murray who was sitting at the piano ready to accompany them as they sang the hymn, 'There is a green hill far away'.

The green hill made Freya think of Maidenhope and then her thoughts turned to Andro. His word was law. Lizzie and she did what he told them without a murmur. Andro was the boss. And now it seemed that God was part of it all. God, the father, and Andro, her dad, were somehow the same person. Maybe the only difference between them was that she could see Andro and she could not see God. And Andro could touch her and hurt her inside. She must have done something very wrong for Andro to punish her the way he did, though she did not know what it was.

Playtimes were already a trial to Freya. At first the other girls had excluded her, going into a tight huddle on their own. Mostly they pretended to ignore her, though no detail of her appearance escaped them.

That Tuesday, having lingered as long as she could in the schoolroom, she decided to go to the toilet. The two netties, one for the boys and one for the girls, were in a small building round the end of the schoolroom, close by the coal shed and the gate to Miss Murray's garden. In order to segregate the sexes, a high wall separated the two doors. Anxiously, she looked around for the other girls, but they were nowhere to be seen. She slipped inside and closed the door. Now she felt safe, so she took her time, musing about what Mr Dogberry had said, staring up at the cobwebs and tendrils of ivy clinging to the rough rafters.

When she emerged into the bright sunlight, they were there, waiting. Elsie Gordon detached herself from the group and stepped up close. She poked a finger at the letters on the pocket of Freya's slip. "And what might I ask is these?" she asked disdainfully.

"My mam sewed them, they stand for my name - Freya Man," Freya replied.

"Oooh!" shrieked Elsie in mock admiration. "Freya Man eh? What a clip! What a fashion plate! And just look at them boots!" Then Elsie did a sort of jig which involved lifting one foot and rotating her ankle so that everyone could admire her feet. "And what d'you think you're doing here all done up like that?" Elsie went on. "Is your mam the queen or what?"

Someone sniggered, then they all moved in closer, forming a circle around Freya.

"Right lassies! What are we going to call her?" asked Elsie.

"Fancy Man! Fancy Man!" chanted Cissy Young who was always quick with an answer.

Soon they were all joining in. Freya stood stock-still, trapped inside the circle of chants. She had been so proud of her new clothes. Maybe all this would never have happened if she had worn her ordinary clothes. Did her mam not know what would happen as soon as the other lassies saw all her new things? Could she not have guessed?

Freya stood her ground, determined to hold back the tears.

With arms akimbo, Elsie thrust her face forward so close to Freya's that their noses were almost touching. "Oh deary me, you're not going to greet, are you? Go on then! Run to Miss," she taunted.

Freya would not yield to tears. She never had in the past. It was only when she was alone that she allowed the tears to flow.

"She'll not greet!" said Cissy. "And d'you know for why?" There was a pause while Cissy enjoyed the suspense she had created. "Who nivver greets, eh?"

Nobody answered.

Cissy looked round the circle triumphantly, then with eyes flashing she said, "A witch! That's who!"

The girls gasped. Cissy's pronouncement had thrilled them to the core.

"Right lassies, we'll let her go!" said Elsie, taking charge. "I'll count to five, then we'll be after her!"

Elsie stood aside to allow Freya to escape. She began to count, but Freya did not move. It was not because she did not want to run away, but because there was nowhere to run to, no secret place to go. Just as Cissy was about to shout five, Freya turned and walked away. The other girls could not run after her because she had not taken flight. They would have looked silly. Freya had somehow outdone them by not playing the game, by not turning tail and running, so they stayed where they were and made do with watching to see where she went.

The playground was a small yard and beyond it there was a triangular field where the children were allowed to play. It was bounded on one side by a small stream. Across a tiny bridge stood a clump of chestnut trees beside the bend in the road. Freya walked slowly around the edge of the field the boundary of which was marked by gnarled hawthorns. She could find no refuge, nowhere to hide. She crossed the bridge and looked up at the trees. There were no low branches to climb on, no dense undergrowth to crawl into. The earth beneath the trees was bare with only the occasional tree root raising a sinewy joint above the earth which was trodden smooth and hard by the passage of children's feet.

Freya stood with her back against the biggest tree, thinking to put its massive trunk between her and the eyes of her tormentors. It was all she could do. As she waited for the bell to signal the beginning of afternoon school, she gazed longingly at the narrow road that led up the hill back home.

The hardest work had been done in the morning after Mr Dogberry's departure. The children worked in separate groups according to age, with Miss Murray moving between them. The oldest ones had notebooks and pencils and were working on something called reduction which involved lengthy sums designed to turn a massive number of ounces into tons and hundredweights.

Freya and the other younger children had slates and slate pencils and they were learning how to write down numbers and say them out loud.

Freya had pressed so hard on the pencil as she copied the figures that the pencil had collapsed into tiny shards on the slate. She had been oblivious of a girl called Jenny who was sitting motionless beside her. Jenny was terrified because she did not know what she was supposed to do.

Freya's concentration was broken by the noise of splashing on the flagstones. As quick as a flash a hand had shot up in the row behind them and a voice, jubilant at the prospect of a break in the tedium, said, "Please Miss? Can you come over here, Miss? One of the new ones has wet their selves!"

Everybody stopped work and stared at the front row where Freya, Jenny and Billy, the prime suspects, were sitting. While Freya and Billy went pale at the possibility that they might be thought guilty, Jenny was behaving as if nothing had happened. She was clutching her pencil like a dagger, moving it vertically across her slate, making a jagged squiggle.

"I want you all to go on with your work," said Miss Murray firmly. Hearing a snort and a few repressed sniggers, she added, "Just ask yourselves whether such a thing has ever happened to you or perhaps nearly happened to you?"

At these chastening words, heads were bent forward once more with no more than the odd sidelong glance as Miss Murray led Jenny from the room.

By the time the children came back into the schoolroom after dinner, the floor and seat of the desk had been washed so that only a damp patch marked the site of Jenny's humiliation. Freya had not seen her at dinner time. Grace had taken her into the house to try and dry her sodden underclothes.

It was Grace's habit during the final part of the school day either to read or tell a story. Sometimes it was a tale of events that had happened many hundreds of years earlier in their native Northumberland. On other occasions she transported them to distant lands, to Asia Minor, Eygpt or Ancient Greece.

"This county where we live was not always called Northumberland," she began. "Many hundreds of years ago it had a different name, it was called Bernicia and its king was called Ida."

"But Miss, Ida's a lassie's name!" objected Cissy.

"Yes, Cissy, it is now. But names are not to be relied upon and we should not jump to conclusions as to whether a name belongs to a man or a woman. Do you know the name Ashtoreth?"

"No, Miss," said Cissy, beginning to regret her interruption.

"When you know your Bible better, Cissy, you will find that Ashtoreth is mentioned several times in the Old Testament along with the names of other gods such as Baal."

"Oh aye Miss! I know who he was!" interjected Stilty Mary, one of the older girls. "The people made a golden calf for him and was busy worshipping it and singing and dancing and that, when Moses came down from off the mountain with the tablets."

"Don't be so daft, Mary! Tablets is what you get from the doctor!" interrupted Elsie.

But Mary was not so easily deterred and, for good measure, she added, "and Baal was a false god!"

"Very good, Mary. Some of what you say is correct, but I think that the Bible does not give us the names of the gods on the occasion you mention, though the golden calf is indeed a symbol of the worship of Ashtoreth. You see I had always assumed that Ashtoreth was a male god just like Baal. But I was wrong. Through reading and studying I have learned that Ashtoreth was in fact a goddess, the Queen of Heaven in fact, and that before the time of Yahweh, or Jehovah as we call him, many of the people in the Holy Land worshipped her. So we must be careful because I believe that it is important to know whether the person we are talking about was a man or a woman."

Freya was thinking about the picture of the woman in the dark wood, wondering whether, perhaps, she was a goddess. Freya's hands were lying palms down on the sloping plank of the desk. She did not notice that Jenny had moved her hand so that it was almost touching Freya's. Just as Grace was holding up an engraving of the great rock fortress of Dinguardi, explaining how Ida's grandson had renamed it Bebbanburgh after his wife, Freya felt a finger interlock with hers.

Apart from Grace's kindness, this was the first friendly gesture that Freya had experienced since she had come to school. She did not look at Jenny, she did not dare, for fear that the gift, the promise of friendship, might be withdrawn.

10

If it had not been for Jenny, Freya would probably not have gone to school the next day. She very much wanted to be there in her seat listening to Grace Murray's soft, clear voice speaking of other worlds, other places beyond Herontop and Eidonhope, but her longing was overshadowed by her fear of Elsie and the other girls. She had no idea that, by not taking flight the day before, she had robbed them of victory. And when it occurred to her that she might pretend to be ill, she thought of Andro. Although he had not yet come to her in her bedroom, she did not feel safe there. So in the end she took courage from the thought that Jenny would be at school, that she would have a friend.

On the second morning Lizzie had walked with the children as far as the old still. After that they walked all the way on their own. Progress was slow because Billy was easily distracted.

On the Friday morning he spotted some bummelkites, juicy blackberries. In his efforts to get to the berries he scratched his legs and stung himself on some nettles.

"Quick! Get a docken, Freya!" he said urgently.

Freya soon found a suitable leaf and handed it to him. Billy squatted down on his hunkers, spat on the spear-shaped leaf and began to rub it on his leg.

"Docken in! Nettle out!" he chanted over and over again.

"Come on, Billy! We'll be late!" Freya insisted, but Billy was not to be hurried.

"I'll just give it a bit more rub, just to be on the safe side," he said with a smile.

The children were unskilled at guessing the time. Until this period in their lives, time, or rather the time by the clock, had had little meaning. At Glittering Shiel the days followed one another in a smooth, unhurried rhythm. The children rose with the sun, did what jobs they were given, played when they could and ate when they were called. No one referred to the clock, to a precise hour of the day. Time pressed only when the weather threatened, when it became a matter of urgency to lead the pikes of sweet-smelling hay to the stack in the yard and make it safe before the approaching storm. Time was a loose and easy thing which divided the year into the lambing, dipping and clipping, hay and harvest.

Both Lizzie and Rose had impressed on the children that they must be in the school yard ready to line up when Miss Murray rang the bell at nine o'clock. Unlike Billy, Freya realised that she did not have an accurate sense of time, so because they had been delayed, she insisted that they run all the way down the hill to school.

Freya did not see Jenny hovering near the chestnut trees beside the bend in the road. As soon as she saw Freya, she came running to meet her, a broad smile on her face.

Jenny was a thin child, much smaller than Freya. She would have been plump and full-cheeked if she had had the benefit of good food such as the crowdie, the milk and oatmeal porridge, that Lizzie prepared for breakfast every morning, but she was lucky if she got a cup of weak tea and a scrap of barley bread.

Jenny was the youngest of ten children. Her mother had died of pernicious anaemia shortly after she was born and she had lived with her granny for as long as she could remember.

Her granny earned a little money by keeping a few hens and selling the eggs. Her other occupation was knitting. It was dark inside her cottage and, since candles cost precious pennies, she would sit outside her door in all but the harshest weather, knitting socks. She made the heels and toes out of hard-wearing blackface wool while the rest was made of the softer Cheviot wool. However, in recent months, she had made fewer pairs than usual. Her workmanship was as fine as ever, but her fingers were becoming less nimble and speedy.

Elsie, Cissy, Stilty Mary and the other Herontop girls had abandoned the nickname 'Fancy Man' in favour of Cissy's idea that Freya was a witch and from then on their imaginations were fired and their inventiveness knew no bounds.

That morning as the girls were dawdling along on their way to school, they lighted upon a clump of cow parsley growing by the roadside. At first they were attracted to it for its beauty. The pale, gilded stalks, delicately ridged and crowned with filigree umbels, were standing tall and motionless in the chill morning air. The prickly stalks were brittle and snapped easily, so they picked some and began to wave them around their heads, showering themselves with golden seeds.

Stilty Mary was the first to think of putting one of the stalks between her legs and pretending it was a hobbyhorse. Soon they were all doing it. Gleefully they hitched up their skirts and went prancing and cavorting about.

A little later, in the playground, Elsie noticed that Freya was watching their antics. "See this!" she shouted excitedly. "This here is my broomstick and I'm off! Over the hills and far away!" As she left the yard, she turned her head and shouted at Freya, "Ha! Ha, Freya Man! See, we've taken all your bunewands, so you'll not can ride to meet the devil tonight!"

Soon Cissy was careering off around the field after Elsie. "Horse and hattock, Horse and go!" she sang at the top of her voice. "Horse and pellatis, ho, ho!"

Freya was a witch, that was settled. But since Jenny and Freya were always together, the Herontop girls had to decide what sort of creature Jenny was. She could not be a witch as well. One witch was a thrill, two were a threat.

At dinner time the Herontop girls saw Freya and Jenny sitting quietly at the edge of the field, so they trooped over and sat down in a circle close enough to Freya and Jenny to ensure that their conversation would be overheard.

"Jenny! She's not a proper lassie!" said Elsie, pretending to speak in confidential tones.

A frisson rippled through the group. They wriggled with excitement, leaning forward on their haunches to listen.

"What d'you mean, Elsie?" whispered Alice Strang. "How come?"

"Why, it's clear as day! Have you not noticed what a puny bit thing she is, always greeting? And it's a known fact that she cannot control herself neither! Fancy peeing on Miss Murray's floor!"

There was a general sniggering.

"My big sister, her what lives down by Hyldetron once knew a bairn just the same," Elsie went on authoritatively. "And it died, just like they said it would!"

The girls were aghast.

"You're not saying Jenny's going to die, are you?" asked Stilty Mary, who had gone quite pale.

"How do I know?" Elsie shrugged. "It all depends on her da and you know who he is?"

None of the girls had ever seen Jenny's father, so they shook their heads.

Elsie waited, savouring their rapt attention. "Why the devil of course!" she said dramatically.

The girls gasped.

Elsie allowed a few more seconds to pass before elaborating. "My sister said that the bairn what died was a changeling!"

"What's one of *them*?" asked Stilty Mary.

"It's when Satan carries a bairn away and puts his own creature in its place!"

"Aye, that'll be it!" said Cissy, nodding her head sagely. "And because she didn't want to go and live with her granny, her da had to drag her by the lips! That's why she's so long-lipped!" she concluded, delighted at having invented an explanation for Jenny's protruding lips.

At this point their deliberations were cut short by the bell for afternoon school so they got up and made their way back to the playground.

As soon as they had gone, Jenny began to sob. "I'm going to die! Elsie says I'm going to die! And... and she says I'm a..."

Freya put her arms around Jenny. "Don't!" she said fiercely. "It's lies, all lies made up to scare you, to scare both of us! You can ask your granny when you get home. She'll tell you it's not true!"

Jenny turned a tear-swollen face to Freya. "And what about you, Freya? They're saying you're a witch!"

Freya looked away, out beyond the tiny field to the distant hills. "Well, what if I am?" she said in a calm voice. "Witches can do things ordinary folk can't. They can make spells! Hannah told me. And they can fly through the air like a bird. Aye, and they can even leave their bodies if they choose!"

That afternoon the children had to finish the writing task they had begun before dinner. Freya particularly liked this activity because it was the only occasion on which the younger children were allowed to write on paper with pen and ink. The white china ink pots had to be filled from a big jug and the pens distributed before the exercise could begin. Then they got out the piece of paper Miss Murray had given them on Monday. It was white and silky smooth with pale pink lines and a fine black margin. There were three words, pandemonium, Zoroastrianism and xenogenesis, printed on it with ten or so empty lines under each word where the scholars could practise their penmanship.

"Please Miss? Is this word we're on with now something to do with the Bible?" asked Stilty Mary.

"Well Mary," said Miss Murray, always pleased to see evidence of independent thought, "Genesis with a capital G is the name of the first book of the Old Testament and that is what Mr Dogberry has been talking about this week. But when it has a small letter, it means how things and human beings come about, er, are created."

"We know all about Adam now, Miss, and how he came about like!" interjected Tom Nesbit, who was keen to make up for the ignorance he had shown earlier in the week. "God made him after he made the world. Aye, Mr Dogberry even gave us the date!"

"Excellent!" said Miss Murray.

Tom glowed with pride and was about to resume his work when he realised that Miss Murray was waiting for him to tell her the date. The colour rushed to his cheeks and he thought hard for a moment. "It was four thousand and four years before the birth of Jesus! Aye, I'm sure that's what Mr Dogberry said!"

"Don't you forget about Eve!" interjected Stilty Mary. "God made her as well!"

Freya remembered what Mr Dogberry had said about Eve, how God had taken a rib from Adam while he was asleep and made her. What was better, she wondered, to be made from a handful of dust like Adam or from a rib like Eve?

At this point Will Coulter, whose father was an elder in the church and who was in the habit of reading passages from the Bible to his family after supper, spoke up. "My dad knows his Bible as good as the next man and it's his opinion that what the minister was calling the Fall of Man is nothing of the kind. He says that if you look carefully at what's written down, you can see it was all Eve's fault!"

Will was warming to his subject, sure of his words because they were his father's. "Eve's the one to blame for the both of them getting sent out of the garden and the menfolk having to sweat all their lives in the fields instead of just picking the fruit. Da says by rights they should have called it the Fall of Woman, that would be ..." Will stopped the second he saw the expression on Miss Murray's face.

Freya was thinking about serpents. The only snakes she had ever seen were the adders with their zigzag patterned skin. She had seen them sunning themselves on a flat rock in the summer time. God had cursed the serpent for what it had done. He said it would have to go on its belly from that day on. That must be why Andro cursed them too. Freya had never seen them do any harm, though Hannah used to warn her about their bite. Freya wondered if she had ever seen a picture of a serpent. Maybe there was one in the picture of the woman in the wood and she hadn't noticed it. She would look as soon as she could. Maybe the woman in the picture was Eve? No, that could not be.

According to Mr Dogberry, Adam and Eve had taken leaves from the fig tree and stitched them into aprons to cover themselves. Freya's woman was fully clothed, magnificently dressed, and anyway there was no man in the picture.

Freya had learned something very important from Mr Dogberry. Eve had sinned. It was Eve's fault that God had sent her and Adam out of the Garden of Eden. And because of this first sin committed by *one* woman, God had decided that *all* women were wicked and not to be trusted. Mr Dogberry had gone on to tell the girls how women should behave. Wives were to submit to their husbands. Women were to keep quiet. Women were on earth to help men and not the other way round. None of this was new to Freya. At Glittering Shiel everything was the way God said it should be, yet in her heart Freya felt that it was wrong.

Mr Dogberry came into the schoolroom at the very moment of embarrassed silence which followed Will's outburst. Soon he was leading the boys outside with their pencils and drawing boards to begin work on a scale drawing of the front elevation of the school. He planned to sit them down under the chestnut trees and instruct them in the laws of perspective before he allowed them to put pencil to paper.

As soon as the boys had gone, Miss Murray told Mary and Elsie to go to the cupboard and get out the sewing things. The girls always had their sewing lesson while the boys did drawing and the first task of the school year was to learn how to sew a flannel patch.

This was the only time in the week that Grace Murray saw the girls on their own. It was her habit to gather them at one end of the schoolroom where they would sit in a circle around her with their legs crossed like itinerant tailors.

At first they would chat to each other in a companionable way, but as a more intimate atmosphere was established, they would ask her the questions they dared not ask in front of the boys. At these times Grace seemed less like a schoolmistress and more like a friend, sharing her thoughts and reflections with them.

It was an unwritten law that the girls never spoke about what she said, neither amongst themselves nor to their mothers, but everything was remembered, carefully wrapped up and stored away like a precious gift. And as far as the School Board inspector was concerned, the words that passed between Miss Murray and her scholars during sewing lessons were of no concern. All that mattered to him was that the stitches on the flannel patches were neat and orderly at the time of the annual inspection.

"Please, Miss," began Cissy. "Are fig leaves big?"

"What a strange question, Cissy! Why do you ask?"

"Well, I was wondering how much work it would be for Eve to make them pinnies in the garden of Eden and I was just wondering how she went on for a needle and thread!"

Grace laughed. "Oh, I see! Yes, now there's a problem. I've never seen a fig tree or eaten a fresh fig. Miss Gilderoy once brought my mother a little basket of dried figs which I think came from Turkey. And as for a needle, well you all know what the fruit of the flower we call shepherd's needle looks like. It's like a long beak. Well I've heard it called Adam's needle because people believed that's what Adam and Eve used to stitch the first garments!"

Cissy, being of a practical turn of mind, found this explanation unsatisfactory. She decided that Eve must have had a hard time of it with only a seed pod for a needle. But, since she idolised Miss Murray, she would never have dreamt of criticising, so she simply nodded and said, "Oh."

"Now then girls, I have something to show you," said Miss Murray a little later. "Mary, there's a cardboard tube on my desk. Please will you get it for me?"

As soon as Mary returned, Miss Murray began. "Apart from the story of Adam and Eve which of course we, as Christians, believe, there are other much older stories of how the world and the men and women in it were created. You see, girls, in ancient times people did not understand the part a man plays in the miracle of how a baby is made."

The needles stopped and the girls held their breath, hoping that Miss Murray was going to speak to them of *that* secret.

"People could see that woman was the bringer of life because it was women who gave birth, so naturally they worshipped a goddess," Miss Murray went on. "Our patroness, Miss Gilderoy, has had the good fortune to travel widely in the ancient world and she has in her possession a small terracotta figurine which I believe is Ishtar or Ashtoreth, the Queen of Heaven."

"Has she got clothes on, Miss, or is she bare like Eve before she made the pinny?" asked Elsie.

"No, she is naked."

Grace Murray was reluctant to linger over the details of Ishtar's nudity or her curvaceous body, so she returned to her theme. "At the time of which I am speaking, arrangements between men and women were not as they are today. There was a people called the Lycians and according to Herodotus - he was a historian - if a Lycian was asked who he was, he would give his mother's name. You see, girls, it mattered little if the father's name was not known. The important thing was that every mother knew her own child. Property was owned by the women and was passed on through them." Then, thinking of the circumstances of her own birth, Grace added quietly, "In some ways it must have been a golden age, when there was no shame in a child not knowing who its father was."

Then Miss Murray took a picture, Botticelli's 'Birth of Venus', from the cardboard tube and unrolled it. "You see, girls, I wanted you to know that there are many stories of how the world and the men and women in it were made and, in the very earliest of these, creation is the work of woman, of a goddess."

"And is that her?" asked Stilty Mary, pointing to the woman in the picture.

"Yes, she is known as Venus, or Aphrodite, the goddess of beauty. There's a serpent in her story too. He was called Ophion and together they produced the egg from which the world was made."

"So her and the serpent was the best of pals, not like Eve?" commented Mary.

"That's right, Mary. Serpents, and women too, have had a bad reputation ever since the events in the Garden of Eden, but things were very different before that. People believed that serpents were wise, that they could tell the future."

"But, Miss, both stories can't be true, can they?" asked Freya, her timidity forgotten.

Grace Murray looked into Freya's earnest face and saw eyes bright with hope. Grace's heart was heavy at the answer she knew she must give. "No, Freya, it's just a story that people believed once upon a time. For the last thousand years, ever since Queen Ethelburg brought Saint Paulinus to this wild north country to baptise our ancestors, we have believed in the word of God, believed what is written in the Bible," and then, to show she understood Freya's hope and shared her sadness, Grace added, "though the burden the Christian faith lays on women is sometimes beyond bearing."

11

Cast out from the community of the Herontop girls, Freya and Jenny were left alone together and so their friendship deepened. The knowledge of who they were had been given to them by the Herontop girls. How they should behave was gleaned from other sources, from Jenny's granny and from what Hannah had told Freya. Gradually the girls came to play the game that Elsie and Cissy had begun. They cultivated the wickedness that had been attributed to them, and became strong.

All their free time was spent together talking quietly in some corner of the little field. However, the Herontop girls could not leave them in peace and frequently sought them out.

Each week Miss Murray gave the children some lines of poetry to learn by heart. She always chose a poem that had some connection with what she was teaching. In the first weeks of the autumn term she had been telling them about the early Saxon kings of Northumberland. She had spoken of Bamburgh castle, the mighty fortress by the North Sea which, set on its massive rock, towered above the sweeping bay. She explained that the rock was part of the Great Whin Sill which lay across the county of Northumberland like the backbone of the biggest giant they could imagine.

One clear afternoon, mounted on her donkey, she led the children up one of the soft green hills that lay to the south of the school from which vantage point they could look to the east and see the great fortress for themselves.

"According to legend, that is the castle of Sir Lancelot du Lac," she said, pointing towards the castle which none of the children had ever visited. "It was called Joyous Gard and Lancelot asked that his body should be brought back there after his death." Then she drew a small, leather-bound volume from her coat and read them the final pages of Malory's *Mort d'Arthure*, which tell of Lancelot's return to Bamburgh.

Freya was enchanted. She closed her eyes and imagined the procession as Lancelot was carried home across the hills. She saw the flames of fifteen torches, blue tar lights on poles, dancing in the wind. Did they, perhaps, rest for the night on the gentle slopes of Eidonhope before crossing the lowland plain to the castle? Could the warrior, her warrior, be Lancelot, the spirit of Lancelot, somehow taken shape in the landscape? Then she saw him in his coffin, his waxen face uncovered for all to see. But to her surprise, his face was not that of a grown man but of a boy. It was Sam's face just as she had seen it that day in the parlour.

The following day Miss Murray wrote on the blackboard some lines from Lord Tennyson's poem, 'Sir Launcelot and Queen Guinevere'. She told the children to copy down the poetry and then to learn it by heart. Freya had committed it to memory even before she had written it down. However, Jenny found it difficult to learn things by heart, so at dinner time she and Freya went outside to practise.

They were sitting under one of the chestnut trees. Jenny was concentrating on her task, eyes closed tight while Freya spoke the lines so that Jenny could repeat them: "'Then, in the boyhood of the year, Sir Launcelot and Queen Guinevere, Rode thro' the coverts of the deer, With blissful treble ringing clear...'"

Suddenly a voice intruded into their small world, shattering the picture in Freya's mind and breaking Jenny's concentration.

It was Elsie.

"So what's going on here then?" she asked. "Are you practising your spells or what?"

Freya remained silent. It was Jenny who recovered first.

"Aye Elsie, that's it," said Jenny, nodding. "We're just finishing saying the Lord's prayer," and then, with a gleam in her eye, she added, "backwards, of course!"

Not knowing that this was a feature of a witch's repertoire, Elsie was taken aback.

"So, if it's all the same to you," said Jenny, seizing the advantage, "I'll just finish off." And with a skill that surprised and delighted Freya, she took a deep breath and said slowly, "heaven in art which Father Our."

This was too much for Elsie, who turned on her heel and hurried off to find her friends.

"And then we're off over yonder," shouted Jenny at the retreating Elsie, "to slake our thirst with some black heather water!"

From that day on, whenever Elsie or one of the other girls tried to torment either herself or Freya, Jenny was ready with an answer. She and Freya almost believed that they did indeed have magic powers, for there was no doubt that what they said had a powerful effect. Of course witches were wicked and they would much rather have been good. But ever since Mr Dogberry had told them about Eve, they could not see much difference between a woman and a witch. According to him, no matter how good women were, how hard they tried, they could not undo that first sin. And it seemed that even Miss Murray could do nothing about it.

One morning before school Jenny came rushing up to Freya. "Granny says witches've got an extra tit!" she whispered into Freya's ear so loudly that it tickled. "She says it's so they can give suck to their imp!"

"What's an imp?" asked Freya, remembering that Rose sometimes called Violet an imp.

"Oh! I forgot to ask! I'll mind on to do it tonight."

It was not long before Jenny thought of having a look to see if either of them had an extra nipple and, since it involved undressing, they decided that the only safe place was the netty.

The more Freya considered the plan, the less she liked it. Undressing anywhere other than in her own bedroom frightened her. Sometimes Andro made her take her clothes off in some hidden place, inside the wall of a sheep stell or in the shadow of the crags. And she was afraid that if Jenny saw her body, she would see some tell-tale sign of what Andro did to her, so she compromised, suggesting that they only search above the waist.

After they had eaten Freya's dinner and drunk the bottle of milk, they went and sat with their backs against the end wall of the schoolroom from where they could see the entrance to the girls' netty. They waited until Elsie and Cissy had been before they made a move.

They pushed open the door and squeezed into the dark space, fastening the door behind them. It was gloomy inside with the only light coming from a tiny pane of glass set high in the stonework and the row of holes cut into the door.

They had agreed that Freya would be first. She sat on the seat, a broad wooden bench with an egg-shaped hole cut in it and began to undress. Jenny was standing in front of her in the space between the bench and the door. Soon Freya's slip with its initialled pocket was lying on the bench and she was fumbling nervously with the buttons of her blouse.

"Here, let me give you a hand!" offered Jenny and, before Freya could say anything, Jenny's deft fingers had undone the blouse and she was pulling it off. Only a flannel liberty bodice remained, then Freya's top half was uncovered. Her skin was porcelain pale in the half light and she was leaning forward, her long white arms gripping the edge of the seat.

"Right then!" said Jenny in a businesslike way. "Let's have a look! It's that dark in here, I can hardly see." She ran the tips of her fingers to and fro over Freya's goose-pimply skin. When she came to her pale biscuit-brown nipples, she smiled at Freya regretfully. "It's a shame these don't count, eh? Now then, lift your arms!"

Freya obeyed.

"No," said Jenny, shaking her head, "there's nothing there."

Freya could tell Jenny was disappointed. "Maybe there's one on my back," she suggested. She stood up, turned round and knelt on the seat so that she had her back to Jenny. Facing the wall with her head bent, she was soon assailed by a nauseating smell.

"What's this?" squealed Jenny excitedly. "Here! On your shoulder! Can you not feel it?"

Freya could feel Jenny's finger on her skin, but she had no sense of a nipple. All of a sudden she felt sick and trapped. She wanted to get away from the foul hole and out of the enclosed space. She had an overwhelming desire to push aside Jenny and her probing, poking fingers and escape.

"No," she stammered. "I didn't know it was there. Jenny!" she said urgently. "I want out or else I'll be sick!"

Jenny was crestfallen. She could not understand why Freya was not thrilled at her discovery. "Aye, all right then. Here's your things. I'll give you a hand." As she helped Freya get down from the bench, she too caught a whiff of the smell. "I know what's wrong!" she said, pinching her nose. "It's Elsie's shite what's done that to you!"

Freya was the first to emerge into the fresh air. Her legs felt like jelly and her eyes were dazzled by the light. When she had recovered a little, she looked around. There was no one to be seen. "It's all right, " she called softly to Jenny. "You can come out."

Freya was deathly pale and dishevelled. Jenny took one look at her, then took her arm and led her like a docile ghost round the corner into the schoolyard. There was nobody there either.

"Oh Freya! The bell must have went! How come we didn't hear it? What'll we do?"

Now Jenny felt sick. They were standing wondering what to do when Miss Murray came out of the girls' door, an anxious look on her face. As soon as she saw them, her expression changed to one of annoyance.

"Where *have* you been?" she asked. "Didn't you hear the bell? I rang it almost ten minutes ago!"

"It's Freya, Miss! Please Miss, she's feeling sick, Miss!" stammered Jenny.

Grace looked at their pinched, earnest faces and her irritation gave way to concern. It had not escaped her that Elsie and Cissy were doing everything they could to make their lives a misery.

111

However, it was an unspoken rule at the school that what went on outside the schoolroom was the children's affair. They had their own ways of sorting things out and only very rarely did they bring their troubles to Grace.

"I see!" said Grace, nodding. "Jenny, take Freya into the schoolhouse and give her a drink of water. Then you can stay with her until she's feeling better."

The Herontop girls never actually made friends with Freya and Jenny, but after the day that Elsie found the figure, an uneasy truce was established.

It was just after school. Freya and Billy were halfway up the hill and Jenny was a lone figure, making her way across the fields to Herontop. She chose to walk over the fields in order to avoid the Herontop girls.

As usual the Herontop girls were in no hurry. They joked and chattered as they dawdled along the road, sometimes walking backwards, waving their arms about in the air. Elsie put her hand into the pocket of her coat, then she stopped dead in the middle of the road.

"What's this?" she cried, horrified.

The other girls quickly gathered round to look at the object Elsie presently drew from her pocket. At first she thought it looked like a small, misshapen hedgehog because of the mass of thorns that had been planted deep into its pasty flesh, but then she saw the shape beneath the prickles. There was no doubt about it. It was a human figure crudely fashioned out of a piece of uncooked bread dough with a rudimentary head, arms and legs.

Ugh!" exclaimed Cissy in disgust. "That's horrible!" She was silent for a while and then she exclaimed, "Elsie! I think I know what it is!"

"Go on, then! Spit it out!" said Elsie impatiently.

"It's you! That thing's meant to be you!"

"What're you on about?" Elsie shouted at her aggressively. But as soon as the meaning of Cissy's words had sunk in, she clasped her free hand to her throat as if she was choking. "What d'you mean? Me!" she gasped

"That witch's put a spell on you! That's what! And those thorns are there to harm you!" Cissy explained with an unmistakable touch of satisfaction.

Elsie let out a groan, then hurled the figure to the ground. She was just about to grind it into the road with the heel of her clog when Cissy grabbed her arm and pulled her back.

"Don't stamp on it!" she said urgently. "You don't want to get yourself crushed to death!"

Nothing was ever said about the figure, but from then on the Herontop girls were more circumspect in their dealings with Jenny and Freya. Their animosity did not vanish, rather it was contained, ready to irrupt when circumstances allowed.

The Herontop girls often needed Jenny and Freya to make up the numbers for one of their games. On such occasions Cissy or Elsie would send an emissary to ask Jenny and Freya to join in. In games where someone had to be "It", this role would invariably fall to Jenny or Freya, which was the price exacted for being allowed to take part.

By the second week in November, the Herontop girls were beginning to get bored with witches. Halloween had been and gone and so they began to play a game called 'Stealy-clothes', otherwise known as 'Scotch and English', a game which had its origins in the Border forays of earlier times. Freya and Jenny were issued with an invitation to take part.

As usual Elsie had taken charge and was organising everybody. "Right Cissy!" she said. "Knot those two ropes together for the line."

Cissy did as she was told and laid the rope along the ground to mark the borderline between the territories of the opposing sides.

"Now lassies, me and Cissy with Jeannie, May and Mary'll be on the English side and the rest of you is on the other side. Go on then, put down your wad!"

Each girl removed an article of clothing and laid it at the prescribed distance away from the rope line. Most of the girls took off a clog, but Freya was wearing boots which took a long time to undo, so she took off her slip instead, folded it and laid it on the grass. Elsie put down her hat, a large red tam-o'-shanter with a huge scarlet pompom, of which she was extremely proud. Elsie was standing opposite Freya ready to give the signal for off. Each player had to attempt to seize an article of dress from the opposing team and carry it back safe to her own territory. If one of the players got caught, she was taken prisoner and branded a 'stinkard'.

"Now for the onset!" shouted Elsie, using the ancient language of strife.

"Here's a leap into thy kingdom, dry-bellied Scot!" yelled Cissy, making a bee-line for Jenny's clog.

Mayhem ensued as the girls dived, squealing and shouting into the *mêlée*. Freya was quick off the mark. Elsie's beret was the obvious target, being close to her slip, which she had to try and defend. She darted forward and snatched up the beret and was turning round ready to run back to her own territory when Elsie saw what she had done.

"You'll not take my tammy, Freya Man!" roared Elsie as she flung herself at Freya's ankles.

The girls fell struggling to the ground with Freya clutching the beret to her chest. Elsie grabbed Freya's plait and pulled her head back while she tried to wrest back the beret. When they finally separated, Elsie had regained her hat. However, her triumph was short-lived for she soon realised that the pompom had come off in the struggle and was still in Freya's clenched fist.

Elsie was mad with rage. "I'll get you for this! You see if I don't!" she yelled, brandishing a fist at Freya. Then she threw her beret back into her own territory and made off in the direction of Freya's slip.

Freya did not pursue Elsie. She felt sick at the damage already done, so she simply stood by and watched.

With eyes blazing, Elsie now did what she had secretly longed to do from the very first day that Freya had come to school. Like a magician about to perform an astounding feat, she held the slip up aloft for all to see. Then she grasped the embroidered pocket and ripped it off with a flourish. Then, her revenge complete, she dumped the pieces unceremoniously on the ground.

As soon as the other girls realised that genuine warfare had broken out, they suspended hostilities. Jenny had been captured by Cissy, but now she came back to her friend's side.

"Don't look at me like that, Jenny!" said Elsie defensively. "It's not my fault! She started it! She didn't ought to have pulled the pompom off my tammy!"

"I'm sorry about your hat, Elsie," said Freya quietly. "I never meant it to happen."

Jenny, knowing that an apology would do no good, went into the attack. "Elsie, you know fine well it was an accident, not like what you just did to Freya's slip!"

Elsie went red.

"Freya'll tell her mam what you did as soon as she gets home and then you'll be for it!"

"See if I care what she tells her mam! Anyway her mam's not her mam, so there!" riposted Elsie, who was never more dangerous than when she was trapped.

"What are you saying, Elsie?" demanded Jenny. "That cannot be right!"

"Just you ask certain folk round here and they'll tell you! Her mam's no more her mam than her da's her da!" And with this final broadside, Elsie flounced off the battlefield.

Freya was in a state of numbed turmoil. Jenny, who knew the pain such accusations caused, did what she could to comfort her.

"Of course your mam's your mam! How could she not be? She's there waiting when you get home, isn't she? She cooks you your breakfast and your dinner," said Jenny, thinking of her own mother whom she had never known."

Freya was remembering how Mr Dogberry had told the children that everybody needed to know who they were and where they came from. Freya had thought she knew these things, but Elsie's words had sent her hurtling into a black emptiness where there was nothing to hold on to.

Pale and expressionless, Freya sat beside Jenny through the afternoon lesson. Though her body was in its appointed place, her mind was adrift. Jenny had made her put her slip back on and had tried to tidy her hair. Jenny had dropped the crumpled garment over Freya's head, drawing her limp arms through the armholes as though she were dressing a doll or a small child. As soon as the slip was on, Jenny saw that Elsie had ripped a gaping hole in the body of the garment. Freya seemed indifferent to the damage, but Jenny knew that Miss Murray would be sure to notice.

Grace did notice. She was also aware of an uneasy calm among the girls as if some storm had raged that now was over, leaving behind a trail of devastation. Elsie and Cissy were unusually quiet, almost penitent. Grace decided that something would have to be done, that she would have to find out what was going on.

Grace was sitting on her chair and a large globe, which she had borrowed from the library at Heron Hall, was standing on the desk in front of her.

Freya watched the multicoloured ball spin round. She knew that the oceans were blue and that the different patches of colour represented countries. But as the globe spun faster and faster, the colours lost their separateness and merged into one another. She concentrated on it, willing it to spin faster and faster, taking comfort from the movement and the unresolved chaos of colour. But soon it began to slow down as she knew it would.

"Do you see where it's stopped?" asked Grace. "It's very clever, it always stops in the same place. It's where we are!" She stood up and came round to the front of the desk. "You see this tiny patch of red here, that is Great Britain and we are here," she added, pointing to the North of England.

Freya looked away, preferring the blank wall. She did not want to be reminded of where she was. The lesson continued, but

Freya did not pay attention. Only the occasional word penetrated her troubled mind - the British Empire, red, red, red like Elsie's bonnet, spreading, getting bigger and bigger, covering everything. She closed her eyes and tried to shut it out.

She did not realise when the lesson was over and it was time to go home. Jenny tugged her sleeve, shaking her as if she had been asleep.

"Come on, Freya! Come on! It's home time!"

Grace watched them leave and resolved to speak to Freya the following day. The girl looked ill, desperately unhappy, and Jenny was obviously very worried about her.

Jenny stood with Freya in the schoolyard until Billy came running up.

"What's wrong?" he asked, as soon as he saw Freya.

"The other lassies was tormenting her at dinner time and her slip got ripped!" explained Jenny.

Billy nodded sympathetically for he understood better than anybody what terrible trouble torn clothes could cause.

Jenny stood under the chestnut trees, watching Freya and Billy walk away from her up the hill. As she waved one last time, she little realised that she would not be seeing her friend for four months.

12

The sun had already disappeared behind the Cheviot hills, so Billy knew they must hurry if they were to get home before dark. Every afternoon the children found that they had to walk a little faster in a race against the coming darkness. Usually it was Billy who had difficulty keeping up with Freya who would stride off in front of him, turning her head from time to time to urge him on. But today was different with Freya walking at a slow rhythmic pace as if she was carrying a great burden.

"Come on, Freya! Get a shift on! Me mam'll put us over her knee if I'm late!" But no matter what Billy said, Freya continued to walk at the same even, trance-like pace.

The valley bottom was so thick with shadows when they came to the old still that they did not see the pony and cart until they were almost upon them.

Andro and Tom Pagon were standing at the ruined doorway, talking. They did not hear the children approach but the collies picked up the metallic click of Billy's tackety boots on the stony track and they began to bark.

The children saw that the pony was Polly and, realising that Andro must be nearby, they stood quietly and waited. Soon Andro's voice came to them. "And about time too! I've been stood here talking to Tom for twenty minutes or more waiting for the pair of you!" Then they heard him say, "We concluded our business long since, eh Tom?"

"Aye, right enough!" Tom replied, feeling in his pocket for the silver coins Andro had handed him a few minutes before.

Andro picked up a grey hen from inside the still, walked down the slope and lifted it into the cart, wedging it securely in one corner. "Now then, Billy, my lad, you can sit beside me and Freya can ride in the back!" Andro was surprised when Freya made no move to climb into the cart, neither did she react when

118

he put his hands around her waist and swung her up over the side rail.

Billy was overjoyed to be sitting at the front next to the driver. Andro too seemed to be in good humour. He was disposed to talk, being well pleased with his day's work.

"I've been over to Hoarstones taking Bart Dunne's brockie-faced ram back," he volunteered with a quiet chuckle. "But I fear Bart'll find him just about done for - for this year anyway! Yon fine beast has worn himself out on my ewes! Aye, and a good thing too. It's no more than what he deserves. I offered him a fair price, did I not? But oh no, he wouldn't have it!"

Billy had little idea what Andro was talking about. His eyes were fixed on Polly's ears which were pointing forwards in eager anticipation of getting back home.

Andro turned to Billy. "So what's been going on, lad? Why were the pair of you so late?"

"It's Freya, sir."

"What about Freya?"

"There's something wrong with her. Her friend, Jenny, told me that the Herontop lassies was tormenting her at dinner time."

"What d'you mean tormenting her?"

"I don't know." Then it occurred to Billy that he ought to be more forthcoming. "The lassies from Herontop have got it into their heads that Freya's a witch!"

"How come?"

"I don't know! Maybe it's her name, they think she's got a queer name. They think she's...different!"

Freya's back was resting against the front rail of the cart, her cloak was wrapped tight around her with the hood pulled up over her head. While Andro and Billy were looking westwards up the valley where the last vestiges of light were receding from Maidenhope, Freya was looking in the opposite direction, over an already darkened landscape.

The cart came to a halt in the farmyard. Billy leapt down and went to Polly's head, ready to take her out of the shafts and lead her off to the field.

"Down with you, Freya!" ordered Andro.

Freya did not move. Andro went to look and saw that she was slumped forward. "Well, if she's not dropped off to sleep," he said to himself. He lifted the flagon of liquor out of the cart and carried it into the house, thinking that Freya would be sure to wake now that the cart had stopped moving.

A minute or two later Lizzie came outside to see what was going on. She saw immediately that something was wrong with Freya. She ran her fingers over Freya's forehead. It was cold. Then she took hold of Freya's hands. They were limp and chilled. "Come on, Freya! Wake up!" said Lizzie gently. But there was no response.

Andro came back out of the house.

"Give me a hand, Andro!" said Lizzie urgently. "There's something wrong with Freya! She's ailing. We'd best get her to bed!"

Freya did not open her eyes nor did she speak for three days. She was feverish, tossing about in bed and mumbling incomprehensible things. Lizzie was very worried and tried to convince herself that Freya had caught the influenza which was going the rounds.

A week earlier they had heard that the Dunne family was struck down with 'flu. Lizzie had wanted to go over to Herondale to see what she could do to help Agnes Dunne, but Andro had refused. Then, a day or two later, Andro had come into the house and said with barely concealed delight, "Well now! If the Lord hasn't showered his bounty on us today! Would you believe me if I told you I found Bart Dunne's brockie-faced ram doing his business in among my ewes up on the marches? The Lord has surely given us a helping hand and we can look forward to a fine crop of speckle-faced lambs this spring!"

Lizzie had thought that it was probably more accurate to say that the Lord helps those that help themselves, but she said nothing. They both knew that the ram would have to be returned, though Andro was in no hurry. Twenty-four hours passed before he loaded the animal into the cart to take him home. Lizzie, happy to have the chance to be neighbourly, gave him a basket of freshly-baked scones and bread for the Dunnes.

Andro had found Bart and Philip in bed in the kitchen. Agnes was over the worst of it, but it was as much as she could do to keep the fire going and get them all something to eat. Andro fetched some water and saw to the animals. Bart was grateful for this and for the return of his prize ram, though he was at a loss to know how it had got out. He distinctly remembered shutting it into the little field at the back of the house, because it was the last thing he had done before taking to his bed.

Lizzie decided that Freya must have caught the 'flu from one of the children at school, though she did think it strange that Freya's slip should have got torn on the very day that she fell ill.

The next evening Lizzie sat by the fire and mended the slip. Andro made no comment except to say he had decided that Freya would go to school no more that year, that she should stay at home until the days began to lengthen. Lizzie, who had hoped to arrange for Freya to lodge at Home Farm as Sam had done, accepted his decision. She was too worried about Freya to argue about school.

It was three days later, on her first visit of the day to the tiny back bedroom, that Lizzie found Freya awake. She was lying on her back staring up at the ceiling. Lizzie felt a surge of relief.

"So you've come back to the land of the living at long last!" she said, sitting down on the edge of the bed and stroking Freya's forehead. "I've been that worried about you, lying here, tossing and turning and not a single word I could make sense of!" She looked into Freya's eyes. "Tell me how you're feeling. Will you not tell me what's been the matter?"

There was silence for a minute or more, then Freya turned her head away towards the window.

"They said you're not my mam," she said in a flat emotionless voice.

"What d'you mean, they said I'm not your mam?"

121

Freya turned to face her. "Elsie said you're not my mam and my dad's not my dad."

Lizzie had feared that this might happen. After all, plenty of folk knew about Felix and the baby and when Sam died Andro had said publicly that Lizzie could not have children. Andro and she had never discussed what they would say if Freya did find out. Lizzie's first impulse was to say the story wasn't true, but she found that she could not. There was something in Freya's steadfast gaze that required her to tell the truth.

"It's right what they told you, Freya. I'm not your mam, but I love you as much as any mother could! You must believe that!"

Once more the globe with its chaotic colours was spinning in Freya's head. The only way that it could be stopped would be if Lizzie told her who she really was.

"But who *is* my mam? Where did I come from? Who *am* I?" she pleaded.

Lizzie could not bear Freya's unflinching gaze. She looked away and folded Freya's slender fingers in her own, holding them tight while she told her all about Felix's visit eight years before.

Freya listened. So that was it, she had come from the sea, from the sea foam like the girl in Miss Murray's picture. But what about her home, her true home? She was from another place across the sea, the North Sea, the same sea that broke on the shore beside Lancelot's castle. That was why she had a strange name, because she came from a far-off place.

Lizzie mistook Freya's silence for disbelief. As she had heard herself telling the story, she had been struck by how incredible it sounded. It was like a fairy tale. Then she remembered the newspaper Hannah had left in the bothy. Lizzie had only looked at it briefly, but she knew it was all about the March storms, columns and columns of it. She had intended to ask Andro to read it to her, but once the paper had been put away in the bottom of the drawer in the dresser, she had forgotten all about it.

"I'll tell you what! Now that you've been to school and got yourself a bit of learning, you can read all about it for yourself! It's in the paper, the newspaper, all about the storms and the ship!

The *Freya*! It must be there. I'll fetch it for you when I bring your porridge up. You'll take a bit of porridge now, won't you?"

Lizzie hurried off to fetch the newspaper. On reflection, she doubted whether Freya had learned enough to be able to read much of it, but she decided that the important thing was to give Freya some sort of proof that what she had said was true.

The paper lay under Freya's pillow for many days. She was content to keep it there, a treasure-chest to be opened and explored when she was ready, when she felt strong enough.

In the meantime she went over and over what Lizzie had told her. She asked Lizzie questions and several times she asked her to repeat the whole story so that she was sure she had got every detail correct.

There was another country which was called Norway. The *Freya* had sailed from there. But where was Norway? What was it like? They had trees there because the *Freya* had been carrying pit-props. And then there were the dangerous rocks, the Black Middens. Freya tried to imagine the ship smashed and broken, yet with a tiny room left whole, with the fire still burning and the cat asleep beside it. Lizzie had told her they had found the ship's log which was a sort of diary. It had been lying open beside the charts, all tidy and up to date.

Once she was satisfied that she had learned everything Lizzie could tell her, Freya went to the shelf in her room and took one of the precious pieces of silky smooth paper she had brought home from school. She put the side with writing exercices face down and wrote carefully on the back '*Freya* Norway Black Middens'. These were to be the signposts which would guide her through the maze of newsprint.

The newspaper never left the tiny bedroom. Whenever she got the chance, Freya would slip upstairs and get it out from under her pillow. It was too big to hold like a book and so she laid it on her bed. Then as if she was about to say her prayers she would kneel down on the bare boards, rest her elbows on the bed and pore over it.

The paper was huge. It lay across her bed like a stiff blanket. On each page there were five long bands of tiny black print each divided into sections with a few words in capital letters in the space between. The paper was yellow at the edges and in some places it had got wet so that there were uneven patches where the print was blurred and illegible.

The work was slow and laborious. The first headline said simply 'GALE AND FLOODS', and below it 'NUMEROUS WRECKS'. That was the problem. A great many ships had been lost that night and the paper seemed to describe them all. Finding the *Freya* was like looking for a needle in a haystack. But she was determined. Day after day she unfolded the paper and studied it. Many a time she wished that Miss Murray was there to help her but she told herself that it was her search, her story that was lying hidden in the thousands of words and that she would find it for herself.

By the middle of December she had found the account of the wreck of the *Freya*. It was near the bottom of the last column on the second page under the headline 'WRECK OF A VESSEL AND LOSS OF THE CREW. The condition of the ship was described in minute detail including the state of the cabin with the fire still in and the ship's canary in its cage, though she could find no mention of the cat Lizzie had told her about. The editor of the paper had included a translation of the captain's last entry in the ship's log. Trembling with emotion Freya read it.

> Blowing a fearful east gale, sea terrible, hourly expecting to go onshore, can do nothing for her, tried to sail several times. She won't bear it. Have told crew what to expect tonight. God grant the wind may veer in time to save us. Soundings in twenty fathoms, rock, so now there is no chance. Expect to go ashore between Ferns and Coquet. No chance of saving life with this sea. Have done all I can to keep her off, but cannot carry canvas.

Praying the Lord have Mercy on our
souls and take us to Heaven.

At the end there was a list of the crew members who had been found washed up on the beach, but nowhere could Freya find any mention of a baby.

13

It was the winter solstice. Early in the morning Freya stood at the boulder by the gate and gazed at the warrior. She watched the sun rise behind his head, turning his rugged profile into the teeth of a giant saw blade. The sun, a huge disc of fiery bronze, moved solemnly in its appointed course along the line of the hills, casting long shadows over the moorland.

The next morning, a day of pinching cold, a mugger, a pedlar man, wound his way up Eidonhope. His donkey was carrying two panniers packed with earthenware crocks purchased in Newcastle market, horn spoons, some besoms and a small bundle of rowan sticks for good luck. The man had spent the night within the ruined walls of the old still, making himself a roof with a piece of oilskin laid across a corner of the building and weighted down with stones.

He led his placid cuddy up the lonely track and, having come almost to the gate of Glittering Shiel, he turned off and went down to the burn so the donkey could have a drink and he could take his ease in the morning sun.

Freya, who was out collecting kindling, crossed to the north bank of the burn some hundred yards downstream of where the pedlar was sitting and began to make her way back up towards the house. So intent was she on her task that she did not see the pedlar sitting there, a grey-coated figure, his back resting against a boulder of paler grey, his face turned to the sun.

He saw her first, a slender figure clutching a bundle of twigs, pale sunlight shining like a golden aureole around her loosely-gathered hair.

"What lovely vision is this?" he cried in the gentle tones of the borderland. "Have I landed up on Huntly Bank and is this not the Queen of Elfhame come to bid an old man follow her to fairyland?"

His voice was soft and melodic and Freya was not afraid. She had never heard of the Queen of Elfhame, but it did not matter. She knew she was a delight to the old man.

"I dare say there's some fine pebbles in yon burn," the old man mused.

Freya laid down her bundle of twigs and felt in her pocket for the quartz pebbles she always carried. Timidly she came up to him and held out her hand.

His brown eyes twinkled when he saw the pebbles. Then without a word he got up and walked a little way down the burn to a boggy place where some tussocks of reed were growing. He got a penknife out of his pocket, opened it and sliced through a handful of the pithy stalks. Then he came back to where he had been sitting and, with dextrous fingers, he began to weave the dark green strands together.

After a time he turned to her. "Now then, my fairy queen, will you trust old Jock with your bright pebbles?"

With the beginnings of a smile playing on her lips, Freya dropped the stones into his cupped hand.

He smiled at her. "I know what!" he said laying the pebbles on the grass while he delved in one of his capacious pockets. "See here, fair maiden, just take a look at my babby-boodies!" In his hand lay an assortment of brightly coloured pieces of pottery and mixed among them were coloured beads made of amber, jet and glass. "Since you've been good enough to trust an old tinker man with your treasure, you shall choose from mine! Go on, choose! Take any one you like!"

Freya would have dearly liked to touch them all, to turn them over, examine the fragments of pattern on the pottery, feel the weight and texture of the beads, but she was too shy, so she pointed to an oval glass bead of uneven shape. It was an intense turquoise, the colour of a damsel fly on a summer's day.

He winked at her. "Aye, lassie that's a good one. I've had it many a long day and I don't mind telling you I'm very fond of it. But like I said, you can have it! Mind, be sure you take good care of it, for the man that gave it to me said it came from an ancient tomb and for all I know it has magic powers!"

Jock slipped the bead and Freya's pebbles into the goblet of reeds that he had woven and then he deftly closed it up. As he handed it to her he shook his head apologetically. "I fear you're too big a lassie to be given a baby's rattle! But never mind, you've Jock of Coverdale's word on it, that bead in there will bring you good fortune!"

By the time Freya had finished collecting firewood and got back home, Jock had gone. He had called at the bothy where Rose had made him welcome. While he warmed himself by the fire and drank some tea, he chatted to Rose and gave her news of her old friends at Roselaw where he had called the previous day. Later, after Rose had bought an egg spoon for Violet and a brown glazed mug for Billy, Jock brought the conversation round to life at Glittering Shiel. He listened intently to everything Rose said, showing as much interest in her concern about Violet's chesty cough as her comments about the farm and her opinion of Andro Man.

Jock's run of good fortune came to an end after he left Rose's fireside. It was Andro who answered his knock at the farmhouse. Lizzie only arrived at the door in time to see him disappearing round the corner of the house.

Jock crossed the bridge and struck off north-west across Skirlmoor, carrying into Scotland his wares and the news from Glittering Shiel. By nightfall he would be in Coverdale, warming his toes by Hob Hetherton's fire.

On Christmas Day the following year, Freya received a present. A large brown envelope was lying on the table beside her porridge bowl when she came downstairs for breakfast.

Lizzie kissed her. "Here's a present for you, Freya! Happy Christmas!"

Never having received a Christmas present before, Freya did not know what she was supposed to do.

"Go on then!" said Lizzie. "Open it! It's not much. I wish I could have got you something better."

Freya opened the envelope and drew out several sheets of thin cardboard. The figure of a girl was printed on the first one. She was plump and dimpled with an abundance of brown curly hair with blobs of pink on her cheeks and dark red, heart-shaped lips.

"You have to cut her out!" Lizzie explained, pointing to the thick black line around the edge of the figure. "See here, you cut round these flaps and then you fold them back and then you can stand her up. And then you can put her clothes on!"

Freya looked at the girl. Her body was a featureless expanse of pinkish card with straight, unjointed arms and legs. Freya put her to one side and looked at the next sheet of card which had a plaid skirt, a bright red coat with a white fur collar and a fur hat printed on it.

Lizzie fetched her sewing scissors so that she could show Freya what to do. She cut out the hat and set it on the girl's head. "See! And it'll look a whole sight better when you've cut her out, when she's standing up!"

After breakfast Freya took the sheets of card upstairs to her room. She carefully cut out the figure and stood it on her shelf.

The next morning when she woke up, she lay and stared at it. She could see no resemblance between herself and the figure, though it was a girl and so was she. At first she thought it was because of the girl's face and hair which were so different from her own. Then she decided she had never seen a girl who looked like that, though the blobs of colour on the cheeks did remind her of Cissy the day she brought the wallpaper scraps to school.

Cissy had discovered that if she wet her finger with spit and rubbed it on the paper, the colour, a deep magenta, would come off. In the playground before school she daubed some on her cheeks and lips as if it was rouge. The instant Mr Dogberry saw her, he flew into a fearful rage and called her a Jezebel with a painted face. Cissy had blushed so deeply that the rest of her face turned almost the same colour as her cheeks. Mr Dogberry seized the moment and delivered a hellfire oration about Jezebel and her dreadful fate and after he had done, like Jehovah with outstretched arm, he expelled Cissy from the schoolroom with orders to scrub her face.

A little later Freya realised that there was something else wrong with the figure. Some things were missing. She had no nipples and, more important than that, there were no openings, no place for a man's thing to go. Dissatisfaction with the figure was replaced by anger because it was telling a lie. It was pretending that that place did not exist. She was about to jump out of bed, take hold of the figure and tear it into little pieces, but then she thought of Lizzie. How would she explain what she had done? So instead, she got up and laid the figure face down on the shelf so that she would not have to look at it any more.

A day later she had the idea of making her own figure out of the envelope in which the rejected figure had come. She used the offending figure as a template. However, she stopped when she came to the neck because the head with its mass of curly hair was the wrong shape. She put the template to one side and drew a slender oval face. Then she cut out the new figure. The shape was now acceptable, but the colour, a muddy brown, was not at all like her own pale skin. Seeing some flakes of whitewash peeling off the bedroom ceiling, she had an idea. She went outside to the stable where Lizzie kept a large drum of whitewash. She prised off the lid and dipped a rag into the chalky liquid. Back in her room, she dabbed the rag over the surface of the figure until it was putty white. Then when it was quite dry she took a pencil and marked on those parts of the body that the first figure had lacked.

It was only later that it occurred to her to give the figure a nose, mouth and eyes. This she did with great delicacy, making the lightest pencil strokes on the blank oval of the face.

The original figure had an extensive wardrobe. There was a party dress which reminded Freya of the fine muslin dress Mary Black had worn one Midsummer's Eve. Then there was a long nightdress, voluminous and white, with rows of tucks, billowing sleeves and ribbons at the wrist. Freya tried these garments on the new figure, then set them aside. They were no good.

Having made a new figure, she decided that she would make her some new clothes. There was one piece of card left over from the envelope, but it was too stiff for clothes so she used one of the sheets of white paper from school.

Her first thought was to draw her best clothes, the ones she wore to go to school, but this would have meant drawing the slip with the initials on the pocket and she could not bear to do that. What about Queen Guinevere's dress, the one she was wearing when she rode out with Sir Lancelot? She tried to remember the lines of poetry. Yes it was a gown of grass-green silk, buckled with golden clasps. She closed her eyes and tried to picture the dress, but instead of Guinevere, a different image came into her mind. It was the woman in the wood, the woman in the book in the parlour. All she had to do was go downstairs and get it.

She asked Violet to lend her the packet of wax crayons she had been given for Christmas. Then, using her bed as a table, she began to draw the woman's clothes. The picture was black and white and she could not imagine what colour the different items of clothing should be. She would have liked to use the red crayon, but bright colours did not seem right so she coloured the hood and cloak black. She chose brown for the animal skin shoes and the staff. When it came to the necklace, she looked round the room for inspiration. Lying on the shelf she saw the rattle with Jock's bead inside. She looked at the five crayons and chose the blue one, because it was the closest to turquoise.

It was only when the drawing and colouring were finished that she thought of trying to read what was written below the picture of the woman in the wood. Some of the letters were a strange shape and some had dots and marks on top. First of all there was the word Frigg with a capital letter. Miss Murray said that capital letters were used at the beginning of the names of people or places, so perhaps the woman was called Frigg. She looked again and, written in brackets after Frigg, she saw her own name,

Freya, followed by what she took to be other names, names she had never heard of, like Odin, Njord and Thor.

It did not matter that the words were strange and mysterious. What was important was that this was the second time that Freya had found her name in print, first in the newspaper, though then it was the name of a ship, and now in the book. And that was not all. This time was better because there was a face to go with the name, a face she knew better than her own.

She closed the book and clasped it to her chest, taking pleasure from the hardness of the binding as it pressed against her ribs. She felt at last that she had something to hold on to. Somehow she now held the promise, though unfulfilled, of knowing who she was. In the spring, when she went back to school, she would take the book and show it to Miss Murray and Miss Murray, who knew so much, would surely be able to explain everything.

A year later some two weeks before Christmas, Freya came downstairs one morning and noticed at once that Lizzie had built an extra big fire and that the set pot and the big black kettle were full to the brim with seething water.

Lizzie came bustling into the kitchen. "Freya, as soon as you've had your breakfast, I want you to go over the yard and mind the little ones so Rose can help Billy and me."

Freya nodded.

"Oh, and he's gone off to Hyldetron for the day," said Lizzie, providing the answer to the question Freya was about to ask herself. "I doubt he'll be back till after midnight when he's sure we've finished."

Ever since Lizzie had admitted that Freya was not Andro's daughter, a subtle change had taken place in the way Lizzie and Freya spoke of Andro, a change of which they were unaware, but which nevertheless afforded them a vague feeling of satisfaction. When Freya and Lizzie were alone together, Lizzie now referred to Andro as "he" rather than "your dad" as she had done in the past. It was not long before Freya adopted the same convention, reducing Andro to "he".

After breakfast, Freya wrapped a shawl around her shoulders and went outside. The air was cold and still. Clouds heavy with snow were massing in the sky and the ground was already covered with a light dusting of white. She saw Billy and young Billy standing by the long wall of the byre. The wooden ladder, which normally hung in the stable, was lying on the ground at their feet and they were about to set it up against the wall.

Rose too had a good fire going with steam issuing from the iron kettle. Breakfast had long since been cleared away and Violet was sitting on the proggie mat attempting to play cat's cradle with Hazel.

"Here's Freya come to play with you!" said Rose with a smile. Then turning to Freya she said, "Now then, just for today, for a treat, they can play with the pans and spoons!" Rose brought some enamel bowls and baking tins which she set down on the mat, then she drew Freya aside. "As soon as I've gone out, you can get all the spoons out of the drawer. Then they can make on they're in a band!"

Freya nodded as Rose put on her brown californian apron, the one she used for dirty jobs.

Hazel and Violet were jubilant at being allowed to play with the cooking things. Freya gave Hazel a big wooden spoon and showed her what a lovely noise it made when she hit it hard against an upturned tin. Violet picked up two shallow cake tins and began to clash them together like cymbals. Freya tried to enter into the spirit of the game but through the laughter and din, she could not help listening for the pig.

Twenty minutes later Rose came back into the cottage, flushed and slightly breathless. "You're needed out there now, Freya! Billy, Lizzie and me'll have to get the hairs out and Lizzie wants you to do the stirring!"

Rose picked up a thick piece of flannel and wrapped it round the handle of the kettle. "Bring that gully with you when you come!" she said as she went out of the door.

Freya picked up the knife and went out. Curious, Violet and Hazel watched her go. Then Violet picked the baby up in her arms and staggered over to the window to watch what was going on.

The farmyard was now blanketed in snow and the pig, now dead, was hanging upside down with its back legs tied to the rungs of the ladder.

Normally pig killing was a job for at least two strong men, but Andro never helped with the twice yearly event. He refused to kill a pig. Before Andro had taken Billy on, he had been most particular to ask him if he could kill a pig.

That year Rose and Billy had been invited to the Kern Supper at Roselaw. The harvest celebration was always held at the end of November or at the beginning of December on the night of a full moon. People thought that this was so they could walk to the party by moonlight, but the custom was rooted more deeply in prehistory than they realised.

The feast, the Kern Supper, was held in honour of Demeter, the barley goddess. Her effigy, the kern babby, woven from the last sheaf of corn, was set up in the granary where the supper was held so that she could preside over the festivities. Demeter was also the moon goddess to whom the pig is sacred and for this reason it was thought unlucky to kill a pig when the moon was on the wane. Andro knew all these things and so he calculated the day on which the pig should be killed from the date of the Kern Supper, thus ensuring that the moon would be waxing. He gave Billy his orders, informed Lizzie and organised a trip to Hyldetron so that he would have nothing at all to do with the business.

When all the blood had been collected, the pig was taken down and laid on a bed of rushes on the ground. The bucket containing the blood from which black pudding would be made was lowered into a tub of cold water to cool it and Freya was given the task of stirring it to prevent it curdling.

While Freya stirred, young Billy staggered to and fro from the bothy and the farmhouse, carrying kettles of boiling water to

134

scald the skin. The two women and Billy kneeled on the ground and scraped off the coarse bristles.

Young Billy fetched and carried as he was told. He was impatient, waiting for the moment when the bladder was removed, hoping that he would be allowed to have it as a ball, though he feared it might be kept and filled with lard. When at last the moment came, Billy looked at his son and smiled. "Aye lad, I know what you're after. You shall have it, you've earned it!" And Billy blew the bladder up and made a fine ball.

At dusk they carried the pig into the kitchen, laid it on the table and rubbed it with salt. Billy cut it up and Lizzie packed the pieces of meat between layers of salt and spices in half casks. The sides of bacon would be left for a month or more before they were washed, rolled and hung from the kitchen ceiling.

According to tradition the pig's head was hung on a big nail set into the corner of the farmhouse where for months after there were dark bloodstains on the wall.

14

It was late spring, a blustery day of wind and showers. The sky was a bright, rain-washed blue. The winter snows had gone, the dykebacks were clear, although in the north-facing gulleys and clefts of Cheviot where the sun's rays never shone, there was snow. There it would remain, granular and crystalline, throughout the hot summer. Tender loops of bracken were pushing up through the springy turf. At first the shoots were curled up tight like the fingers of a newborn baby. Later they would unfurl and turn into intricately wrought bishops' croziers and after a time it would seem as if enough of them had risen from the earth to supply all the bishops in Christendom.

Bartholemew Dunne was standing high on Cockslack, the wide fell between Warrior Crag and Maidenhope, on the march between Hoarstones land and that of Glittering Shiel. From this vantage point he had a clear view over the valley of Eidenhope with the farmhouse of Glittering Shiel nestling like a jewel at its centre.

He had been looking his sheep and, finding himself on this extremity of his territory, he had thought to cast his eyes over Andro Man's flock - something he did from time to time.

Bart sat down to smoke his pipe while he viewed the scene. The lambing was over and he was well contented with his crop of lambs. The sheep had thrived that year on the plentiful supply of their favourite springtime food, the succulent shoots of hare's-tail cotton grass. Andro's ewes and lambs were dotted over the fell. Bart could read sheep as well as the minister his Bible and what to the uninitiated were no more than random marks on a sheep's face were like a crisp signature to him.

No more than thirty feet away he saw a sturdy ewe about three years old with her twin lambs. The ewe had two distinctive brown blazes running down her face. Bart nodded ruefully at the sight. "Aye," he said out loud, "breeding will out. It cannot be hid! Yon ewe's her daddy's bairn and that's a certainty!"

The marks on the sheep confirmed what Bart had long suspected, that his fine brockie-faced ram had been sowing his seed in Andro's flock, though the question of whether this had happened by accident or design was another matter. Bart added this suspicion to other, long-standing grievances.

Twice a year the shepherds met together at the Hanging Rock on the northwest flank of Cheviot in order to return stray sheep to their rightful owners. Andro Man was always there and, while he always came empty-handed, he invariably left with one or two sheep. If he did change the mark on any stray sheep that happened to come his way, the case was almost impossible to prove, so nothing was ever said, but the other shepherds had become increasingly watchful and suspicious.

Just as he was about to turn towards home, Bart saw a pair of carriages and several riders progressing up the track to Glittering Shiel. One of the carriages was the phaeton from Heron Hall. He could not tell who was in it, but judging from the bonnets, there were several ladies. He wondered what business the gentry could possibly have at Glittering Shiel, so he watched for a few minutes more before going home to tell Agnes what he had seen.

The approaching visitors were expected at Glittering Shiel. Will Matheson, Orlando de Gilderoy's chief steward, had ridden up to the farm a week earlier to inform Andro that some dozen members of the Berwickshire Naturalists' Field Club would be coming to visit the stone circle at Glittering Shiel.

Augusta de Gilderoy, who had a passionate interest in prehistory and the wealth of ancient monuments to be found in the northern part of Northumberland, would be leading the group. She had proposed the outing the moment she learnt that Dr Julius Blackwell, a Cambridge don and noted antiquarian, was to visit the county. She had written to ask him if he would be kind enough to give her his opinion of the stone circle at Glittering Shiel which she believed to be of the greatest significance.

Dr Blackwell, having read Cobbett's account of his journey through Northumberland in 1832, had embarked on the journey north with considerable trepidation, expecting to find a dreary, treeless place, devoid of interest. However, after a few days he revised his preconceptions and was much excited by what he had seen.

Sir Arthur Avenal, the president of the club, had shown him some curious markings carved on the soft flat sandstone which was exposed on the moorland lying between the Cheviots and the North Sea. Dr Blackwell had gazed through his magnifying glass at these mysterious ciphers and declared himself both thrilled and perplexed. Now he was being led to the granite heart of the county, there to stand in the centre of one of its most ancient monuments.

Since he resented any intrusion onto his land, Andro's first thought had been to tell Will Matheson that the visitors could not come. However, as his conversation with Will proceeded, he realised that Will's visit was a mere formality, a matter of courtesy; Andro's acquiescence had been taken for granted.

The party had lunched at Heron Hall on saddle of lamb and copious quantities of fine claret from Orlando's cellar, after which they had set off up the valley.

The previous day, a Friday, Miss Murray had drawn Freya aside and told her that Miss Gilderoy, knowing of Grace's interest in antiquities, had invited her to accompany the party to Glittering Shiel. Never having ventured so far into the hills, Grace had been delighted to accept and furthermore the visit would give her the opportunity of meeting Freya's father and seeing where she lived.

While Freya was excited to think of Grace coming to the farm, she was also nervous. Home life and school life had hitherto remained separate. Now it seemed that they were to meet and though Miss Murray was never intrusive, she was sensitive and profoundly observant so that Freya was fearful of what she might discover when she met Andro.

Freya was also resentful. As far as she knew, nobody except herself had ever taken any interest at all in the Maidens. Andro always said they were nuisance, that if they were not there he could have made more hay. But Freya loved them. They were her friends, reliable and constant. She often went to the circle to pour out her troubles. But now strangers were coming to stare at the stones and she was feeling defensive.

Freya had stood by the boulder, watching for the first sign of the visitors, but long before it was necessary, she withdrew to the alder grove at the bottom of the garden from where she planned to observe the visitors. Of course she wanted to talk to Miss Murray, but she was overcome with shyness, so at first, like a tree sprite, she hid herself away.

She heard voices in the farmyard, greetings and introductions and then a cry of delight. "My! What a perfectly charming little house! A jewel! And in such a romantic spot! Truly this is paradise! I could write poetry here, the muse would come, I am quite convinced of it!" A few minutes later the owner of the voice came round to the front of the house accompanied by Andro.

It was Maud Avenal, Sir Arthur's daughter, an exuberant young lady with a vivid imagination and a taste for romance. Having immediately singled Andro out as a most exotic personage, she had put her hand on his arm and drawn him round to view the house from the front.

"Quite the prettiest windows and such a charming carving!" she exclaimed as soon as she saw the sandstone carving above the porch. "Now let me see, what is it?" she asked, tilting her head in an elegant pose. "Dear me! The poor fellow, if fellow he be, is quite worn away!" Her curiosity quickly evaporated and she turned away as her thoughts darted off in a new direction. "Tell me, Mr Man, is this not the house in which the great Sir Walter stayed, regaling himself on goat's milk and fish from the burn?"

Augusta had followed them round the end of the house and heard Maud's question. "No, my dear," she said in her deep authoritative voice, "you are mistaken. The farmhouse which Scott visited lies at the head of the next valley at the very foot of

Cheviot. This house was only just being built at the time of Sir Walter's visit in 1791. And the carving you mention, the one above the door, was put there by Jasper Hetherton. You see, it was he who built the house."

Maud nodded. "My goodness Miss Gilderoy, what a veritable fountain of knowledge you are!"

Andro was feeling irritated and uncomfortable. He did not like the gentry. They made him feel ignorant and what was more he disliked being reminded of the Hethertons and the fact that they had once owned Glittering Shiel.

Freya did not see Miss Murray until the party moved off towards the stones. Unable to walk any distance, she had stayed in the farmyard mounted on her donkey ready to cross the ford while the others walked over the footbridge.

Much to Andro's relief, Maud seemed to lose interest in him and walked off to join Dr Blackwell who was deep in conversation with Augusta. Maud had taken a liking to him the minute she first saw him. He was not her usual type, but perhaps his high seriousness, erudition and devotion to the study of antiquities presented her with a challenge, or perhaps she needed a change from young men who talked of nothing but hot air balloons and hunting. Whatever the reason, she had resolved to make an indelible impression on him.

Freya watched their progress. She recognised the tall, slightly stooping figure of Augusta who had visited the school on numerous occasions, though the other members of the club were strangers to her.

There was Mr Trummel, the vicar of Hyldetron, Mr and Mrs Wood from near Alnham, Mr Gillyflower of Crawcester, an ardent campaigner for the improvement of the living conditions of the peasantry, two elderly gentlemen from Berwick upon Tweed, and Mr Tuedie, a ruddy-faced farmer and passionate lepidopterist who had taken it upon himself to lead Grace's donkey. Finally there was Doctor Dobson from Willove and his wife Mary. Andro, wearing his plaid and foxskin hat, and Will Matheson, who was tightly buttoned into a suit which, due to his increasing *embonpoint,* had become almost too small for him, brought up the rear at a respectful distance.

Will did not relish the role that had been imposed upon him. He did not give tuppence for stones except as material for gateposts or stone walls. Managing the Gilderoy estate was his proper business, not acting nursemaid to a party of toffs. He had consoled himself that while his charges visited the Maidens he could make himself comfortable by the fire, have a dram or two and pass the time of day with Andro. But this was not to be. Andro had no intention of letting the visitors out of his sight. What was more, he needed Will to keep him company so that he could listen to what was said without the risk of being drawn into their conversation. In any case there would have been no escape for Will because Augusta had ordered him to carry some rugs up to the stones for the ladies to sit on.

As soon as he reached the stones Dr Blackwell began to walk to and fro, up and down, poking and peering into the heather and bent-grass. He drew a small compass from his pocket which he consulted at intervals. Once he had determined the general disposition of the stones, he opened the leather bag he always carried on such expeditions and took out a notebook, pencil and a circular leather case which contained a long tape measure. He enlisted the help of Dr Dobson to undertake a thorough and accurate measurement of the stones themselves and their distance one from another.

Maud found such scientific rigour tedious, so she drifted, joining this person or that as they herborised, discussed the landmarks visible in the distance or gazed up into the sky in the hope of catching a glimpse of some rare bird - a blue cock merlin perhaps. None of this was of any interest to Maud. Left to her own devices, she went and leant against Meg, the tallest stone, where she struck an elegant pose. She put her kid-gloved hand to her smooth forehead and gazed intently towards the sea, imagining herself a northern Isolde scanning the far horizon for a glimpse of Tristan's sail.

When at last Dr Blackwell had finished measuring, they gathered together in the middle of the circle. The rugs were spread on the ground and the ladies made themselves comfortable.

Augusta finished telling Mary Dobson about the tunnel which was said to lead from the stones to the dark chasm known as Henhole on the north face of Cheviot. Then she turned her attention to Dr Blackwell. "So, Dr Blackwell, what do you make of our stones? Are they not fine?"

Will and Andro were standing some twenty feet away. "Aye, yon fellow'll need to have all his buttons on!" Will remarked with feeling. "Yon's a terrible woman, a perfect pest of a woman and terrible determined when she gets the bit between her teeth!" They listened for a while before Will said quietly, "I'll tell you this for nowt, there's just one question I'd be wanting to ask yon professor fellow!"

"And what's that?" asked Andro.

"Why man, whether or not there's gold buried beneath them stones!"

"Gold! I've never heard tell of gold round here, except for the fool's gold what sometimes glints in the bed of the burn."

"Oh well, folk is always full of tales about druid gold and such like buried beneath stones. My father used to tell a tale about a king's ransom of gold said to be buried beneath the Devil's Stone over by Willove. But nobody's ever found anything except for the odd elf-bolt and maybe a jet bead." Then Will looked shrewdly at Andro and winked. "For all I know, there's a hoard of Hetherton gold hidden under those stones what got forgotten after the troublous times! Why man, maybe you should take a look some dark night. Heaven knows what you might find!"

Andro made no reply, not knowing whether or not to take Will seriously. He moved a little closer to the group, thinking he might do well to listen more attentively to what was said. As he did so, he caught a glimpse of two heads moving along the back of the stone wall near the Maidens.

As soon as the party had left, Freya had emerged from the trees and gone to collect Violet so they could follow on behind at a safe distance. Hidden from the view of those sitting down, Freya and Violet were moving along behind the wall. Once they were out of the visitors' field of vision, Freya planned that they would slip over the wall and approach discreetly from the side.

Dr Blackwell was on his feet addressing the group. "Ladies and gentlemen, this is undoubtedly a druidical temple of great importance, a place of legislation, devotion and sepulture, though not of defence, for I see no ditch or rampire. Of course, much of what I say can be no more than mere supposition. Really, it ought to be dug."

"Do tell us about the druids, Dr Blackwell!" said Mary Dobson. "For example, can you throw any light on the derivation of the word druid? I was wondering if perhaps it came from the Celtic?"

"Yes indeed, it comes from the word for an oak tree, though it is a matter of some debate among etymologists. Certainly the oak tree was of great importance to the rude aboriginal tribes that inhabited this island before Caesar's invasion." Dr Blackwell raised his arm and swept it round in a wide arc. "These great open wastes were once clothed with oaks. But we are in some difficulty. You see, our knowledge of the druids comes to us secondhand, from such writers as Caesar, Strabo, Herodotus and Diodorus Siculus. The druids themselves never wrote down the secrets of their religion. In this they resembled Socrates and Pythagoras. Druid priests had to learn the philosophy of nature and sacred ritual by heart. They were taught in academies and what is more the process could take twenty years or more."

Maud was dismayed, she feared that the talk was in danger of becoming fusty and book-bound, so she interjected. "Do tell us about their rites, Dr Blackwell! I have heard that the druids performed ritual sacrifice!" Then she looked around and shook her head in disappointment. "Though I see no altar here."

"But it is here nonetheless!" replied Dr Blackwell. "It lies outside the circle, almost hidden in the bent-grass. You must

143

understand, Miss Avenal, that the druids believed in the immortality of the soul, that after death the soul ascended to some higher orb and enjoyed a sublime felicity."

"But they *did* perform sacrifices, human sacrifices, did they not?" Maud insisted.

"Yes indeed! They had complex rites of propitiation, augury and divination, and yes, human victims constituted a part of their sacrifices. It is true that their altars streamed with blood. However, the sacrifice was not an act of punishment, but rather it was intended to avert a catastrophe of some sort. The greater the threat, the more virtuous, noble and beloved the victim had to be!"

Maud's eyes widened and she had a vision of a flaxen haired youth, a prince no less, a gold torque around his neck, about to allow his blood to be shed for the good of the tribe.

"The sacrifice was carried out in the depths of a dark grove. The white-robed arch-druid was skilled in the art of garotting, but first the victim was cut in two across the diaphragm. You see the priests made their divinations from the position in which the victim fell, from the course of his blood and from the quivering motion of his members..."

Maud almost swooned, though Dr Blackwell seemed not to notice. His eyes were on Grace who was listening intently, nodding her head from time to time as if she was already acquainted with much of what he was saying.

"And as the votive blood flowed, the victim's groans were drowned amid the clangour of musical instruments."

Maud's pallor increased. She swayed a little as if she was about to faint. Dr Dobson, who was reluctant to disrupt the learned gentleman's discourse, drew a phial of smelling salts from his pocket which he handed to his wife so that she could attend to the stricken Maud.

Having finished what he was saying, Dr Blackwell took advantage of the pause to consider Grace Murray's subtle beauty. Grace had just noticed Freya and Violet standing hand in hand by the wall some forty feet away and had turned to wave to them.

144

Dr Blackwell observed Grace's mutilated foot encased in its special boot and was wondering how such a tragedy could have occurred. He had had no opportunity to talk with her for she had not lunched with them at Heron Hall, nor had she ridden in the carriage which would have allowed him to engage her in conversation.

Augusta was determined to make the most of Dr Blackwell's visit so she put another question to him. "Now then Dr Blackwell, I am always interested in the role of women. What part did they play in these rituals?"

"The position of women? Ah, yes! Well, I could not say. I fear it is not a proper subject for ladies."

"Nonsense, my dear Dr Blackwell! You see before you Northumbrian women. We have stout hearts, unlike our more delicate southern sisters! I must insist that you tell us what you know."

Dr Blackwell, who recognised *force majeure* when he met it, took a deep breath. "Well, I understand that the sacrifice was followed by scenes of mad intemperance."

"I do not doubt it!" snapped Augusta. "But tell us about the women!"

"Well, if you insist! The Britons brought their women naked to the sacrifices!" said Dr Blackwell, the colour rising in his pale cheeks. "Of course what happened in those barbaric days in no way calls into question the continency of British ladies!"

Augusta's gaze was upon him, requiring that he continue.

"Well then, all right. All I can say is that what ensued was neither chaste nor delicate!" At this point Dr Blackwell managed to recover his composure a little and resolved to justify what he had said by putting it in its proper historical setting. "You must understand that acts of this sort, er, what we now might choose to call prostitution, formed a part of the religion of many nations. Think of Jewish women and the Queen of Heaven, think of Persia, think of Armenia! Strabo tells us that there all young virgins were prostituted in the temple in honour of the goddess and only after that could they be given in marriage."

Mr Trummel, the vicar, could contain himself no longer. Such indecent talk could not be allowed to run on unchallenged. It was his duty as a servant of God to intervene and bring the unseemly and heathenish discussion to a rapid conclusion. Accordingly he cleared his throat, looked solicitously at the ladies, all of whom had clearly found Dr Blackwell's words fascinating. Undeterred, he launched off. "Pray do not distress yourselves, ladies. Such barbaric practices belong to the antediluvian past, a past so distant, so lost in the mists of time that it were better to draw a veil over it."

A steely look from Augusta pierced Mr Trummel in mid-sentence. He knew what she was thinking. As members of the Berwickshire Naturalists' Field Club, it was precisely their declared and legitimate business to peer into the mists of time. But Mr Trummel, though bloodied by Augusta's glance, was as yet unbowed. He continued in a conciliatory tone. "We must forgive primitive man. He knew no better. Like the painted savages of the New World, he was but a child, worshipping the sun, the moon, trees, water, fire and rocks and heaven knows what else besides!" Then his tone became more emollient. "But that time of foolish childhood ignorance is past. For the last two thousand years we have had God, the eternal Father, for our guide! And His Word, unlike that of Dr Blackwell's aborigines, *has* been written down. Indeed at this very moment noble mariners are plying the oceans in vessels laden with copies of the Good Book, risking life and limb to bring the word of God to the furthest corners of the globe!"

After that, the conversation became more general with Mr Gillyflower speaking of the scientific achievements of the druids and Augusta telling them that the Gaelic expression for 'Are you going to church?' literally meant 'Are you going to the stones?'

This upset Mr Trummel all over again, so Dr Dobson sought to pour oil on troubled waters by invoking the club's practice of inviting members to show some article of historical interest that had come into their possession.

The next twenty minutes were taken up with an examination of a letter by Sir Humphry Davy relating to safety in mines. Then they looked at a handful of fossilised sea-lilies which were known as Saint Cuthbert's beads and which in times gone by had been much used for rosaries.

They had stayed at the stones longer than planned, so it was decided that the party would return without delay to Heron Hall. Augusta called Will over and conveyed this information to him and he in turn conveyed it to Andro who was glad that they would soon be gone.

Grace, mounted once more on her donkey, gestured to Freya to come over. Diffidently the two girls approached.

"I had hoped to see you earlier Freya, when we arrived," said Grace.

"Yes, Miss Murray, I saw you coming, but..."

Grace smiled. "Yes, I know, all these grand people. Never mind, you're here now! Will you lead the way back down? And then I have something to give you!"

When they got back to the farmyard Lizzie came out ready to receive them. Andro whispered to her that they would not be going into the house for tea as expected. Lizzie thought of the table all set for tea with the finest linen and best china the house could provide, but her disappointment quickly gave way to relief at escaping the ordeal of entertaining such important people.

Before they left Grace spoke to Lizzie. "It is a pleasure to meet you again, Mrs Man. I'm sorry that I have not been able to speak to your husband. Perhaps I may yet have a word or two with him."

Grace looked over at Andro who was talking to Dr Blackwell. She had observed him carefully over the course of the afternoon, noting the fox hat, the leather garter at his knee and his swarthy good looks which contrasted so strikingly with Dr Blackwell's pallor. She thought him an enigmatic man, without doubt a powerful man.

She turned her attention back to Lizzie. "You know, Freya is quite the brightest star in my little constellation at Herontop school. I have high hopes for her!" Then Grace hesitated, undecided whether or not to go on, but then she added, "Though I must confess that I am anxious about her sometimes. She seems so distant. I cannot help wondering if something is wrong. Sometimes she looks as if she has the weight of the whole world on her slender shoulders."

The pleasure Lizzie had felt at Grace's first remark vanished. Had Miss Murray already guessed that Freya was not her and Andro's child? Or was there more to it than that?

Grace gently urged her donkey over to Andro and Dr Blackwell. "I must thank you for your kindness to us today, Mr Man," she began.

Andro nodded in acknowledgement.

"I have just been telling your wife what a fine girl Freya is. She has imagination and a fine intelligence and how clever of you to give her such a wonderful name! Freya! Her pale beauty is quite equal to it!"

"Ah yes!" said Dr Blackwell. "Freya, goddess of love and death who in the earliest time forsook the warm Mediterranean shores to come to the North."

Still Andro did not speak. He had sensed Grace's percipience and was wary.

Grace, undaunted, went on. "And you are fortunate to live in this place. There is something strange and magical about it! Would you not agree Dr Blackwell?"

Dr Blackwell readily concurred. "Yes indeed, few have the good fortune to live near stones such as those we have seen today."

As the procession left the farmyard, Grace turned to wave goodbye. She saw Lizzie standing with Freya, who was clutching the book Grace had given her. Lizzie put her arm around the girl and drew her close. Of Andro there was no sign. He had already disappeared.

15

It was a Sunday in the middle of July. The top hayfield, the one by the Maidens, was a ripple of wavy hair-grass, sweet vernal-grass and meadow-grass, while down beside the stell in the wet bottom field, the grasses were threaded through with ragged robin, meadow cranesbill and buttercups.

The scythes had been taken down from their hooks in the barn and the long curved blades honed sharp and bright. Haymaking was to begin next day when Andro and Billy would mow the sweet-smelling grasses. Then Lizzie and Rose, helped by Freya and young Billy, would turn the hay and when it was ready they would heap it into pikes. Later Polly, pulling the flat cart, would lead the pikes to the farmyard where the stack was to be built. Freya and Billy would not go back to school until the stack stood finished and thatched with reeds.

Sunday, however, was a day of rest. Rose and Billy had gone over to Hevensgate to attend a simple service in the farmhouse. They were to stay for tea afterwards and return home in the early evening.

Freya was supposed to be playing with Violet and Hazel. They had gone to a narrow sandy shore up the burn with the intention of playing 'houses', Violet's favourite game, which involved collecting some small stones which were arranged in a rectangle to mark out the living room of a house. A broken slate brought specially for the purpose was mounted on more stones to provide a table and tiny pieces of twig were heaped up at one end of the room for a fire.

"You can get on and make a cake for the tea, our Hazel!" ordered Violet, knowing how much Hazel liked to make mud pies and decorate them with dried leaves and flowers. "Me and Freya'll do the mam and dad!"

Making a mother and father to sit at the table involved searching for two straight, thick sticks and two thinner ones with bends in the right place, which could be bound together with a reed to make a cross. Then they would wind sheep's wool round and round the top of the cross to make a head. Finally the simple dolls would be clothed in leaves and grasses.

Freya did not move when Violet suggested they went in search of twigs. Violet looked and saw that Freya was sitting staring into the burn and immediately she knew that it was pointless to insist. Freya often sat still like this for a long time without saying a word. In the past Violet had tried to rouse her as she would someone in a deep sleep, but now she left her alone, knowing that even if she could persuade her to join in the game, it would be a drab, joyless affair.

Freya's thoughts were miles away down the valley in the schoolroom. It would be silent and empty now, but tomorrow most of the children would be there, except those like herself who had to stay at home and help with the hay.

She pictured the front row of desks with her seat beside Jenny empty. Mr Dogberry would be there after break. She would miss the 'Flood'. That was a pity. She would think about Jenny tomorrow just as they had promised and Jenny would think of her. When Freya had gone back to school that spring she and Jenny had sealed their friendship by pricking their thumbs and mixing blood. Freya looked down at her thumb, remembering the tiny spot of blood which had welled up into a big, glossy blob.

Freya sighed. She thought of the book Miss Murray had brought the day of the visit to the Maidens. It was a slender volume with a red cloth cover entitled *Tales and Legends of the Borders*. There was a list of contents at the front which promised stories of fairies, witches, monsters and ghosts. Freya read slowly and carefully and, because she was determined to make the stories last as long as possible, each day she reread the pages she had read for the first time the day before and only then did she move on. Sometimes she read in the evening before she went to sleep but the stories rarely brought her sweet dreams. Freya did not have dreams like other girls, she had nightmares and though Andro's face did not appear in them, they were thick with his presence.

At school there was no longer any need for Freya and Jenny to pretend they were witches and they could simply be friends, but at Glittering Shiel it was different.

Freya felt guilty and miserable because of what passed between her and Andro. He would use soft cajoling words before, and praise her afterwards, but that only made it worse. She could not understand why such things were happening to her. She knew from Mr Dogberry that all women and girls were wicked because of Eve, but other girls did not suffer as she did. There had to be a reason. Perhaps the Herontop girls were right. Perhaps she really was a witch. She told herself that everything would have been different if she had known who she really was, who her mother and father were, that all her problems came from that. But the chances of finding out the answer to those questions had been smashed on the Black Middens along with the *Freya*. Whenever she turned these thoughts over in her mind, she always came back to the same idea. She must deserve to suffer such misfortune and the only reason she could think of was that she was a witch. It was not long before she decided that she should use her magic powers at Glittering Shiel just as she had done at school.

So she had collected together the hardened droplets of tallow from the candle she carried up to her room every night. Before she went to sleep she held them in the palms of her hands, rolling them to and fro, warming them until they were soft and malleable. The ball of tallow gradually grew bigger and bigger until it was the size of a peewit's egg. When she thought that it was big enough to shape into a human figure, she remembered something that Jenny had told her. If the magic was to work, something from his body had to be included. Jenny said that parings from fingernails or toe nails were best, but Freya had never seen Andro cut his nails. She wondered whether a strand or two of his hair might do instead. She might find one inside his fox hat, but it rarely left his head.

One day when there was no one else in the house, she crept into Andro and Lizzie's bedroom. She went round to Andro's side of the bed and with trembling fingers she drew back the covers and bent forward to examine the pillow, searching for stray hairs. The smell of him rose from the rough flannel and made her feel sick. There was nothing on the pillow so she pulled the sheets back and found two or three short hairs. Wiry, angular and black, she knew they were his. They looked like black print that had been lifted off a white page and then imperfectly straightened. Carefully she picked them up and carried them off to her room. That night she bedded them into the tallow which, for the first time, she shaped into human form. She hid the effigy in her room and every night before she went to sleep she got it out and stared at it.

Then one night after Andro and Lizzie had gone to bed, she slipped out of bed and reached for the figure. Noiselessly she opened her door and glided down the stairs. It was dark in the kitchen except for the dull glow of the fire. Barefoot, she stood on the stone flags in front of the fire with the figure in her hand, deciding where to put it. There was a dusty cushion of burnt peat in the grate and she carefully laid the figure on top. A puff of fine ochre dust billowed out before being drawn up the chimney. The figure lay like some strange, dusty, forgotten object. She waited. At first nothing happened, then slowly the tallow softened and began to spread until the figure lost all semblance of human form. Then at last there was a sudden crackle followed by a burst of flame as the figure was consumed. Stony-faced, she watched until nothing remained and the fire was quiescent once more. Then she turned and left the room.

In the days that followed, she watched and waited for a sign that the magic had worked, but there was none and life went on as before. In despair, she went up to the Maidens and spoke to Meg. She told her what she had done and asked her why it had not worked. Then it came to her that perhaps she had not done the thing properly. Jenny said that witches had special words that had to be said when they cast spells. How was she to find out what they were? Jenny might know but she dared not ask her, because that would mean telling her what she was planning to do.

Freya emerged from her reverie for a few moments and saw Hazel shaping some mud into a gingerbread man. It reminded her of the day she had been in the bothy with Rose and the other children.

Rose's mother had sent them a box of fairings, ginger biscuits from Willove fair. There were six of them, piled up one on top of another with sheets of shiny blue paper between. Their shape had reminded Freya of the cut-out doll Lizzie had given her one Christmas. The biscuits had the same straight legs, though their arms were folded over their chests. They were almost as featureless as the cardboard doll except they had two currant eyes and a collar and buttons made of blobs of sugar icing.

Rose saw the look of fascination on Freya's face as she unwrapped the package and handed a biscuit to Violet and then one to Hazel. Freya hung back. "Here Freya, take one!" Rose had said. "There's plenty!"

Unsmiling, Freya had accepted the gift. Hazel and Violet had already licked off the icing and bitten into the hard gingery biscuit. Freya had no appetite for hers. Instead she had carried it off to her room and stood it up on her shelf. There it remained for several days until the damp air made it go soft.

At last she had taken it down and laid it on her bed. As she had looked at it, something had crystallised in her mind. Perhaps it was the sugary line of the gingerbread man's waistcoat or something to do with the way he had stood on her shelf looking at her with his dark eyes, but suddenly the humble biscuit was transformed into a second effigy of Andro. She shivered as the familiar feelings of disgust and loathing overcame her. Then she bent forward and dug the nail of her index finger deep into the biscuit, gouging out one of his currant eyes. She stared for a moment at the black shrivelled thing lying in the palm of her hand before putting it into her mouth where it left a bitter, burnt taste on her tongue.

Later she had carried the gingerbread man to the burn. Sitting on the alder bough, she had held him at arm's length above the water and pulled off a leg, crumbling the soft dough between her fingers, then she had done the same thing to the other leg and then the head and finally the trunk. The steady stream of brown crumbs dropped down into the burn and was carried away downstream.

That evening Andro had come into the house in a rage, with blood streaming down his cheek. He burst into the kitchen, flinging his stick down on the table with a clatter. Lizzie was in the scullery. He shouted to her to fetch a bowl of salt and water to clean the wound.

Freya was in the parlour. Curiosity drew her to the kitchen. Andro had his back to her and Lizzie was bending over, washing the blood from his face. Neither of them noticed her standing silently by the door.

"The devil take that bird! It very nearly had my eye out!"

"What d'you mean?" asked Lizzie, solicitously.

"I was down checking the dipper when this pair of hoolits came screeching and circling over my head, so I waved my stick at them to drive them off, but one of them would have none of it! Then while I'm looking up to see what they were going to do next, I put my foot down a hole! You know what a scene of holes there is down there! Well down I went, splayed out all over the place and before I know what's happened one of them takes a swipe at me with his beak!"

"They must have a nest close by with little ones in! You must've worried them!"

"I'll be giving them something to worry about in the morning! I'll be down there with the gun, aye and they'll get both barrels. I'll make the feathers fly!"

Freya had gone down to the dipper the following afternoon. Andro had been as good as his word and wrought a terrible vengeance on the pair of short-eared owls. He had blasted them with shot and hung them by the neck from a twisted hawthorn branch as if they were common vermin.

She had combed the surrounding ground, searching for their nest, hoping to save the nestlings. While Andro's injury gave her a bitter satisfaction, her eyes were full of tears because of the owls. She grieved for them. They were not wicked. All they had been trying to do was protect their young ones. Had she made this happen? Was she guilty of this too?

Ever since that first day up on the fell when Andro had hurt her so badly, when by some miracle she had been able to leave her body and take flight with the pipit, the birds that lived by the burn and on the hills had become precious to her. There was the dipper that always flew down the burn, keeping her company on the way to school, the broon kitty, the wren, who busied herself by the water when she came to sit on the alder bough and the peewits and pipits which were her constant companions on the open fell.

She had learnt how to leave her body when Andro made it uninhabitable. No matter how Andro took her, whether her face was turned towards the earth or towards the sky, she knew what to fix her mind on. If it was the earth, she looked for a stone and concentrated on its cold, hard indifference. "You cannot get blood out of a stone!" Hannah used to say, so Freya became like a stone so that Andro could not harm her. If it was the sky, she sought a bird to lift her spirit free. And if there was neither stone nor bird she closed her eyes and called them forth in her imagination.

Freya's reverie was broken by Violet. "Come on, Freya! Mam and dad'll be back from the meeting soon. Come and look!"

Freya got up and walked over. Two stick figures were planted in the soft sand close by the slate table upon which lay a dollop of mud, a cake ready for tea. There was a blanched sheep bone lying on a bed of grass and feathers by the fire which Violet informed her proudly was a baby.

"Aye, I can see you've got all the family there," said Freya in a strange, flat voice. "The two of you can go back on your own," she went on. "I've got to gather some wool for my mam."

"We can give you a hand if you like!" offered Violet.

"No!" said Freya, so sharply that Violet felt rebuked for her kindness. "It's time you took Hazel home. It's getting late."

Freya watched them go. She waited until they had crossed the bridge and disappeared into the farmyard before she looked again at the childish arrangement of sticks and stones.

Tight-lipped, she brought her clog down on the fire and the baby in its cradle. She swivelled on her heel driving them deep into the ground. Then she looked at the result. No, it would not do, it was not what she wanted, so she prised them out of the sandy mud and then kicked them, sending a shower of sand, bone, grass and twigs up into the air. She went on and on until every last fragment of this fantasy world had been sent spinning back into the chaos from which it had come and when she had done, no pattern, shape or order remained on the ground.

16

The day after haymaking finished, a letter arrived addressed to Mrs A. Man. Lizzie did not receive regular news from Seamouth, she assumed that all was well unless she heard to the contrary and it was only on rare occasions that Andro wrote a letter to Felix, asking for some money for Freya. She stared at the envelope, beset by fears about what the letter might contain. Letters had a tendency to turn the world upside down. She associated them with important news, the sort of news that changed lives.

It was early afternoon. Freya was at school and Andro and Billy were out digging drainage ditches. Even if she opened the letter she would not be able to read it, so she slipped it into her pocket and went to work in the garden which had been neglected during haymaking.

Rhythmically she hoed down the rows of beans and carrots. The regular movement was soothing and gradually she became calm and able to reflect. She remembered a day several months earlier when a feeling of foreboding had come upon her, lodging itself in her chest like a hard, round stone. She was sure that it had something to do with Felix. The closeness they had shared in the womb had never been destroyed. No matter how great the distance between them, a vestige of that early intimacy survived, the possibility of wordless communication. Something had made her go outside and she had looked towards the coast where the sea and sky were welded into a broad, steel-grey band. She had known then with utter certainty that Felix was at sea and she wondered if at that moment he was thinking of her as she was of him.

Nine months had passed since that day and Lizzie had waited, daily fearing to receive news of Felix's death at sea. No news had come, yet she had continued to live with a presentiment of loss. Now with the letter in her pocket, the fears came flooding back.

Freya was first home that evening. As soon as she had hung up her cloak and come into the kitchen, Lizzie took the letter from her pocket and laid it on the table.

"This came today!" she said. "Here's a knife. Open it and read it for me, please!"

Freya inserted the blade and sheared through the cheap paper. Inside there was a single sheet of thin writing paper. As Freya drew it out of the envelope, a small package fell onto the table. She unfolded the letter and read out loud.

> *Dear Lizzie,*
> *Mam is sadly badly. She is asking*
> *for you. Come as quick as you can.*
>
> *Your loving Da.*

Freya looked up. "What does sadly badly mean?"

"Oh, it's just da's way of saying she's bad, very ill. But why didn't Felix write? I doubt da's ever wrote a letter in his life. And what's this?" Lizzie picked up the package and undid the screw of paper. Two silver shillings fell jingling onto the table.

Freya looked at the bright coins. "They'll be for the train, so you can get there quickly!"

"But I cannot go! What'll *he* say? There's that much work to be done, what with the cooking and then there's outside, the garden and everything." Lizzie looked at her hands, a residue of fine soil in every crevice and a dark arc under each fingernail. Then she thought of something else. "And you, Freya! How will you get on? Will you be all right, with him, I mean?" Lizzie's voice betrayed an anxiety that was more than concern about the practicalities of daily life.

Freya looked at her. Had the colour risen in Lizzie's pale cheeks? Had her vigilance faltered and allowed something long kept from conscious thought to rise to the surface and make itself known? Fleetingly their eyes met in mute recognition of the truth, though neither was able, nor would have wished, to give voice to it.

It was Freya who spoke first, her voice lacking conviction. "I'll manage. It'll be all right," she said hesitantly.

As soon as Freya had read the letter she felt sure that Lizzie would go to Seamouth and her first thought had been to ask Lizzie to find out more about the wreck of the *Freya*. Surely there must be a clue at Seamouth which would help to solve the mystery of where she had come from. But she soon rejected the idea; the subject was painful to her and she was reluctant to raise it again. In any case she had never told Lizzie what she had discovered in the newspaper and Lizzie had never asked. Besides, now was not the time. Lizzie's mind was elsewhere, occupied with other more pressing worries.

Later Lizzie told Andro about the letter and by supper time everything was settled. To Lizzie's surprise Andro raised no objection to her going, indeed he even offered to drive her to Hyldetron station first thing next morning so she could catch a southbound train.

Lizzie's departure suited Andro's purposes perfectly. Dr Blackwell's visit, or more particularly what Will Matheson had told him on that occasion, had sown the seed of an idea which in the ensuing days and weeks had pushed its roots deep into every recess of Andro's mind, so that he was able to think of little else.

He had begun to dream about the stones and the hoard of gold concealed beneath them. In his dreams the stones were light as thistledown, the merest breath of air upon them and they lifted free from the earth and floated off into a sky of dazzling brightness. Then the moist, earthy smell of peat would assail his nostrils and his arms would be plunged armpit-deep into the earth where they fastened round an iron-bound kist. It was heavy, as heavy as the stones were light, heavy beyond lifting, full to the brim with gold, Hetherton gold that had once bedecked Hetherton women - glittering booty, dazzling proof of prowess and daring. But every time the moment came for him to unlatch the chest, the sky turned pitch-black and a mighty whirlwind blew up. It whisked his fox hat from his head and sent it spinning off into the darkness. It wound his plaid tight around him, pinioning his arms and legs like bands around a newborn babe. Then a tall figure mounted on a monstrous, shaggy mountain goat with great, curving horns loomed up before him and he found himself trapped in its shadow, helpless, unable to move. A monkish cowl hung over the creature's face, yet something told him it was a woman. Once he fancied he glimpsed her profile and thought maybe that it was old Mrs Hetherton come to torment him as she had sworn to do.

Far from putting Andro off, the dreams only strengthened his resolve. He became even more convinced that there was gold beneath the stones, there for the taking, but he kept his plans to himself. During haymaking, as he and Billy strode up and down the top field swinging their scythes through the long grasses, he had studied the stones and planned how he would go about the digging. He told himself that he would have to hurry. Had that professor fellow not said that the place should be dug? And if what Will said was anything to go by, that Augusta was a terrible woman, a right horsegodmother of a woman, forever poking her nose into other folks' affairs. If she got it into her head to do something about the stones, all hell would be let loose.

He decided to dig at night, so no one would know. Not that he felt like a felon, not at all. Glittering Shiel and whatever was buried on it was rightfully his and he had a perfect right to do what he liked with it. But some instinct told him he must do the work under cover of darkness, despite the fact that he knew that it was not the time to be tampering with ancient things, for like everyone else Andro believed that such places had their vengeful spirits, ever watchful and quick to repel an invader.

Then there was Lizzie. He did not want to tell her of his plans. Although they had never discussed it he knew she did not think of the farm as his property, far less her own. To her way of thinking it still belonged to the Hethertons. Lizzie did not know about Will's remarks the day of the visit and even if she had known, he doubted whether she would have believed the story. And if there was gold beneath the stones, it was better by far that no one except himself should know of it.

So Andro could hardly believe his luck when Lizzie told him about the letter, which he took as a favourable omen. His generosity was boundless and when Lizzie broached the subject of Freya, he even said she could go to school as usual. Lizzie was relieved because she had feared that he would insist on Freya staying at home to cook and clean.

The following morning the four of them, Lizzie, Andro, Freya and young Billy set off down the valley. Lizzie said goodbye to Freya at the bend by the school. Not wishing to prolong the moment of parting, she took Freya in her arms for only the briefest moment. "Take care, Freya. I'll be back as soon as I can! I promise!"

The first few days after Lizzie's departure passed without incident. Andro was in high good humour. Freya worked hard before she left for school, feeding the pigs and getting the breakfast for herself and Andro. He complimented her on the porridge saying what a grand little wife she made, but he did not so much as lay a finger on her. His mind was engaged on other matters.

At the end of their daily stint digging the drains, Andro and Billy carried the mattock and spades back to the stable. They were working on Skirlmoor, the rising tract of fell studded with rocky outcrops, which lay to the north of Glittering Shiel. The trackway into Scotland led diagonally across it, forking on the top by Dumb Crag. One route led down to Hevensgate in the next valley, while the other wound round the foot of Maidenhope and up over the shoulder of Cheviot into Scotland. This was the route taken by Jock, the tinker, and the Hethertons when they had come for Sam's funeral.

Fortunately for Andro, the vast acres of Skirlmoor were Billy's hirsel. Billy was onto his beat almost as soon as he had climbed the slope at the back of the bothy, so he had no cause to pass the Maidens. Of course he could see them in the distance, but they were too far away for him to see what was going on.

Every evening, as soon as Freya had cleared away the supper things, Andro told her to go to bed. She needed no second bidding and was glad to escape to her room where she lay in bed trembling lest he came upstairs to her. She listened for noises that might indicate what he was doing. At first there was silence. Then after half an hour or so she would hear the back door close quietly. Since no noise followed, she concluded that he had gone out. For several nights she tried to stay awake, listening for the chimes of the clock in the kitchen, waiting for his return. She never heard anything, but he was always there in the morning, weary and unshaven with a fevered glint in his eyes.

The weekend came. Billy had asked Andro several times if he could take Rose and the children to visit his parents who lived in a village between Roselaw and Willove. Andro had always shaken his head and mentioned some task that had to be done. Then suddenly on the Friday afternoon without Billy asking, Andro told him that he and Rose could go away on the following afternoon as soon as the regular jobs were done and that they could stay away overnight and return on the Sunday evening.

As soon as the Lillicos had gone and with only Freya left at Glittering Shiel, Andro no longer felt the need to act discreetly.

Freya and he were sitting in the kitchen at dinnertime eating cold mutton and boiled potatoes. Andro pushed his empty plate away and looked at Freya.

"You've been up to those stones!" he said, accusingly. "Did you think I didn't see you this forenoon slinking along the back of the wall?"

Freya went pale. The day Lizzie had left, Andro had told her sternly that she must not go near the Maidens. But that morning she had indeed disobeyed him and gone to visit her friends. She had found a neat pile of turves stacked near each stone. The earth had been cleared down to a depth of some three feet from the base of the five stones that were still standing. She had gazed at the scene in horror. The freshly exposed stone was darker than

162

the rest with a tidemark indicating where the earth had been. She was afraid that Meg, the tallest and most slender of the stones, now deprived of her earthly support, might topple over. Then she saw that a deep trench had been dug from one stone to the next and several stones, long hidden beneath the earth, had been uncovered. She stood in the middle of the circle where Augusta, Miss Murray and the other ladies had sat only a few weeks before and looked around. Soon the trench would be complete, there were only another eight or so feet left to be dug. She walked round the edge, counting the stones. Eleven. There were eleven of them.

Freya did not know what it all meant, but at least she had discovered what Andro had been doing every night while she slept. He had not moved any of the stones, not yet. Then the dreadful thought struck her that he might be planning to destroy the circle.

Freya hung her head and waited.

"Never mind that now," said Andro, disinclined to make an issue out of her disobedience. "Away and fetch me a dram!"

She went and fetched the bottle and Andro poured himself half a tumbler of the pale liquor. He took a mouthful or two, then leaned back in his chair. "I'll finish it tonight!" he said contentedly. "Aye, and then we'll see!"

While Andro sat by the fire drinking, Freya began to clear the table.

"Aye, I'll bet my boots on it!" he mused. "There's twelve of yon beauties! No doubt about it! Aye, twelve! And you know that twelve's a lucky number, eh Freya? Have they not told you that down in yon school?"

Andro believed that when the twelfth stone was uncovered, the treasure would be revealed or at least the knowledge would come to him of where it lay. So far his exertions had yielded little. He had come upon a thin layer of blackish material which he took to be charcoal lying a foot or so beneath the surface. There had been an exciting moment two nights before when he had come across the hard straight edge of an object. After feverish digging, he had held the object in his hand. It was a sharping stone, a long discarded whetstone which he had cast aside in disgust.

Sitting by his own fireside, fed on mutton from his own sheep, a bottle of the finest whisky uncorked at his elbow, Andro felt like a lord. And if it pleased him to do so, he had only to step outside the door and cast his eyes over the wide, wild hills. His, all his and no man to say different and in a matter of hours his labours were to be crowned with gold.

The day was almost spent. The sun had begun its descent through the summer sky and soon it would vanish behind Cheviot. At last Andro judged that the time was right. He threw some peat onto the fire, poured a finger of whisky into the glass and was about to toss it back when he changed his mind. He would leave it until he came back. It would be a celebration.

He picked up his stick and went outside. Freya was nowhere to be seen. She had slipped out of the house more than an hour earlier with Grace's book tucked under her arm and was sitting on her alder bough above the water, reading. She would have preferred to take the book to her secret garden, a secluded place of tumbling waterfalls she had discovered upstream from the Maidens, but she did not dare because it would have meant going close to the Maidens for a second time that day. What was more, Andro had given her strict instructions that she was to be close at hand at all times in case he needed her. She knew he would be angry if she did not instantly appear to do his bidding.

She was reading about some celebrated Northumbrian witches who she was surprised to discover had the most ordinary names such as Ann Baites, Ann Armstrong and Lucy Thompson. However, what happened to them and the things they did were strange and magical.

She read how, at Ridingbridge End, Ann Baites went riding about in egg shells and empty wooden dishes that had never been wet. The witches had marvellous feasts when all they had to do was pull on a rope and ask for what they wanted and down it came - plump capons, plum broth, ale, wine, beef, flour and butter, as much as they wanted. And sometimes after they had eaten their fill, they amused themselves by turning into a cat or a hare. Ann Baites had even turned herself into a greyhound and then a bee. They did all this to impress the man they called their saviour and protector. He was the devil, a long black man, mounted on a fine bay galloway. They danced with him and sought to impress him by telling tales of what they had done.

Andro went to the stable to fetch the mattock and a spade. Leaving the farmyard, he crossed the footbridge and took the path to the Maidens. Freya heard the metallic noise of the tools clinking against each other. After a few minutes she slipped out from her hiding place and set about the evening chores, going first to the field to milk the cow.

When she had finished outside, she went back indoors and busied herself in the scullery. She poured the milk into the big shallow dish which stood on the slate bench. Later, when it had cooled, she would skim off the cream and add it to the cream already in the jar which Rose would churn into butter next week. A few root vegetables remained in the winter store. She fetched a wrinkled turnip, an onion or two and some carrots which she peeled and chopped. She added them and a handful of barley to the mutton broth that was already simmering in the yetling. By the time she had finished it was almost dark.

She lit the lamp and sat down to wait. Her book lay unopened on the table beside Andro's glass of whisky. She gazed at the fire, watching the fibres of peat glow red, then fade and crumble. The clock struck nine, then ten and still there was no sign of him. She listened as the minutes ticked by. Her arms and legs were stiff, her mouth was dry with nervousness yet she could not bring herself to move, so apprehensive was she.

At last the back door burst open and a gust of air rushed along the corridor, pushing open the unlatched kitchen door. She turned. A second or two later he appeared in the doorway. Febrile, his face gleaming with sweat, he seemed huge, like a giant.

"Fetch the lamp!" he ordered. "I need light!"

Instantly she leapt to her feet and moved towards the door. As he turned to leave he saw the whisky bottle on the table. "And fetch yon bottle!"

Freya went to the scullery and lit the byre lamp. Then, with one hand around the neck of the whisky bottle and the other holding the lamp, she went outside. The sky was dark and thick with cloud and the wind was beginning to stir in the topmost branches of the wych elms.

After a time Freya's eyes became accustomed to the darkness. Andro moved off in front as soon as she appeared. They followed the path until they came to the Maidens. Freya needed the light then, to cross the battlefield that Andro had created.

In his eagerness to get on with the task, he was twenty yards or more ahead of her. "Over here!" he shouted.

She guessed that he was digging the last section of trench which would link the stones together in an oval like the beads of a giant necklace. Slowly she picked her way across.

He made her stand close to him. "It cannot be long now!" he breathed. "See this?" he said striking a large, recumbent stone with his stick. "This is the eleventh stone just like I told you! Now then, stand here and hold the lamp while I get on and uncover the twelfth!"

She held the lamp up as high as she could. Seeing the bottle in her hand, he took it from her, uncorked it and took a mouthful, then he wiped his mouth on his rolled-up shirt sleeve, spat on his hands and picked up the mattock. He abandoned his earlier practice of cutting and stacking the turves tidily so that they could be replaced later. Instead, he began to hurl the earth and stones over his shoulder at random. The digging became more frantic and uncontrolled. Over and over again he raised the mattock high above his head and brought it down hard into the earth. After about ten minutes he encountered something hard.

"Closer! Bring the lamp closer, I cannot see!" he said, his voice trembling with excitement.

Now he abandoned the mattock for his bare hands and crouching in the trench he began to scratch at the earth like a

166

terrier at a foxhole. A few minutes later he gave out a hoarse shout. "No! No! It cannot be!"

Freya tensed, fearful of what he had discovered.

More digging followed accompanied by mutterings that she was unable to decipher because she had to turn her head away to avoid the shower of clods. Suddenly all activity stopped and she heard a strange noise, a growl of pain, more animal than human.

Andro climbed out of the trench, straightened up, then reeled for a few seconds before staggering the two or three paces to Meg. With his eyes closed, he leaned against the stone for a minute or two. After a time he seemed to come to, he pulled off his hat and wiped his gleaming brow.

"Damnation!" he fumed. "Damnation to the lot of them!" He turned to face Meg, clenched his fist and brought it down hard on her grainy surface. "Thirteen! There's thirteen of the damned things! Oh if it's not a blasted coven I've turned up!"

Andro's mounting rage sought a channel of escape and he remembered his dreams and the creature mounted on the goat. "Oh aye! I see it all now. It's yon Hecate's fault!" he railed. "She's the one to blame! Did she not swear to take vengeance on me for what I did! The bloody Hethertons! Will I never be shot of them?" He seized the whisky bottle and drank. "Aye and while I'm about it, a curse on yon horsefaced woman Gilderoy as well! Her and all her fancy friends! Why if she hadn't come ameddling, this would never have happened!"

Andro's diatribe was addressed to the night air. He seemed to have forgotten Freya who had not moved since setting the lamp down at her feet as soon as Andro had left the trench.

Eventually the flood of invective ebbed and Andro remembered that she was there. At that moment, the moon, a slender crescent, emerged from a tatter of clouds. As Freya looked up at it, a lull in the wind caused the lamp to burn more brightly, reflecting light off Freya's smooth forehead and finely sculptured chin.

To Andro she looked as cold and unfeeling as a stone statue and the sight gave his anger a new impetus and direction.

He took a step towards her. "Have you nowt to say, then? No words of comfort for a man what's slaved these last nights in vain?" he growled. Then young Billy's words came into his fevered mind. "Wicked eh? A wicked witch! Oh aye! I know what they been saying! Well maybe you are and maybe I've been on the wrong track and she what's to blame for my misfortunes is standing right here in front of me!"

Freya was terrified, unable to find a word of defence. She looked first at the ground and then at the moon. Perhaps it was an effect of the flickering light, but Andro could have sworn he saw the beginnings of a smile on her lips.

"What's this I see? Do you dare to smile?" Now his anger was unbounded and, throwing the bottle aside, he seized her by the shoulders. "D'you know what they do with the likes of you?" he asked her ominously.

There was no response.

He shook her. "Do you? Do you?" he insisted.

Freya managed a mute shake of the head.

"Well I'll tell you! They send for the pricker! That's what! He knows how to wipe the smile off a witch's face!" he said triumphantly.

Restored, jubilant in the knowledge of his power and what he was about to do with it, Andro locked one arm round Freya's body, while with the other he felt for the hem of her skirt. But before he could do more, Freya, overwhelmed, made her escape. She fainted, leaving him holding her limp, impassive body.

168

17

The next morning Freya woke in her bed unable to remember how she had got back home and at first she thought that the events of the previous night had been a nightmare. She stirred a little, moving her body under the warm blankets. She was sore and bruised and then she knew that last night had been no dream but a reality.

She lay very still and tried to think. She had heard Andro tell her that he knew what Cissy and Elsie had said about her, that she was a witch. Did that mean he knew about the wax figure and the ginger biscuit man? She shivered. He had been so mad with rage last night that she had feared for her life. What would he do with her now he knew? Elsie and Cissy said that they filled witches' pockets with stones and threw them into a deep pool. The thought terrified her. She must get up, get away from him, run, run as fast as she could. She tried to sit up, but her head began to swim and she sank back down helpless into the bed.

Panic-stricken, her eyes darted about the room. She saw her familiar things: the jam jar on the window ledge with the wild flowers she had picked the day before, ragged robin, harebells, cranesbill and the delicate green-veined flowers of grass-of-parnassus. Jock's rattle, the green reeds now faded to brown, was lying on the shelf. She wished she could hold it, along with Miss Murray's book which was beside it. Soon, fear and the effort of trying to think overcame her. She closed her eyes and shut everything out - Andro, the room, everything.

Sleep came at once. Late in the morning she woke and again her mind started to work. Andro had failed last night. He had disturbed the Maidens in vain and when he had failed to find what he was looking for, he had blamed her. His fury would have destroyed her, but he had failed in that too. He could never have destroyed her there inside the necklace of stones surrounded by her friends. And she was glad there were thirteen of them - five awake and eight asleep like in a fairy tale.

She got up at noon and looked out of her tiny window at a blue cloudless sky. The outline of Maidenhope was sharp and clear and she remembered walking to the summit one Midsummer's Eve when she was very small. She had often dreamed of the fire and the wild, prancing figure clothed in animal skins. Suddenly it came to her that the man had been Andro! Then she thought of Miss Murray's book and the long dark man who came and danced with the witches beside the bridge. He was their master, the devil. The women had danced behind their leader that magic night. Did that mean that Andro was the devil?

There was a little water in the blue-rimmed jug with its transfer-printed cornflowers. She poured it into the basin and splashed her face. The water was cool and refreshing but it was not enough. She was overcome with the desire to bathe in the burn. Today she felt like a survivor. She was strong, nothing would stop her, today she would go to her special place.

Her clogs were not in her room and so she went barefoot down the stairs and out of the back door. Andro's hat and stick were not on the peg but she did not notice, so intent was she on her purpose.

As she crossed the bridge, she did not turn to see if her broon kitty was in the alder trees. She took the path to the Maidens. It was not until she was level with them that she looked around to see if Andro was watching. There was no one, only the occasional ewe looked up as she passed, staring at her with a look of indifference or effrontery. Instead of crossing the burn, she continued on upstream. There was no path but she was sure-footed, knowing every clump of reed, every grassy hummock, every rise and fall in the ground. With increasing speed, she threaded her way through the thistles and bracken.

A twisted hawthorn marked the entrance to a narrow defile through which the Eidon Burn tumbled and splashed in a series of small waterfalls. It was the only such place upstream from the farm. The burn, which had its source in a wide, boggy dish of land at the foot of Maidenhope, slapped and clatched its way downstream until it came to this place where the ground dropped suddenly and the water was forced to find its way through great shoulders of granite. No one looking across the valley from Skirlmoor would have guessed the place existed and it always came as a pleasant surprise to the rare walker who chanced upon it. Of course Andro knew it was there. He walked near it every day on his way to look the sheep, but he had only climbed down by the water to search for lost sheep.

Freya turned and looked behind her once more before she dropped onto all fours and began to scramble up the warm rocks until she came to her special place.

The burn flowed over a mossy lip and slid into a large pool. On the south side a large rowan tree spread its branches down over the rock. The brown water massed almost motionless in the sunless corner and just above the foamy rim of the pool a dense carpet of mosses and tiny ferns grew in the cool shade. When Freya had first discovered the place, she had crept under the overhanging branches and pressed her hand on the bed of tiny plants, a tapestry of bright stars, miniature parasols and verdant, feathery fingers. Dark green liverwort clung to the stones by the water's edge, its leathery leaves marked with lines like the footprints of some tiny diluvian creature.

Once the water had rounded the darkened bend, it emerged into the sunlight and flowed along the side of a rock. The bottom of the pool was dappled amber, while on the surface danced the glinting yellow reflection of the craws taes which grew on a grassy cushion close by. At the sunny end of the pool there was a second rowan tree, younger than the first, with a lustrous gunmetal trunk which grew out of a cleft in the rock. Beneath the rowan and above the water there was a deep, rocky ledge. It was to this place that Freya retreated.

Panting slightly, she sat down and drew her knees up under her chin. Then, like a sea creature seeking the sanctuary of a rocky crevice, she folded herself up and withdrew as far as she could. No one could see her here and at last she began to feel safe. She closed her eyes and listened to the soothing song of the water.

Later she took off her clothes and laid them on the rock. The water was icy. She gasped as it closed around her chest. Her feet, as soon as they touched the stones on the bed of the pool, sent up a cloud of fine particles. The water became cloudy, her limbs vague and lost. Step by step, she made her way into the shady part of the pool where the water was deeper. She held out her arms and slowly bent her knees until she was totally immersed in the water. For a few seconds she held her breath, then trembling with the cold, she emerged and climbed down to a flat stone at the foot of the waterfall which cascaded down from the pool.

There, she basked in the warm sun. Later, she thought of washing her clothes. The sleeves of her blouse ballooned out as they filled with water. She did the same thing with her skirt, holding the hem like the rim of a wide-necked funnel. Then she twisted each garment to wring out the water, finally draping them over a rock to dry.

The sun and the sound of the burbling burn gave her comfort and gradually she began to feel better. A pair of meadow pipits were fluttering and singing high above her. Her white, water-wrinkled hands were resting on a smooth stone beside a clump of horsetails that looked like a forest of fairy Christmas trees. She bent over to look more closely at the miniature landscape, examining the flowers of tormentil with their enamel-yellow petals and next to them the delicate mauve flowers of marsh willowherb. She picked a strand of sweet vernal-grass and rolled it in her fingers, releasing the sweet perfume of new-mown hay.

Freya left the place at the same time as the sun. She made her way up the steep side of the defile, stopping only to pick a handful of inky bilberries. A sheep track with short, velvety grass ran through the heather and bracken down towards the Maidens. She paused briefly to look at them. Andro had been there. Much of the earth had been replaced, but the work was not finished. Boldly she walked over to Meg and touched her. Like Freya, she had survived. She was still there, staunch as ever, her foundations once more bedded safe in the earth.

When Freya got back the farmyard was a bustle of activity. The Lillicos had recently returned. Billy waved as he went off to look the sheep and Violet and Hazel came running up the moment Freya appeared.

"Here Freya! You can have one of our bullets!" said Violet, holding out the cone of paper which her grandmother had given her. It had been full of boiled sweets, but now there were only four or five stuck together in a lump at the bottom. Freya prised one loose and put it in her mouth.

"Where's your clogs?" asked Violet as soon as she noticed Freya's bare feet.

Before Freya could answer, Rose appeared carrying a pail of milk. Freya hurried to take it from her and carry it into the scullery. There was no noise inside the house though Andro's stick and hat were there. Freya dealt with the milk and then she tiptoed nervously into the kitchen.

Andro was bent over the fire which was piled high with smouldering peat. Freya looked in surprise at the table which was set ready for a meal with a loaf of barley bread, two plates, two glasses and a bottle of Lizzie's ginger ale.

Andro sensed that she was there and turned round. "So there you are at long last!" The words were uttered with an air of concern not criticism. "There's no need to look so scared," he went on equably. "I was mad with rage last night, I know that, but tonight everything'll be different. Tonight I'll show you my true colours and you can give yourself over to me."

Freya, though reassured by Andro's tone, was instantly anxious as to what his words meant.

"Don't just stand in the doorway, come in and sit yourself down! I've prepared a dinner fit for a queen!"

Freya did as she was told while Andro continued to busy himself with the fire. She sat and waited. After a time he took a poker and pushed the peat to one side. Then he inserted a large metal fork and lifted an object like a large oval, biscuit-coloured stone out of the fire which he carefully lowered onto a plate which was warming on top of the set pot.

He smiled at her. "You've never seen the like of this before, have you?" He lifted the dish onto the table, took the big horn-handled gully and inserted it into a crack in the clay. The casing fell away and a delicious smell of chicken filled the air. As he carefully lifted away the shards, Freya saw that the bird's feathers were bonded into the clay and once the casing was removed, the chicken was ready to be carved.

Freya looked in amazement. Chicken was a special treat which they only ever had at Christmas and she had never seen it cooked in such a strange way.

Andro began to carve. "It was grand when I was a laddie," he told her, "and my mother cooked a bird like this, excepting of course she did it outside. Aye, and then it smelled even better!"

Freya said nothing. Andro's behaviour was bewildering. She had never heard him mention his mother before and, as for cooking, he had never so much as touched a spoon. Her relief at his mood gradually gave way to a sense of foreboding about his intentions. There had to be more to it than putting the rest of the earth back around the stones. He must have other things in mind, things that involved her.

Andro gave her a generous portion of meat which was so delicious that she could not help thinking it was probably the sort of food witches ate at their feasts.

"So tonight, we'll have a christening up by the stones!" Andro informed her when they had finished eating.

He saw her look of incomprehension. "Why lassie, you've never been properly named! Yon Felix saddled you with the name of Freya and what sort of foreign nonsense name is that? It's high time I took the matter in hand."

Still she had no idea what he meant, but he was not disposed to say more. He simply told her to be ready to leave at nightfall.

Over the course of the afternoon a feeling of calm and strength had grown inside Freya and even now it did not leave her. She had weathered the storm the night before. The night to come could surely not be worse.

At nightfall a thick blanket of cloud descended on the hills and there was neither moon nor stars. They left the house at ten o'clock. When they got to the stones Andro told her to hold the lamp while he worked. He laboured steadily, shovelling earth back into the trench. Finally he shuffled and stamped on the turves to settle them back into the ground.

"There!" he said standing back to admire his work. "That'll soon grow back! In a week or two even yon nosey Gilderoy woman'll not can tell the difference." There was a pause and then he turned to Freya. "And now, lassie, it's your turn!"

Freya felt a twist of fear, for Andro's words were uttered in the soft persuasive tones he used when he was about to do something unpleasant.

"Like I said last night, I know that they say you're a witch. Now then, there's nothing wrong with being a witch, nothing at all. The only thing is, it has to be done right! And I'm the man to see to it. You see, I know all about such things and the first thing is that you can only be a witch if it's of your own choosing. So it's up to you! If you *do* decide, then you have to do certain things what I can instruct you in and afterwards you can enjoy all the benefits of the craft. Now then what d'you say? Will you take the vow? Aye, and get yourself a new name, a good solid name what I'll give you?"

Freya could scarcely believe her ears. Andro was saying that it was all right to be a witch. He was even offering to help her become a proper witch with a new name. He seemed to know all about it. And as for choosing to become a witch, why she had made that choice long ago at school and had confirmed it by her actions several times since.

Andro was waiting, willing her to say yes.

"What's it to be then?" he asked gently. "Will you make the vow? Will you do the things I tell you?"

She wanted to ask him how it was that he could do this. Yes, he *must* be like the long dark man in Miss Murray's book. There could be no other explanation.

She said nothing and he, taking her silence for acquiescence, stepped over, took her by the hand and led her outside the circle of the stones and down to the Eidon Burn. She heard the gentle music of the water and was reassured by the thought that it had flowed through her secret place only minutes before.

From the folds of his plaid Andro drew a candle, darker and thicker than an ordinary one, which he lit and set on a stone. Then he took off his plaid to reveal a shaggy goatskin draped around his shoulders with the black cloven feet of its forelegs hanging down over his chest like hairy braces.

Freya made a sharp intake of breath. Something about the hairy pelt reminded her again of that distant Midsummer night and she was surer than ever that Andro was the prancing man of Maidenhope.

"Now then," he began in a loud stage whisper, "take off those clouts!"

Slowly she undressed, but he could not see her naked body because the candle gave only a meagre light and there was no moonlight. He wanted to touch her, but he could not, not yet. He told her to kneel down. Then standing in front of her, he took her hands in his and began to speak in a sonorous ceremonial voice.

"The Master bids you welcome."

A series of questions followed, uttered in the same voice.

"Do you come to this place of your own free will?"

The stage whisper prompted her. "Say aye, Lord!"

She managed to produce an acceptable sound.

"Do you gainsay your baptism and your belief in the god what calls himself the Almighty, the god of the Jews, him what sent down the tablets off the mountain?" intoned the official voice.

Freya could not understand why Andro was asking her about her baptism for they both knew that she had never been baptised. And as for the Almighty, she had no difficulty forsaking him. He was Mr Dogberry's god, the god who had said such terrible things to Eve.

"Will you make solemn paction with me, to obey me as your lord for seven years and to do my bidding in all things?" There was a pause before he continued. "Aye, and in exchange for this I swear to give you long life and prosperity."

Freya did not know what paction was, but she did understand that she was promising to obey Andro for seven years. Later, when she had had time to think about it, she decided that she preferred Andro's god to Mr Dogberry's. Mr Dogberry's took everyone's obedience for granted, he did not give people a choice and he assumed that they would obey him for ever.

Then Andro took hold of her arms, raised her to her feet and whispered further instructions. She did as he told her and, putting one hand on the crown of her head and the other on the sole of her foot, she hesitantly repeated what he had said. "I swear to give over to you all what is between my two hands."

Then he drew her to the edge of the burn and told her to get down on her knees. With one hand on her breast and the other in the middle of her back, he began to push her down towards the water.

Fear gripped her and she thought that the dinner, the kindness had all been a pretence. He was as wild with fury tonight as he had been last night except that now he was calm and in control. Was this his vengeance, to push her head under the water until she could breath no more? Instinctively she fought against the pressure of his powerful arms which were forcing her down closer and closer to the water.

For a second, he held her face under the water, then pulled her back. For several seconds she spluttered, gasping for air and then she heard him say, "And I baptise thee Issabel!"

A short time later he uncorked his liquor flask. "Now then, take a drop of this unholy fire water!" he said in his normal voice. He put the flask to her lips and tipped it so that a rush of whisky filled her mouth. Somehow she managed to swallow some.

177

"Good lassie!" he purred. "That's what I like to see, a body what can take their liquor!"

He had a nip or two himself while he waited for the drink to take effect. From the moment that the fear had started to mount within her, when Andro had forced her down into the water, Freya had begun to withdraw. Now the process continued, aided by the strong liquor. Very soon she became detached, removed from her body so that it was as if she was watching what happened next from across the water.

Andro put his hands on her shoulders, bent over and began to suck the skin behind her right shoulder. He sucked and sucked until the spot was numb. "And now, Issabel," he said in a satisfied tone, "you bear upon your body your master's mark just like the sheep on the hills!"

Next he ordered her to go down on her knees. "There's just one last thing and that's the kiss!" he said in a husky voice. "To seal the pact and for to show your obedience to me, you must kiss my body wheresoever I direct you! Do you understand what I'm saying?"

Freya saw her nod.

"First, you must kiss my backparts!"

Naked apart from the goatskin, he turned his back towards her, bent over and said in a playful, sing-song voice, "Come on then Issabel, put them sweet lips on my backparts. Quick now! Don't keep your lord waiting!"

Freya saw her do the thing.

He turned to face her. "And now the belly button! Put your sweet lips on my belly button!"

Freya saw her bend her head and do the thing.

"And now, my Issabel, put your sweet lips to my man's thing!"

Freya's throat was dry as she watched her obey. Then she thought she heard Andro say that he was going to take her for a ride, that a true witch liked nothing better than to ride the same way as Adam's other wife, Lilith. After that there was nothing.

18

A week passed and then another with no word from Lizzie.
Freya went to school every day. Grace became increasingly
worried about her and on the Monday morning after Andro had
baptised her, she and Billy arrived late for school.

Freya's face was ashen as she sat forlorn and lifeless in her
desk. At break, when Grace asked her if anything was wrong,
she looked blankly into Grace's face. Grace thought she
discerned a flicker of emotion in the depths of Freya's blue eyes
and for a second there was a movement of the lips as if she would
speak, but the moment passed and her face composed itself into a
mask of resolute silence. It was a look that Grace had not seen
before and it was one that she did not understand.

It was Jenny who told Grace that Lizzie had had to go to
Seamouth because her mother was very ill. Thus Grace realised
that Freya would be doing Lizzie's work before she left for school
in the morning and no doubt it was the same when she got home
in the evening. But that did not explain the broken and
demoralised state into which she lapsed when she thought herself
unobserved. So Grace began to suspect there was more to
Freya's state than simple tiredness, that the girl was being
mistreated in some way. Grace had no proof of cruelty and, even
if she had, she did not know what she could do about it. It was
unthinkable for her to go and see Andro. A man's home was his
castle, his wife and his children were his property. No one, and
certainly not a mere spinster school mistress, had the right to
trespass onto his territory and meddle in his affairs. So all Grace
could do was watch and wait.

Grace had other things on her mind. The school inspector was
about to make his annual visit. It was an anxious time because
the amount of money the school received the following year
depended on the scholars' level of achievement in the current

year. The little infants, the big infants and standards one to seven had each to perform a variety of tasks for the inspector which were all set out in an official document known as *The Revised Code*.

The inspector, Mr Greated from Newcastle, arrived first thing on Friday morning. A striking figure in a black tailcoat, he was tall and thin with a long, flowing beard. By the end of the morning the children had christened him Elijah. The awe and reverence he inspired was so great that, to Grace's deep despair, he was at first unable to get much more than a single syllable out of the children.

Throughout the day they underwent rigorous tests in mental arithmetic, written arithmetic, mensuration and geometry. Hesitantly, in indistinct and monotonous voices, they recited the poems they had learned. They told him on what latitude he would find Lake Titicaca, Lake Victoria and the Dead Sea, what the population of India was, where whalebones came from and what they were used for. When the time came for them to display their religious knowledge, Tom Nesbit confused arithmetic and the Bible by proudly explaining that a gross darkness was one hundred and forty-four times thicker than ordinary darkness. They demonstrated their penmanship, they took dictation, they parsed, punctuated, composed and reduced to the very limits of their ability for they all wished to do their best for Miss Murray.

With due ceremony, Mr Greated recorded the results of the tests along with his comments in a large, shiny black ledger which the children thought looked as impressive and weighty as the Lord's book on the Day of Judgement. There was a universal sigh of relief when, a little after three o'clock in the afternoon, he closed the tome. For a few seconds his pale grey eyes rested on the earnest faces before him and then, without a word of either encouragement or criticism, he bade the scholars of Herontop School a solemn farewell.

Grace went outside with him and when she returned she found two of the boys standing on their desks. They had climbed up so they could look out of the windows and watch Elijah's departure.

Great was the jubilation when they reported him riding away down the road to Herontop. Grace was no less relieved to see him go and so, to celebrate, she told the children that they could go home early.

It was a hot summer afternoon. For once there was no need for Freya and Billy to hurry off up the hill. Freya and Jenny stood in the shade of the chestnut trees and waited for Billy. Jenny intended to walk a little way up the road with them so that she and Freya could spend a few more minutes together. As the three of them turned to go, they did not notice a person in the distance coming along the road towards the school from the direction of Herontop.

The children had felt cool when they first came out of school, but the stifling heat and the uphill walk soon made them feel hot, so once the steepest part was over they stopped for a while. Billy immediately went off to see if he could find a chaffinch or bluetit's nest while Freya and Jenny sat down in the long grass in the shade of the hedge. Jenny picked some harebells which she threaded into Freya's hair. Then after a few minutes she reluctantly got up, said goodbye and walked back down the hill.

As Freya stood and watched her go, she noticed that someone had just come round the bend by the school and was beginning to walk up the hill. The person was carrying a large bundle. She looked as if she wanted to wave but could not because of the bundle. Freya assumed that it was someone Jenny knew, but to her surprise the two passed each other without stopping. It was only then that the stranger laid the bundle down on the ground and waved.

Freya turned to Billy. "Look! Down the road! Somebody's waving! Who is it?"

Billy emerged from the hedge. "Oh it's just some old woman with her bits of things, maybe it's Martha, her what comes about this time of year, her with the ribbons and thread. She'll be going to call on Mrs Matheson. Come on Freya, we'd better get going!"

"No! She wants us to wait! Look, she's trying to run!"

Sure enough, the woman was running a few paces, then dropping back into a walk. Gradually she came closer, a black-clothed figure in a bonnet.

"Why it's your mam!" Billy exclaimed.

Freya began to run back down the hill. It *was* Lizzie and Freya could hear her calling out breathlessly, "Freya! Freya! It's me!"

Even when they were face to face, Freya felt as if she was meeting a stranger. It was certainly Lizzie's voice, but apart from that, Freya could hardly believe that it was the same woman who had kissed her goodbye only three weeks before. Lizzie seemed smaller, older. Perhaps it was the clothes. Freya had never seen them before. They were made of a thick dark material more suitable for winter than high summer and they were worn and patched.

"I'd thought to meet you out of school!" Lizzie gasped. "I came as fast as I could, but it's that hot and I've had to walk nearly all the way. I set off early before the sun was up. Oh dear, I'm fit to drop, as weak as a kitten!"

Freya took the bundle from her and drew her into the shade so she could sit down.

"No! No! I dare not! If I sit down, I'll never get up again! No, if you'll carry my things, I'll just keep going." She smiled bleakly. "We can take a rest when we've got a bit farther up the road."

They plodded on wordlessly. Lizzie had no breath to spare for talking. The effort of walking was enough to make her breathe heavily and she had to stop frequently to get her breath and then, more often than not, she coughed a dry rasping cough.

Lizzie's head was swimming with fatigue. It seemed as if her journey had lasted a lifetime, as if it was years ago that she had stopped to watch a gang of bondagers in their bright red and white checked kerchiefs and uglie bonnets labouring in a field of turnips. She found that whenever she closed her eyes for a moment to shut out the sun, black patches, the shape of the keel boat or the church on the dunes, danced before her eyes.

182

From time to time Freya stole a quick glance at Lizzie. Lizzie had never had pink cheeks like Rose, but in the summertime her face was always brown and freckled. Now neither the heat nor the effort of walking had brought any colour to her cheeks and her pale skin was beaded with sweat.

They walked through the gates of Heron Hall along the avenue of whispering limes round the corner past Home Farm and on into the dappled darkness of the wood. Fortunately the Matheson's dog was not tied up by the back door so there was no barking to alert Lilian who was doubtless indoors resting in the cool parlour after the exertion of cooking Will's dinner.

As they emerged from the wood, the wide fells, shimmering and hazy in the heat, opened out before them. Lizzie paused for a moment, her eyes rediscovering the contours of Maidenhope and Cheviot.

She sighed. "That's better! I'll be able to breathe easier now. I didn't know how much I'd missed the hills!"

Billy was skipping along some fifty yards ahead and as soon as he came to the ford by the still, he darted down to the edge of the burn and took off his boots and socks.

Freya expected Lizzie to insist that they go on, but she said a rest would do her good before the last leg of the journey. They went down to the water and with cupped hands they drank their fill and splashed their faces. Afterwards they found a shady place beside the tranquil burn. Here and there clumps of orange mimulus tumbled over the stones and from time to time they caught a glimpse of Billy moving stealthily along the bank on the lookout for a trout to tickle.

Lizzie's attention was drawn to a black-faced sheep which was rubbing its head compulsively on the gnarled boss of a hawthorn trunk. She could see raw flesh exposed at the base of its curving horns. "Is the flies bad then?" she asked dully.

Freya was disappointed. She was hoping that as soon as they stopped Lizzie would tell her what had happened at Seamouth. "Aye," she said, replying to Lizzie's remark, "he says it's the hot weather that's made them worse. Him and Billy were on last

183

weekend putting tar round the blackies' horns and tying caps on the Cheviots, but there wasn't enough so he told Rose and me to get cracking and make some more."

Freya remembered how she and Rose had sat stitching the little calico caps the whole of the previous Sunday. Rose, who was most particular not to knit or sew on the Sabbath, had been most reluctant to break the Lord's commandment. She did not argue though she did mutter and complain at length while they worked, but when Andro appeared she gave him a bright willing smile.

Lizzie nodded her head mechanically. "Aye, that's right enough. The headflies is always worse in hot weather."

Again there was a pause and Freya hoped that now the conversation would turn to Seamouth.

"So everything's all right, is it? Up there?" asked Lizzie with a nod in the direction of Glittering Shiel.

Freya said nothing.

Lizzie turned to her. "And you, Freya, are you all right?"

Freya nodded hesitantly. Though she had no intention of telling Lizzie anything about Andro and the stones, she was worried about Lizzie's store of clean cloths some of which she had used and then burned on the fire.

The bleeding had started one afternoon the previous week. On the way home from school, she had felt a strange pain in her stomach and by the time she got home, the bleeding had started. The blood frightened her because she did not know what it meant. One of the things Elsie had told her was that witches did not bleed and now that she was a proper witch she could not understand what had gone wrong. Perhaps Andro had made a mistake with the vow? And if he had, did that mean she wasn't a witch after all?

Freya tried to find the words to broach the subject of the cloths. Her skin went hot and prickly. She took a deep breath, but the words that came out were not the ones she had intended. "What about your mam?" she stammered.

184

"My mam?" There was a long pause. "Mam's gone and Felix and all."

"Gone?"

"Aye, gone! Mam's gone to heaven," said Lizzie, adding bitterly, "always supposing there's more justice in the next world than there is in this one." Wearily she began to explain. "We buried her yesterday, da, and the rest of us."

Freya waited while Lizzie gathered the strength to go on.

"Those last few days near broke my heart. She was lying there dying and she kept on and on asking for Felix as if she'd forgotten where he'd gone. Da just kept saying, he's doing his best, Meggie. He's on his way, he'll be here before long. But there was no way he could get him back, was there? What with him being round the other side of the world."

The other side of the world! Freya had no idea what lay on the other side of the globe, thousands of miles from the red patch that was England.

"He's been gone near enough ten months now. I *knew* he'd gone. I knew it *here*!" said Lizzie vehemently, putting her clenched fist to her breast. "One morning, without so much as a word of warning, he went off to Newcastle and signed on. Da told me the name of the ship, but I cannot mind it now. Anyway, the vessel was bound for Sydney. That's in a country called Australia. There's a lot of folk from Tyneside gone there. He told da there was nowt for him here. You see, he always said he'd never go down the pit and with the herring fishing done for, what else could he do? Boats and the sea is all he knows."

Lizzie fell silent. She was thinking about the fishing. As well as caring for her mother, she had done her best to take her place. Every day she had sat on an upturned creel, her back against the tar-crazed boards of the boat and baited lines, a thousand hooks a time, and before the sun was up she had gone down to the shingle beach with the other women and helped launch the cobles. Fully clothed, they waded waist-deep into the water to push the boats off the beach. She wished her father could have stayed at home with her mother, but she did not say a word. She knew that the work had to go on or they would surely starve.

Lizzie's eyes fell on the bundle lying on the grass in front of her. It was tied with a stout piece of hemp rope which her father had looped into a handle so it would be easier to carry.

"Da gave me some of her things. He said he wanted me to have them." She tried to undo the knot but it was too tight. "You've got nimble fingers, Freya. Open it will you?"

Freya pulled the bundle towards her and quickly undid the rope. As soon as it was released, the bundle unrolled itself on the grass. It was a quilt, its colours much faded and in some places it was completely worn away, revealing the old curtain with which it had been stuffed.

Lizzie gazed at it affectionately. Her childhood lay before her like an open picture album. Apart from a broad border of dull pink cotton, there was little pattern or design to the quilt. The patches were triangular and of different sizes, having been cut from old clothes in such a way as to make use of every square inch of unworn fabric.

"Those colours were bright once," she remarked, shaking her head sadly. "Mam got scraps of clout wherever she could. She used to take fish regular to one of the big houses and the housekeeper was always kind to her. She would give her an old skirt or maybe a blouse what nobody wanted. Oh aye, mam was a dab hand with a needle! See this?"

Lizzie pointed to a pale green patch which was almost threadbare. "That was once the prettiest little blouse you ever saw. I can't have been more than four or five when she got it and cut it down to fit me. She was over the moon with it, she said it was silk like what fine ladies wore. That's why it's all worn away, too soft for the likes of us." Then she added fiercely, "You see that's why I wanted new things for you when you went to school. I wanted better for *you*!"

The quilt was not completely unrolled, so Lizzie eased herself up onto her knees and gave it a push. Two objects were revealed, an orange and something wrapped in a scrap of yellowing lace.

Lizzie retrieved them. "This is for you!" she said, handing Freya the orange. "Da got two for mam. He was hoping to tempt her but she didn't want any. A drop of water was all she'd take."

Freya had never held an orange in her hand. She pulled her fingernail across the skin and grazed the surface, producing a tiny jet of fine mist and a bitter sharp smell.

For the first time Lizzie smiled. "Go on then, peel it! I nearly did on the way. I could've done with it many a time, I was that parched."

Freya began to peel the orange.

"Once you've got the skin off, you have to put your thumbs in at the top and pull it open."

Freya did as Lizzie said, then carefully distributed the segments one by one.

"Shouldn't we give some to Billy?" asked Freya.

"No, Freya! We'll share it, just the two of us, just this once!"

After they had eaten the orange Lizzie turned to the lace package lying in her lap. Her fingers were sticky with juice so she delicately took hold of one corner and shook it gently.

"It was the only nice thing she had, bar her wedding ring of course, and she went to her grave with that on her finger. Da was loathe to see gold put useless in the ground, but she made him promise."

A large, oval brooch with a bunch of flowers carved on it lay in the palm of Lizzie's hand.

"She got this when they were first married and da was earning good money as a keelman. He took her on holiday to Whitby and he bought her this brooch as a souvenir. It's made of jet! She was so proud of it, on Sundays she used it to put it on her dress on top of this bit of lace so she would look smart when she went to church."

19

Life at Glittering Shiel went on as before. Andro said little when Lizzie returned, seeming neither glad nor sorry to see her back. Rose remarked to Billy how weary and dispirited Lizzie looked. They put it down to grief and the sleepless nights she had spent caring for her mother. Lizzie told Rose only the bare facts concerning her mother's death and Felix's departure. Unaccustomed to speak of her feelings, she did not say that Felix had taken a part of her away with him the day he had sailed out of the Tyne.

The week after Lizzie came home, school closed for the summer holidays. As usual on the last day of the school year the children gathered in the little field for their annual sports. Mr Dogberry was there to organise the races and see fair play. Augusta came down from Heron Hall in a pony and trap bringing the prizes for the winners and a hamper full of iced cakes, scones, sandwiches and lemonade for the tea afterwards. A handful of the children's relatives, those who did not have to go to work, came to watch and cheer the children on.

Grace knew that Lizzie was back. On the day of Mr Greated's visit, after she had released the children early, she had gone to sit quietly in her parlour. Looking out of the window, she saw Lizzie go past the school and on up the hill towards Heron Hall, but like Freya she had not recognised her at first. By the time she had realised that it *was* Lizzie and that she might take the opportunity of speaking to her, it was too late. Grace could only move slowly so that by the time she got outside, Lizzie was too far away.

Grace was disappointed, though not surprised, when Lizzie did not turn up for the sports. It was a long way to walk just for an hour or two and she had never seen Lizzie riding a horse.

When the festivities were over and Augusta had presented the prizes, and after the food and drink had all been consumed and God thanked for his bounteousness, everyone went their separate ways.

Grace called Freya over before she left. She had chosen several books from her small library, which she had tied in a bundle with a stout strap. She handed them to Freya, saying that she could have them over the holidays. The books were a pretext to enable Grace to see Freya. She told Freya that although she would probably not need them, if by chance she did, she would send word so that Freya could bring them to her. Grace really wanted to tell Freya that she could come to her at any time if the need arose. However, that would have meant suggesting there was a problem and Freya had never confessed as much.

The summer ran its indolent course. The grass grew thick and lush and the sheep thrived. The Eidon Burn was reduced to a trickle and the trout had fewer places to hide from Billy's deft fingers.

During August Andro decided to build a shieling. He had the idea when he and Billy were cutting and stacking bent-grass on the open fell which was something they did every year in order to have a supply of extra fodder for the sheep in the event of a harsh winter. They were working close by the old peat cuttings on Cockslack, the sweep of fell which lay between Warrior Crag and the foot of Maidenhope.

As soon as they had finished stacking the bent, Andro sent Billy off to the other side of the valley to start cutting and stacking there, while he started to build the simple shelter. He told Billy that he could not think why he had not built one long ago since the nearest shelter, a stell, was a good half mile further down towards the Maidens. The shieling would provide a useful shelter for man and beast against the winter blast.

There were almost no trees on the open fell suitable for building a shelter so Andro had to go down into Freya's secret garden to find birch and rowan saplings. He cut brushy bundles like giant besoms and brought Polly to haul them to the place he had chosen. It was right in the middle of his hirsel, in a natural bay at the edge of the thick blanket of peat which clothed the top of the fell. There he set about weaving the supple branches together into walls and a roof which he thatched with heather.

Every day Andro told Lizzie to send Freya up with his dinner so he could get on with the work. At noon he would plant his ram's horn stick in the wall of peat by the entrance to the shelter and draw Freya inside onto a bed of dry bracken where he was ingenious in finding ways for her to prove her obedience to him.

He called her his sweet Issabel, dividing her name into three syllables so that it sounded more like a message than a name. He would linger over the double 's', pause after the 'a' and finish with a resonant 'bel'. "Bel means beautiful," he would tell her. Of course he never called her Issabel in the house, though sometimes when Lizzie was out of the room or he thought she was not looking, he would cast a meaningful glance at Freya, stroke his nose with his index finger and say softly 'sss' as if he were ruminating on some plan or other.

Freya never returned his look, never smiled at him. It was no longer a question of hating him or not. She had made a choice which bound them together and so she did what he told her.

Freya had long since abandoned the hope of being like other girls. She was two people. When she was with Andro, she was called Issabel. From the moment of her baptism, Andro had treated her as a person in her own right, something he had never done before. But at other times she was Freya, the girl who sat cross-legged at Grace Murray's feet listening to her speak of strong, beautiful women.

Freya was allowed more time to herself than ever before. In the past Andro had given her innumerable tasks just as he did everyone else on the farm, but that summer, because of her compliance, she enjoyed certain privileges. He never questioned what she did or where she went during her free time. For Lizzie's sake, she worked in the garden, picking and preserving the fruit and vegetables. She milked the cow and fed the pigs and hens. Over the weeks Lizzie became more cheerful, more like her old self, though Freya noticed that she did everything more slowly than before. Sometimes she would sigh quietly as she summoned up the strength to go on with whatever task she was engaged on and several times in the afternoon Freya had found her asleep in the leather chair in the parlour, her hands still holding the sewing she had been doing before sleep had overcome her.

In those quiet moments in the afternoons, Freya would go upstairs and choose one of the books Miss Murray had given her. There was *A Book of Golden Deeds* by Charlotte Yonge, Lord Tennyson's *Idylls of the King*, Mrs Loudon's *Entertaining Naturalist* and a bundle of booklets, six-penny periodicals entitled *Border Miscellany*, which contained stories, ballads and poems, some by Sir Walter Scott and others by lesser known poets.

Freya had stood the books up on the shelf in her bedroom. The sight of them sitting there, waiting to be read, pleased her. At first she moved from one book to the next, reading a line here and a line there, sampling them like a butterfly seeking the best nectar. She liked the Border poetry though she found it difficult to understand. However, she discovered that if she read the lines out loud, she could grasp the meaning. Sitting on her mossy seat on the alder bough, words flowed from her lips, more perhaps than she had uttered in her whole life. Many of them sounded strange, but through them came the unmistakable rhythms of borderland speech and thought.

After Walter Scott's *Marmion*, Freya came to a poem about a man called Thomas the Rhymer. There were two versions of the story, the first was by Sir Walter and the second was anonymous. The first lines of Scott's poem made her think of Jock, the tinker, who had come to Glittering Shiel one frosty morning just before Christmas and given her the turquoise bead and the rattle. She remembered the words with which he had greeted her and the delight in his voice. 'What lovely vision is this? Have I landed up on Huntly Bank and is this not the Queen of Elfhame herself?'

Freya had often wondered who the lovely Queen of Elfhame was. She had wanted to ask Miss Murray but she had never found the courage. Perhaps Jock's bead was indeed lucky because, without her asking, Miss Murray had given her what she wished for. The answers to her questions lay before her, printed on the pages of the book.

From Sir Walter Scott's poem Freya learned that the Queen of Elfhame wore the finest silk and velvet and rode a milk-white steed with fifty silver bells and nine jingling in its mane. Thomas the Rhymer was the name of a man who met the Queen of Elfhame at a place called Huntly Bank, though at first he thought she was the Queen of Heaven. The Queen and Thomas made a pact and the Queen said to him, 'If ye dare to kiss my lips, Sure of your bodie I will be.' And Thomas had done the thing, he kissed her lips beneath the Eildon Tree. And then the Queen said to him, 'And ye must serve me seven years, Thro' weal or woe as may chance to be.'

After that they went on a long journey, the Queen and Thomas. They left the living land and came to a wide desert. The Queen pointed to three roads, the first was the path of righteousness, the second was the path of wickedness and the third, which is the one they took, led to fair Elfhame. They rode through deep rivers and streams of blood with neither sun nor moon to light their way until they came to a garden with an apple tree. The Queen picked an apple and gave it to Thomas saying, 'Take this for wages, true Thomas. It will give thee the tongue that can never lie.' At this point the poem came to an abrupt end without saying what happened to Thomas and the Queen.

Freya was deeply disappointed because she very much wanted to know more about Elfhame. She thought she could guess what Huntly Bank was like because the poem said it was in the living land. She decided that it must be over the border. She knew that the Eildon Hills lay to the northwest of Cheviot and had decided that the Eildon Tree must surely be near them. Huntly Bank, she concluded, was probably a place that Jock knew well. After all, he came from Coverdale which was also on the other side of Cheviot, in Scotland.

Fortunately the anonymous second poem supplied what was missing from the first and Freya was able to discover that Thomas had had to leave Elfhame. It was the Queen who ordered him to go. One day she came and told him that the foul fiend of hell was expected soon and, according to custom, he would choose a victim. The Queen, fearing that the fiend would take Thomas because he was such a fine man, commanded him to return home.

The night after Freya had finished reading the poems she had a dream, a dream she was to have so many times in the coming months that she came to believe that one day the events in it would become a reality.

Freya was the Queen of Elfhame and Andro was Thomas. Andro kissed her and gave his body to her for seven years. Freya chose the road they would take from the desert, the road that brought them to Elfhame and when the seven years had passed and the time came for the foul fiend to claim his victim, she mounted her milk-white steed, took to the hills and left Andro to his fate.

In the autumn Andro and Billy went off up Maidenhope to search for wild goats which they gathered like sheep, selecting two or three to be killed and salted down for the winter. In September all the sheep were gathered and sorted. The six year-old ewes were sent to the market at Willove. The lambs born the previous spring, having been separated from their mothers in August, made the same journey.

Billy and Rose looked forward to this time of year because they received some cash. Billy's lambs were given a separate mark from the other sheep and they too went to market where, according to tradition, they were sold without commission. The auctioneer would say to the assembled buyers, "Now then gentlemen, these here are the herd's lambs!" In this way the buyers knew what was expected of them and they always made sure that the herd's sheep made a shilling or two more than the master's.

After the sale Rose and Billy spent many an evening deciding how the money should be spent. Most of it would go on staple foodstuffs: wheat, oat and barley meal, dried beans and peas and some dried fruit. There was always a long list of other essentials such as salt, paraffin, vinegar, black lead, polishing paste, washing soda, saltpetre, not to mention material for clothes and some hessian so Rose could make a proggie mat during the winter months.

The only other occasion when the Lillicos received a sizeable sum of money into their hands was when they were paid for the fleeces from their sheep which were sold to Mr Moffat, the wool merchant from Hawick. The fleeces had been particularly fine that year and yet they had received less than the previous year. As he handed the money to Billy, Andro had neglected to mention Mr Moffat's remark that the fleeces from Glittering Shiel had been, as he put it, "terrible wet", by which he meant to imply that their weight had been deliberately increased by the addition of water.

Freya was thirteen that September and about to begin her last year at Herontop school. Cissy and Elsie had left a year earlier, Cissy to work as a scullery maid at Heron Hall where she spent her days scrubbing pans and blacking the ranges and Elsie to work on the land as a bondager where her first task had been to pull up couch grass.

On the first day back at school Freya and young Billy were joined by Violet. She should have started school a year earlier, but Rose and Billy had decided to keep her at home for another year to help look after Hazel. Hazel would have to wait until Billy left before she could have her turn at book learning since the Lillicos could not afford to send more than two children to school at the same time. Young Billy was impatient to leave, hoping that the happy event would happen when he was twelve, the age at which he could expect to find work on a farm.

20

The winter was not severe, though it rained almost every day, so that everywhere was miserably cold and damp. The stone walls of the scullery were moist to the touch and it was warm nowhere except in front of the fire.

Soon after Christmas everyone was struck down with a virulent influenza. They were ill in rotation, with the able-bodied caring for the sick, before they in turn were forced to take to their beds.

Lizzie suffered last and longest. Freya heard long bouts of coughing in the night. As soon as it started Lizzie would get up, go downstairs and sit by the fire rather than disturb Andro. He was tolerant enough at first, but when she failed to mend, he became impatient. He spoke to her sharply, telling her to pull herself together. Lizzie nodded and looked apologetic, but the truth was that she had tried. There was nothing she could say to herself, nothing she could do to overcome the lassitude she felt in every fibre of her body.

Freya tried to lighten Lizzie's workload. Lizzie would go to the scullery and find the potatoes ready peeled, the milk things washed and put ready for the next milking. Anxiously, Freya watched and waited, hoping to see an improvement, but with every passing day Lizzie seemed to become more wasted and worn.

Freya decided to speak to Andro, to try and persuade him to do something to help Lizzie, so one day after Andro had lured her into the stable and taken his pleasure, she broached the subject.

"Will you not send for the doctor for mam?" she asked gently. "She should have mended by now!"

"No!" replied Andro sharply, who disliked sickness and whose way of dealing with it was to ignore it. "I doubt it would do any good." He shook his head with an air of finality. "I know a piner when I see one. No, there's nowt to be done!"

Freya felt an icy chill run down her back. She knew that a piner was a sheep which would change in a matter of weeks from a healthy animal to a sad dejected creature with its fleece hanging off. All the usual remedies failed to cure the malaise and in the end Billy or Andro, unable to bear the wretched sight a moment longer, would put the animal out of its misery.

Through January, the land slept. Towards the end of February, there were several clear, bright days and as the hours of daylight increased, there was a quickening among the birds, an eagerness in their movements, an exuberance in their song. The cry of the curlew was heard once more on the open fell.

Many a year the snowdrops bloomed unseen beneath a blanket of snow, but this year they jostled together in clumps by the front door. Freya knelt down to look at them. From a distance she thought they looked like delicate white glass lampshades or fairies' skirts, but on closer inspection she found the long petals more like miniature newborn lambs' ears, silky and white.

At the beginning of March, Andro too became restless and, without a word of explanation, one afternoon he rode off to Willove. When he got there he led Polly up the narrow passageway at the side of the Three Half Moons and saw her stabled. Then he proceeded to divide his time between the Three Half Moons and Kitty Jobson's alehouse in Windy Row.

He found a bright fire blazing in the taproom of the Three Half Moons, the friendly clink of pewter, air thick with tobacco smoke, laughter and plenty of talk. The place was full of drovers and loose men whiling away the days until they could find work after the long, lean winter months. Travelling folk came and went, collecting the latest news which they took with them on their way. Within a day or so the information that Andro Man of Glittering Shiel was holed up in Willove had spread throughout the surrounding countryside, reaching as far as the Hethertons in Coverdale.

Old Janet Hetherton had died a year earlier and on her deathbed she had made Hob swear to see justice done and Glittering Shiel returned to the Hetherton family. From the outset Janet had been unswerving in her belief that Andro Man was guilty of Sam's death and probably also that of her son, Will. Hob too became convinced when certain evidence came to light some two or three months after George and Hannah left Glittering Shiel.

One day George and Hob had met at Kelso market and George had handed Hob a package. It was a black sheepskin which had been given to him by Bart Dunne. Bart had found the headdress at first light the day after Halloween, hanging on a tree above the place where Sam had died. Though the presence of such an object struck Bart as strange, he would have thought little more about it had he not spied Andro Man coming over the fell not a half hour later. Bart had watched as Andro combed the burn below Ruffie's Loup, obviously searching for something, though Bart noted that he had gone away empty-handed.

The black sheepskin now lay across the back of a chair in the Hetherton kitchen, a constant reminder of unfinished business. Hob did not know by what means he would settle the score with Andro Man. For the time being he was keeping watch from a distance, learning what he could about Andro and Glittering Shiel from travelling folk such as Jock, the tinker. As soon as he heard that Andro was drinking in Willove, he knew that it was a chance not to be missed, so he quickly decided to send his son, Rob, to learn what he could.

In Kitty Jobson's establishment Andro found four or five drovers discussing the railway which was coming closer to Willove every day and which they feared would deprive them of their livelihoods by transporting cattle and sheep to the markets in Morpeth, Newcastle and Carlisle. There was even talk about a mart being set up in a field near where the station yard was to be. Then there were two or three normally abstemious farmers who were well on the way to drinking the proceeds from the sale of a pig or a calf. Andro chuckled, thinking that by late afternoon

197

they would be past caring what their wives said when they staggered home penniless. He noticed a game of nap in progress at a table in the corner, so he got a guinea out of his waistcoat pocket, bought himself a pint of ale and a whisky to chase it down, then settled down to some serious gambling.

Andro had arrived in Willove on Tuesday afternoon and by Thursday morning, he was almost out of funds. In the middle of the morning, he decided to take a turn along the High Street, thinking that a walk might clear his head before he decided what to do next.

In the Market Place he came upon a straggle of disconsolate people, mostly lads and lassies. Then he remembered that it was the Runaway Hirings, the day on which farm servants who had recently gone to a new master and not found themselves suited, came to town to seek a different place.

Strolling along the street, idly jingling the few remaining coins in his pocket, Andro reluctantly came to the conclusion that the time for going home could not be long delayed. As he walked, he ran a critical eye over the young men and women who had come in search of work, deriving a certain pleasure from the fact that he was now a master and no longer a servant.

His sense of self esteem demanded that he have something to show for his visit to Willove and it occurred to him that he might return home with a spare pair of hands to help about the place. Yes, that would surely please Freya and what was more it looked as if he could get somebody cheap.

It was then that he saw Rob, who was sitting dejectedly on a doorstep wondering how he was going to tell his father that he had not even managed to set eyes on Andro Man.

Rob, with his collie at his side, had set off the previous afternoon and spent the night in a barn five miles to the north of Willove. At first light he had walked the last leg of the journey and as soon as he arrived in the town, he went straight to the Three Half Moons to look for Andro. Having drawn a blank there, he went to Kitty Jobson's and when he saw that Andro was not there either, he made enquiries, only to be told that Andro had paid his bill and left not an hour earlier.

Andro thought that Rob was in Willove for the hirings and for some reason he was drawn to the lad though he could not have said why. He was finding it hard to think straight, his mind was fuddled with drink and lack of sleeep.

"Good day," said Andro as he approached, "and what work is it you're after?"

Surprised, Rob looked up. It was several seconds before he realised that the man standing before him was none other than Andro Man.

Quickly he pulled off his cap and leapt to his feet. "Anything, sir!" he said. "But it's herding I do best!"

"Well now, there's a rare coincidence!" said Andro. "I could do with a lad about the place." Then he added in a grave confiding tone, "You see, my wife's not been so grand lately."

Sensing a change in his master's fortunes, the collie's ears pricked up and its moist nose twitched with interest.

"Well, sir, I can do most things on a farm and if there's something I cannot do, you'll find I'm more than willing to learn!"

Andro looked the lad up and down, assessing his physical potential. He was fifteen or sixteen, almost as tall as Andro, supple and loose-limbed like the young dog at his side. In a year or two, he would be even stronger, a real asset.

"What's your name?"

"Rob, sir!" There was silence until Rob realised that Andro was waiting for his surname. Things were moving so fast that Rob almost said Hetherton, but he stopped himself just in time. "My name! Er, it's Atherton, sir. Robert Atherton."

Andro seemed satisfied. "Well then, Rob Atherton, you look like you could do with a bite to eat! We'll just step into the Three Half Moons here and see if Bessie Lamb can fettle you up and then when you've got some food in your belly, we can get down to business! Now what d'you say?"

Rob readily agreed. He could hardly believe the change in his fortunes. What better than if he went to work at Glittering Shiel!

Andro ordered two plates of ham and eggs. Rob ate hungrily, though Andro noted that the lad was careful to give some generous scraps to his dog.

"What about my dog?" asked Rob, suddenly realising that Andro might not be willing to take a dog. "He's a good dog and I couldn't think of getting rid of him." Rob regretted the words as soon as they were uttered, thinking perhaps that he had thrown away his chance.

Andro was thinking that the two collies at Glittering Shiel were both bitches and that a dog would surely cause no end of bother, but he could tell that on this point the lad was determined. "All right," he said, "you can keep the dog, but I'm warning you I cannot pay much. You'll get a bed and your meat and drink."

A few seconds later Andro was pressing his last silver shilling into Rob's hand and the bargain was struck.

Andro left Rob standing in front of the inn while he went off to buy a bottle of tonic for Lizzie. Rob knew that this would be his only opportunity to leave a message for his father, but the problem was that he did not know anybody in Willove. Finally he decided that there was nothing he could do and that, when in a day or two he did not return home, Hob would be sure to come looking for him and then someone in the Three Half Moons would tell him what had happened.

They arrived at Glittering Shiel in the middle of the afternoon. Rose glanced out of the window as they passed and her heart sank. She guessed immediately that Andro had taken the lad on. It was a bitter blow, for she and Billy had often talked about how in a year or so they might ask Andro to employ young Billy.

Lizzie and Freya heard the clatter of horseshoes on the cobbles in front of the stable and came to see who was there.

The walk had cleared Andro's head and he was in good humour, well pleased with his visit to Willove. He handed Lizzie the tonic and introduced Rob.

Overcome with shyness, Freya hung back. Her eyes met Rob's for only a second before she looked away, but it was long enough for her to feel their warmth and kindness. Because of her confusion she did not notice Lizzie's reaction when she saw Rob. Lizzie put her hand to her mouth in mute astonishment. Andro saw the gesture, but thought nothing of it, putting it down to surprise at the arrival of a newcomer.

Lizzie had experienced a flash of recognition, which she rejected almost immediately, telling herself that it was foolishness, just another of the strange imaginings she had been a prey to since her mother's death.

Over the last few months Lizzie had ceased to trust her feelings and intuitions. She had become self-enclosed, mistrustful of herself and everyone else, fearful sometimes even of Freya who seemed to have found a new strength which Lizzie did not understand. So, although she had the distinct feeling that she had seen Rob somewhere before, she quickly disguised her feelings and uttered some words of welcome.

"Now then, Rob," said Andro equably. "You can bed down here in the stable. There's plenty of dry bracken and Lizzie'll fix you up with some blankets. Aye and Freya here can help you clear the stall next to Polly. There's the burn just down there for you to get washed in and of course you can take your meat with us in the house."

Freya fetched a besom and began to brush out the stall. Her eyes rested for a few moments on the the pile of bracken where she had often lain with Andro. Rob offered to take it away. She watched him plunge the shining tines of the hay fork into the brown heap and then it was gone, whisked away to the midden and Freya wondered perhaps if other things could be changed as quickly, past things swept away in a trice. She experienced then a new emotion. Optimism, frail at first, began to quicken within her. Perhaps springtime had reached into her heart too, but no matter what the reason, Freya felt the stirrings of hope.

Rob's few possessions were rolled up in his plaid which he now undid. A small notebook and a silver coin fell onto the floor at Freya's feet which she retrieved and handed to him.

"Thank you kindly, Miss Man!" he said with his wide warm smile. "I must not lose my book of marks!"

"Book of marks?"

"Aye, sheep marks so I can tell who a sheep belongs to. And this here is my lucky coin! I do not know where it came from, though somebody once told me that it was made in France at the time they had a great revolution. It's got a date. See, 1792!"

Freya came closer to look.

"I found it one day when I was digging in the tattie yard at home," Rob went on. "I always carry it for luck and it surely served me well today!"

Freya smiled and nodded.

Rob looked around and noticed a stone with a hole in the middle which was hanging on a faded red cord high up on the wall. "And there's another bit o' luck!" he said pointing to it.

Freya had never noticed the dusty stone hanging among the disused tools, shanks and pieces of harness.

"It's what my granny called an adder stone," Rob explained. "And, by the looks of it, that one was put there long since. To find a stone with a hole in it brings good luck and it keeps the evil spirits away from the animals, so it'll surely do the same for me!" he said with a laugh.

Freya could not share Rob's light-heartedness. His last words reminded her of Andro and then she was overcome with a sense of loss. Although she had not realised it at the time, while she had been brushing out the stall, she had been happy. It was a modest, innocent, unthinking happiness and now that it was gone, she felt sad.

Rob was so different from Andro. Whereas everything about Andro was shiny black like a raven's wing, with Rob it was broon-kitty brown. He wore worn cord breeches the colour of dry peat and a faded jacket of herringbone tweed - subtly barred plumage of tawny and buff. And his hazel eyes were flecked with amber lights like a darting trout in the summer burn.

Later Freya went to the stable to tell Rob that supper was ready. There was the last of the salted fish which Freya had taken from the barrel early that morning and put to soak in the burn.

Rob followed her to the kitchen door, then stood waiting for Lizzie to tell him where he should sit. Freya felt a surge of tenderness towards him then, standing in the doorway, ill at ease, all arms and hands.

Lizzie pointed to a chair on the far side of the table where Sam used to sit. As they ate, Andro told Rob about the farm and what he would be expected to do. He had decided to give Rob the herding on Maidenhope because it was the most arduous and involved walking the greatest distances. Rob's beat would march on Andro's along the cleugh that ran up between the foot of Maidenhope and Cockslack.

When Andro had finished talking, Lizzie thought she should engage Rob in conversation, but she was in some difficulty. The normal thing would have been to ask him about his home and family, but she was afraid of what her questions might reveal and so in the end she settled on his dog as a safe subject of conversation.

"What's your dog called, Rob?"

"Fine."

"Well I've heard some mighty odd names for a dog but that's a new one on me!" said Andro good humouredly.

"Well, you see I got him from a herd near ... near where I was working. He had the handiest collie for miles around, so when she had pups, I asked if I could have one. They were all spoken for bar the last and it was a poor weak thing. He said he didn't give much for its chances, but I said I'd take it all the same and he said to me, 'Right lad, that'll be fine!' So that was it, I called him Fine!"

21

At five o'clock every morning, Rob, with Fine by his side, strode off up Maidenhope. He was a good shepherd. In order to make sure that his sheep made the best use of the land, at dusk he drove them onto the higher ground where the grazing was poor and in the morning he brought them down to the richer lower pastures.

Andro congratulated himself on his choice of shepherd when he saw Rob's skill at lambing time. When a ewe was having twins Rob knew just how to push one lamb back until the other had been born and he seemed to know instinctively when a high horn lamb, one whose horns had begun to grow while it was still inside its mother, was on the way. Then he would slip a rope over the budding horns and guide the head safely out. Nothing concerning the welfare of his sheep was too much trouble to him and because the hardy black-faced sheep lambed out on the open fell, he spent many a night outside with them.

At the weekends during lambing time, if Rob did not appear at breakfast because he was out on the fell, Freya would spread some butter on a thick slice of bread, fill the tin bottle she took to school with strong sweet tea and set off towards Maidenhope. She never knew exactly where Rob would be, but she could rely on Fine to find her and bring her to his master.

Rob and Freya spoke little to one another up on the hill. Sometimes Rob would give a cold lamb into her care and she would carry it home and put it by the fire until it was strong enough to take some milk.

For his part, Rob thought that Freya was the most beautiful girl he had ever seen. Her natural grace and simple quiet ways pleased him. Sometimes he caught her looking at him, an enigmatic expression on her face, and he would wonder what she was thinking. It was a disappointment to him that she never sought him out just for his company as the Lillico children did. Whenever she appeared, it was for some reason, to bring him a message from Andro or something to eat. Increasingly he became aware of a sadness in her and he decided perhaps that it had something to do with Lizzie, for he could see that she was ailing, wasting further with every passing day.

It was Freya's last term at Herontop school. Jenny was leaving too, though she did not yet know what would become of her. She had never grown strong, so she knew that she was unlikely to find work on the land. Miss Murray was doing her best to persuade Mr Dogberry that his housekeeper needed some extra help, pointing out to him that although Jenny lacked physical strength, she was honest, dependable and good with her hands, having inherited her grandmother's skill with a needle.

But it was Freya who most concerned Grace. One day she asked Freya if she thought her parents might allow her to stay on at school as a pupil teacher. For a moment Freya's eyes had lit up, but then she had shaken her head, saying sadly, "No, my father will never allow it. Mam is poorly and I'm needed at home."

"But Freya, you must think of your future!" Grace had insisted, determined not to let the matter rest. "It's no life for a young woman with your talents, up there in the hills lost to the world."

The future was something Freya rarely thought about. She had tried to imagine a period of seven years, but had given up. She could not see beyond the difficulties of the present and as for a life somewhere other than Glittering Shiel, she could not begin to imagine it.

Almost every day on the way home from school after the children had passed the old still and entered the valley of Eidonhope, first Fine and then Rob would appear as if by magic. Freya was never sure from which direction they would come, but she came to expect them and was disappointed if they failed to turn up. Suddenly she would see Rob, a lone figure standing high on the hill. He would wait until she gave some indication that she had seen him, slowing her pace or even pausing momentarily to look in his direction. It was only then that he would wave before bounding across the fell and down onto the track.

First he would chat with young Billy for a while, then he might tease Violet and make her laugh, but after a time he always dropped back so that he could be with Freya who was usually walking quietly along behind.

He would tell her about the things he had seen and what he had done during the day. She listened, but never asked a question. Then, if he was feeling bold, he would say that it was her turn. But she never said much, just that Mr Dogberry had been or that she had been with Jenny all dinnertime.

Often he had some small thing to give her, something he had found which he hoped might interest her and perhaps even win him a smile. He brought her the first purple orchid to flower in the boggy ground below the stell, a single stem of grass-of-parnassus and the first bunch of hare's-tail cotton grass. Once he carried a handful of bitter-sweet crowberries down from the crown of Maidenhope and on another day it was a dark red stone from the burn which he had burnished till it shone.

One day early in June when they got to the big boulder by the gate, Rob told Fine to sit quietly and wait. Young Billy and Violet had scampered off down the track to Rose, so Freya and Rob were alone.

Rob led Freya a little way across the fell. A pair of peewits appeared and began to call and wheel about above their heads. One landed some twenty yards away and with wings outspread it fluttered clumsily on the ground.

Forgetting her usual reserve, Freya cried out, "Look Rob! Look at the peewit! It's hurt its wing!"

"Don't upset yourself," Rob reassured her. "It isn't hurt, not really. It wants to draw us away, the clever bird!"

"Now then, come over here," he said, taking her hand and leading her carefully a few steps further. "Now, can you see it?"

he asked without giving her the slightest hint of where she should look.

Rob's gaze followed Freya's as she looked along the line of Cheviot and scanned the broad sweep of Skirlmoor on whose fringes they were standing. Two or three clouds were moving majestically across the sky, casting field-size shadows on the fell. Apart from the peewit, Freya saw nothing unusual so she turned and gave Rob an enquiring look.

"Closer, you must look closer! Look, look down there!" he said pointing down at the ground.

Then she saw the eggs, four of them lying neatly on a patch of short grass with the narrow ends pointing inwards so they would not roll out of the shallow depression. In subtle shades of green and brown, they were so well disguised that it would have been the easiest thing in the world to step on them. She gave a cry of delight and knelt down to look more closely, noticing how the peewit had pecked at whatever food lay within reach of the nest, leaving behind a fine scattering of herbage.

By this time the peewit's lamentations had increased and it was tumbling about on the ground, pitifully trailing a wing.

Rob gently took hold of Freya's hands and drew her to her feet. "All that," he said, pointing to the afflicted bird, "is to draw us away! Da used to say peewits are deceitful birds, but it's just their way of looking after their own."

Freya was remembering the short-eared owls and how they had tried to protect their young by attacking Andro. Then she heard Rob say in a strange voice, "Sometimes deceit works best. Sometimes it's the only way."

Still holding her hand, Rob drew Freya close to him. He did not dare to look into her eyes for he was afraid that if he did, he would be struck dumb and the words would not come out. "Freya," he began. "Freya, you know ... I want to tell you ... Oh Freya, I care for you!" He paused, relieved at having told her what was in his heart and before he knew it, he found himself saying, "And so long as I'm here, you've no need to fear."

207

Rob regretted the words almost immediately. They seemed stupid and unnecessary and yet he knew it was true, something was terribly awry at Glittering Shiel. During the short time that he had been there, he had noticed a dozen tiny things which taken together told him that Freya was troubled, deeply troubled.

Freya could not speak. She had heard the words and now she needed time to absorb them. Little by little she realised that they were words of love, words of love for her. She had heard them and now she weighed them in her mind.

Anxiously, Rob waited for an answer.

Freya moved away. A prickle of tears welled up into her eyes and she turned and looked into his caring, candid face. Words almost failed her. "Rob," she stammered, "I'm not what you think! It cannot be! You cannot care for me!"

Rob understood the words, yet something in her voice and in her eyes belied them.

Unable any longer to bear the hurt she was inflicting on him, Freya turned and walked away. The air was cool on her face and she allowed the tears to flow. She saw the familiar outline of the warrior as though through a rain-drenched window and Hannah's words came back to her. 'Good men have always been hard to find'. Oh yes, Rob was a good man. He was good and faithful and true. And he was standing only a few steps away, wanting to love her, ready to love her.

She reached the track. Fine saw her approach and pricked up his ears, waiting for permission to come to her, but she did not even glance at him as she passed by on her way to the burn. She made her way upstream, seeking somewhere private. Finding an overhanging bank, she crouched down and wrapped her arms around her chest. When at last the sobbing subsided, she continued to rock to and fro on her heels, moaning quietly to herself. Gradually the grief ebbed and her aching sense of loss was replaced by anger, anger at Andro and what he had taken from her. How could she ever tell Rob of the bond between herself and Andro? There might as well be a wide ocean separating her from Rob or prison walls as stout and thick as those of Beaver Tower. And if she did find a way to tell him, what would he say? He would surely turn away from her. But then she thought that if he truly loved her, perhaps he would wait and if he waited seven years, then she would be free.

Some two weeks later on a Sunday afternoon, Rob went in search of Freya, hoping to persuade her to come for a walk with him, but she was nowhere to be found. Since the day he had shown her the peewits' nest, he had been especially careful not to impose himself on her, though he continued to join the children as they walked home from school. Freya too had gone on as before, helping him as much as she could by performing small, near wordless acts of kindness.

Rob, who wanted to get to know the surrounding countryside better, had taken to roaming beyond the valley of Eidonhope on Sunday afternoons. His energy was boundless and the prospect of another long walk to look his sheep after supper did not deter him. He had been over to Hevensgate and now he planned to take the ancient trackway that went along the foot of Warrior Crag which would bring him into Herondale.

Soon he came down into Herondale and arrived at Beaver Tower. It was smaller than the fortified pele in Coverdale, but nevertheless the sight of it reminded him of home. He walked around the massive outer walls. Over the centuries some stones had been taken away, but because they had been bonded together with hot lime, most had resisted attempts to prise them free. When the moment came to enter the vaulted chamber Fine sniffed the air and hung back, so Rob entered alone leaving Fine to guard the entrance.

Then they set off up Herondale, following the course of the river. A mile or so above Hoarstones Rob decided that he should strike a course northeast which he calculated would bring him back into Eidonhope near the head of the valley by the foot Maidenhope.

The sun was starting its evening descent behind Cheviot as they came onto the top of Cockslack. Rob took his bearings and set off again, thinking to join the burn about half a mile to the west of the Maidens. Fine was trotting along at his heels as they picked their way through the heather and bright green quaking bog.

Suddenly Fine sniffed the air and made the throaty noise that precedes a growl.

Rob stopped. "What is it, boy?"

Fine growled. They both listened. There were voices not more than fifty feet away over the brow of the hill.

"Whisht Fine! Quiet!" whispered Rob.

They proceeded silently through the chasms and gulleys of the old peat cuttings. The voices became more distinct. Fine looked at Rob. They both recognised Andro's deep tones and soon after that a female voice.

Rob stopped and crouched down in the heather. He knew that he was on Andro's beat and, although Andro had never actually said Rob was to keep off it, he had got the distinct impression that it was forbidden territory. Now that he was actually on it and Andro was so close, Rob felt like a trespasser. Caution told him to retreat, but a more powerful emotion drove him forward.

He ordered Fine to stay quiet while he dropped onto his stomach and worked his way forward, moving in the direction of the voices. He came to the edge of a cliff made of peat. Risking a quick look over the edge, he saw a rough shelter roofed with heather. Its back wall was no more than two feet from the face of the cliff and he could have reached out and almost touched it.

Now the voices had stopped and a noise reached Rob's ears, a noise that he had heard couples make when they thought they were alone, a noise that made him feel even more like an intruder. Instinctively, he flattened himself against the ground, putting his head on one side. He could not have said if it was the beating of his heart or simply his imagination, but the very earth seemed to be shuddering. Then he heard a cry. It was enough! He knew every cadence of her voice. It was Freya, there in the shelter, with Andro, with her father!

Rob's mind froze. He closed his eyes tight, aware only of the involuntary movement of his breathing. A minute or two later he was seized by the desire to escape. He looked down at his hands and saw that he had plunged his fingers deep into the soft, wiry, root-crossed ground. Pushing on the heel of his hands, he worked his way back from the brink and as soon as he thought it was safe, he stood up.

He looked down and saw that he was clutching a twisted root of heather. Shock gave way to a tide of turbulent emotions followed by a surge of unanswerable questions until he felt as if his head would burst. Then through the confusion came the quiet certain knowledge of his love for Freya and gradually his anguish became crystallised into an iron resolve. He took hold of the root with both hands and with one decisive movement he broke it in two. Then, throwing the two pieces on the ground, he turned and walked off towards Maidenhope.

22

Towards the end of July, Freya said farewell to Herontop school, to Grace Murray and to her faithful friend, Jenny. There was to be no summer holiday for Jenny, no breathing space between her old life as one of Miss Murray's scholars and her new one as a housemaid in Mr Dogberry's service for she was due to start work at six o'clock the Monday morning after the end of term.

As soon as Jenny's future was settled, Miss Murray had given her four yards of stout, white cotton upon which Jenny had laboured throughout the rest of the term and by the last day two finely stitched caps and aprons were ready to be worn.

Grace gave Freya a farewell gift. It was a copy of William Aldington's translation of *The Golden Ass*, which Grace had chosen because it contained an enchanting description of the Goddess. In her quiet moments when she was alone, Grace had begun to think of Freya as a special visitant, a manifestation of the White Goddess, whose name she bore.

On the last afternoon Grace contemplated Freya's long oval face, her delicately arching eyebrows and pale blue eyes fringed with fine gold lashes. She sighed. The schoolroom would seem so empty in September. It was not that Freya was memorable for her wit or conversation. On the contrary she had always been quiet and contemplative. Yet sometimes when she happened to look up from some absorbing book or picture, Grace thought that she had an ethereal quality that was not of this world.

A year earlier, when Freya's mother had been away, Grace had been deeply anxious, sensing that the girl was on the edge of some terrible abyss. Then the following September, the crisis, if crisis there had been, had passed and Freya returned to school with a newfound strength. Yet there was something about it that Grace had found disquieting. It was an embattled, almost defiant confidence which seemed to make Freya even more impenetrable than she had been before. In vain Grace kept hoping that Freya would confide in her, but she did not, so that in the end Grace came to accept that Freya was immured with her secret and was likely to remain so. However, Grace consoled herself with the thought that this state of affairs was not due to lack of affection on Freya's part, for Grace was sure that Freya loved her.

Grace had given a great amount of thought as to what she might say at the moment of parting. She desperately wanted to make some arrangement that would enable her to see Freya from time to time, but she could not devise a suitable pretext. Then she thought of giving her some message, some wise sustaining words that Freya could take back to the lonely farmhouse by the stones, words which might act as a sort of talisman.

"This book is for you, Freya," said Grace, when the moment came. "It is my own copy and I want you to have it. You will see that I have made a note of those passages I find most beautiful and moving. I hope they will be a source of comfort and pleasure to you and that perhaps they will remind you of me." She kissed Freya lightly on the cheek as she gave her the book, noticing with a twist of pain that it was her hand not Freya's that trembled with emotion at the giving and receiving of the gift.

Then Grace went outside with Freya and walked with her as far as the chestnut trees. "Remember," she said as evenly as she could, "that I am your friend. I shall always be here if you need me."

Freya nodded slowly, her face pale and impassive. She turned and began to walk away, then for a brief moment she looked back and Grace saw that the mask of composure had gone and in its place was a look of desolation.

For many days after his trespass onto Cockslack, Rob withdrew into himself. He did not come to meet the children on their way home from school and Freya scanned the hills in vain. At supper time she kept hoping that he would look at her and give her some small sign that he still cared for her. However, although he was still quick to lend a hand, he remained quiet and reserved. Their eyes met once, but immediately he looked away. She blamed herself for this. Was it not to be expected? Had she not rejected his love? And yet she was perplexed. He had not behaved in this way immediately after the day he had shown her the peewits' nest. Of course he had been quiet then, but he had not avoided her in the way he did now.

Rob spent his free hours alone with Fine. Sitting by the Eidon Burn, knees drawn up to his chin, he gazed into the brown waters and ruminated about Freya, Lizzie and Andro.

Throughout his childhood Rob had heard his grandmother and parents speak of Glittering Shiel, of his uncle Will, his cousin Sam and, most of all, of the villainy of Andro Man. Rob was by nature a generous lad, reluctant to think ill of any man and when he had first met Andro he had thought the condemnation harsh, for he could see no evidence for it.

That morning in Willove Andro had been the very model of a caring husband whose only concern was his wife's health and well-being. It was true that Andro had driven a hard bargain, but that was only to be expected. Then Rob thought of his journey back to Glittering Shiel with Andro. They had met all manner of folk along the way, herds, drovers, even a small band of tinkers. All had greeted Andro with a smile and were happy to pass the time of day with him. And as for the Lillicos, Rob had not heard Billy or Rose complain. Not that Rob felt he knew them well. They kept themselves to themselves and though Billy was always civil to Rob, he had never invited him into the bothy.

But now everything had changed. Now Rob knew that Andro Man was not what he seemed. His concern for Lizzie was a sham. He never gave her a kind word and most of the time he ignored her. She was a sick woman, anybody could see that. Rob was used to gentler ways. Even when there was a dispute between his parents, his father never spoke to his mother the way Andro spoke to Lizzie.

And then there was Freya. What Rob had taken for a father's love and pride in his daughter, he now saw was lust. He came to hate the satisfied way Andro would look at her as she fetched and carried, obeying his orders, although he wondered sometimes if he did not glimpse a rebelliousness beneath her apparent docility. Did her hands clench white when Andro spoke harshly to Lizzie? Did her eyes stab hatred into Andro's back when he left the room? Or did Rob imagine it because he wanted it to be so?

Mealtimes were a pain and a pleasure to him. He looked forward to being in the same room as Freya, to being close to her, to hearing her voice. When she handed him a plate of food, he would turn it round and run his fingers over the rim so as to touch the place that she had touched. And when the meal was over, he would help clear away, watching as her fingers closed around the object that he had handed her. Sometimes he found himself wishing that a pan would be too hot or too heavy and she would need him to help her. He even imagined her tripping on one of the flagstones and him catching her in his arms. The pain came from never touching her, the pleasure from the knowledge that she was near enough to make such a thing possible.

The deceptive normality of the homely kitchen became an annoyance to him: the polished dresser with its orderly rows of plates and bowls, the smell of ironed clothes or bread fresh from the oven, the bright fireside, the copious plates of food set out on the sand-scrubbed table. All the elements of family contentment, warmth, sustenance and comfort were there. Yet as he watched Freya and Lizzie quietly attending to Andro's needs, he realised that what was missing from the room was love. There was care, consideration, but no love. Neither was there laughter, except from Andro. There were no spontaneous words, no speaking of thoughts, no sharing of inconsequential things. What exchanges there were, were controlled, safe, carefully routine, protective of the web in which the three of them were held.

In August Freya did not bleed as she had come to expect. She took the change as a sign that her magical powers had been restored in full. This was confirmed by the evidence of her dreams which, with increasing frequency, told her that she held Andro in her power. She was the Queen of Elfhame with the power of life or death over him. All she had to do was wait until the time came and then he was doomed.

One afternoon when Freya slipped down to the alder grove to spend a few minutes alone she found a plaited circlet of purple and white clover lying on her mossy bough. A solitary bee had discovered it first and was clambering over the flowers, collecting pollen. She waited until it had flown away before picking the circlet up. It could only be from Rob. Her heart began to sing. Surely this was a sign that he still loved her. She held the circlet in her hands and marvelled at the skill with which he had woven it. She smelled the sweet flowers before she put it on her head and did a little dance of joy on the bank of the burn. Later she carried it up to her room and hid it under her bed.

The circlet was only the first of several gifts. A few days later she found a piece of deerhorn moss and a week after that a four-leaved clover.

Sometimes in the long summer evenings, she would go up to her room and get out the clover crown. Day by day she watched the flowers fade, but that did not matter. Still she treasured it, placing it on her head, enjoying the feel of it. How she wished that it was his hand resting there instead of the love token that he had made! And she wondered what she looked like with it on her head. Like the Queen of Elfhame perhaps, or the goddess in the book Miss Murray had given her.

One evening she fetched the slender volume from the shelf and went to sit on the broad, stone window ledge to catch the last beams of the sun before it disappeared behind Cheviot. The book fell open at her favourite page and she quickly found the words that she was looking for, 'on the crowne of her head she bare many garlands enterlaced with floures...'.

So absorbed was she that she did not see Rob come striding down from Maidenhope. But he saw her, framed in the small window, her head bent over the book, the clover circlet on her pale brow. He stopped, not daring to move for fear that she might see him and move away. Then he seized the precious moment and imprinted her image on his mind.

Autumn came and the bracken turned to gold and then to bronze. The sheep were gathered from the hills and sorted. Rob and Andro drove them to Willove. Then Rob went home for three days, after which he was to return to Glittering Shiel for the winter.

Freya worked hard, making chutneys and pots of amber crab apple jelly. Lizzie helped as much as she could, but mostly she gave instructions as to how the different tasks were to be done

Lizzie, with Freya as her accomplice, tried to hide the extent of her illness from Andro. When the moment came to serve the dinner, Lizzie would be there, ladling out the rich stew from the steaming yetling. But as soon as the menfolk had gone she would sink into a chair, exhausted. With the cooler weather, her cough got worse and her pallor increased. Freya took to lighting the fire in the parlour after dinner, so Lizzie could rest in the leather chair while Freya got on with the chores.

One afternoon Freya went into the parlour to take Lizzie a cup of tea. She found the chair empty and Lizzie standing beside the wall opposite the window. In her hands she held a picture which she had just lifted off its hook. She looked startled, like a child caught red-handed stealing a juicy apple.

Freya knew the picture well. It was David, depicted after he had chosen the five smooth stones from the burn, and the sling, with which he was to slay Goliath, was lying on a rock beside his staff. Freya said nothing as she set the cup and saucer down on a stool by the chair.

"It was fair covered with dust!" said Lizzie, taking hold of the corner of her pinny and rubbing the dull gilt frame vigorously. Then she looked up and gave a little smile. "I was just going to take it to the light to get a better look!"

Freya joined her by the window and they both studied the picture.

"I was told that Will Hetherton was the model for David," said Lizzie.

"Will Hetherton?"

"Aye, Sam's dad. He died before I came here. Of course he was only a lad when this picture was painted. Mary, she was Will's wife, said that the artist who painted it just turned up on the doorstep one day. He was roaming about the countryside looking for romantic rocks and waterfalls to paint. According to Mary he stayed in the house a month or more and being how he didn't have any silver to pay for his keep, he did this painting of Will instead."

Freya looked again at the picture.

"Can you see the likeness?" asked Lizzie.

"What d'you mean?"

"Why, David! Who d'you think he looks like?"

The boy in the picture did not remind Freya of anyone.

Lizzie became agitated. "I know!" she said. "The photo! I'll find the photo and then you'll see what I mean!" Feverishly, she turned the picture over and began to pluck at the thick, brown paper which was on the back. "It used to be here," she said breathlessly. "It was tucked in the back, I'm sure!" At last she came upon a sharp corner of photographic paper. "Aye!" she said, relieved. "Here it is! It's still here! I knew it would be. Now then, will you get it out!"

Freya drew the sepia-tinted photograph from its hiding place. She could see that it was the same boy as the one in the painting except that he was a little older. But still she did not recognise him.

Lizzie looked at her with a mixture of hope and desperation. "Surely you remember Sam? He was the spitting image of his father!"

"Oh yes, I remember Sam, but I can't remember what he looked like. I was very little when he died."

"Oh yes, I suppose you were," said Lizzie, crestfallen. Then her face darkened. "It's going on seven years since that terrible night!"

Then she told Freya about the events surrounding Sam's death, about the Hethertons and how they had come riding over the hills from Coverdale for the funeral.

"Yes, Hannah and me put him in his coffin. It was stood over there!" she said, pointing to an empty space in the middle of the room. "And the old lady, Sam's granny, put a little bunch of greenery into the coffin. That night was pure purgatory! And then in the morning before they nailed the lid on the coffin, everybody had to touch Sam's body. Hob said that was how it had to be, though at the time I couldn't see the reason for it."

Lizzie's face was ashen and Freya was afraid that she would faint, so she drew her towards the chair. Lizzie had no sooner sat down than her hands grasped the arms of the chair as if she would get up again, as if there was something urgent she had to do. Her face convulsed with fear, she turned to Freya. "You see, I'm scared! Scared of what might happen, scared that it's going to happen all over again!"

Freya knelt down in front of Lizzie and tried to calm her. "Don't distress yourself, please! Here have a drink of tea."

Lizzie's hands were trembling and tiny beads of sweat had gathered on her brow. Freya waited until she was calmer, then she looked earnestly into Lizzie's eyes and said, "Please, tell me what you're afraid of."

Lizzie was reluctant to speak and yet she knew that if she could only say the first words, the rest would follow. In any case she knew could not refuse Freya, not when she looked at her that way.

Lizzie sighed. "Aye, all right then. God knows it's past time I spoke up. I don't have much time left. It's all up with me."

Freya took Lizzie's hand and cradled it in hers.

After a time Lizzie began to speak. "I saw Sam that night, the night he was killed. Oh yes, he was killed all right! I was the one who cleaned the wound and it was a dreadful gash, vicious, a mortal blow! And he," she paused to get her breath and gather her strength, "he never did tell me the truth! I didn't dare think it at the time. I pushed it out of my mind. But now, now I'm going to speak! He did it so he could have the land, so it could be his!"

"D'you mean Andro?" asked Freya who had to be sure she understood what Lizzie meant. "Are you saying that Andro killed Sam so he could have Glittering Shiel?"

Lizzie nodded. "Aye Freya, that's just what I'm saying and I'm better for the saying of it. It's tormented me long enough." Then a new intensity came into Lizzie's voice. "But you see, that's not all! When I look at Rob, sitting there where Sam used to sit, it's as if Sam's come back. It's not so much his looks. It's more the way he does certain things or maybe it's the way he speaks, he reminds me of Sam! And then I get to thinking..."

Lizzie stopped, unable to continue. "Oh these wild imaginings," she said wearily, "they're driving me mad. I'd be better off dead!"

Freya comforted her. She put her arms round Lizzie and held her tight. "You mustn't speak like that," she said. "Things'll look different when you're better, you'll see."

Lizzie never spoke of Sam again. Having told Freya what was on her mind, she seemed more peaceful and from that day on she gave up the struggle to conceal her illness and began to prepare for death.

In the ensuing days and weeks, Freya turned Lizzie's words back and forth in her mind. Like the pieces of a jigsaw puzzle, she laid them out and tried to make a picture out of them.

Seven years, it was always seven years. Almost seven years since Sam had died. Her pact with Andro was for seven years. And was it not every seven years that the fiend of hell came to Elfhame to claim his victim? And in the story, because the Queen had sent Thomas away, the fiend chose some other man to die instead? Perhaps Sam had died instead of Andro. Andro knew about such things, so had he planned it? And now another seven years had almost passed. Would Andro, once again, have to find another man to die in his place? And if so, what finer man than Rob? Was it for that that Andro had brought him to

Glittering Shiel? To die? Is that what Lizzie had dimly understood and tried to tell her?

Racked with fear for Rob, Freya began to watch Andro's every word and gesture, looking for a sign of evil intent.

23

Everyone was warning of a harsh winter, yet Andro seemed unconcerned. He had a fine stack of hay in the yard as well as the remains of the one from the year before, and then there were several large pikes of bent-grass dotted about on the fell. The autumn was mild and gentle enough, but the winter, when it came, was one of vengeful winds and driving storms.

One morning Freya woke to see her window transformed into a silvered page of swirling filigree. She shivered as she got up from the warm bed, her breath condensing in the still, cold air like steam from a boiling kettle. She went to the window to look at the frosty pattern, leant forward and breathed gently on the pane of glass. Immediately she regretted her action, for her breath had marred the fragile beauty of the frost. Then thinking to wash, she tiptoed over to the washstand, only to find that the water in the jug was frozen solid.

Billy was crossing the farmyard when Freya went out to fetch water from the spring. "Aye, Jack Frost was about last night, eh Freya?" he called to her. "Like I was saying to Rose, the fire's the best flower in the garden this time of year!" Then he blew on his hands and rubbed them together as he walked up the track, his hob-nailed boots crunching through the frozen crust of mud. The puddles in the ruts had been glazed with cloudy panes, but the Lillico children had already been out and jumped on them before they went off to school.

In the weeks before Christmas, the cold even at noon did not relinquish its icy grip on man and beast. The fire in the kitchen was kept banked high and the curtain at the door was drawn against the draughts.

The cold sapped what little strength Lizzie had left and just before Christmas she took to her bed. Once more Freya pleaded with Andro to send for the doctor, but he was adamant that it was no use, though he did give her permission to light a fire in the little iron grate in Lizzie's bedroom.

Andro moved out of Lizzie's room and into the spare room above the parlour. Freya was deeply disappointed because she had been hoping that when the bad weather came and every square inch of shelter was needed for animals, Andro would say that Rob could move into the house.

On Christmas Eve Andro opened a bottle of whisky and carried two pieces of wood into the kitchen. To Freya's surprise he insisted that Lizzie come downstairs for supper and take a dram. She was not strong enough to walk, so Rob carried her down. Then they all sat around the fire while Andro put the remains of the previous year's Yule log on the fire. It was a rare treat to burn wood. The bright flames danced up the chimney, giving off a sweet smell quite unlike the acrid odour of peat and, when the old log was almost consumed, with due ceremony Andro laid the new log on the ashes of the old. Thus they presided over the symbolic death of the old year and the birth of the new.

They were each enclosed within the privacy of their own thoughts and yet they were united by the fascination of the flames, the shared community of the fire. Once Freya thought she saw a smile play on Lizzie's pale lips. And indeed, for a brief moment, Lizzie's old dream had been rekindled and she was almost able to believe that she had a real family gathered around her.

On Christmas morning Freya was up early as usual to do her chores. To her surprise she found Fine sitting on the doorstep when she opened the back door. He wagged his tail, then to his intense joy she caressed his head and whispered a Christmas greeting in his silky ear. No sooner had she done this than he got up and trotted off round the side of the house, turning halfway to see if she was following him. She smiled at his odd behaviour and made as if to return indoors, but he whined, pleading with her to follow him.

He brought her round the west end of the house to the wicket-gate which opened into the front garden. He sat and waited while she opened it, then streaked off down towards the burn and into the alder grove.

Freya saw the ribbon first, hanging from a branch. Attached to it was a pendant carved out of bone, the vestige of a sheep that had once raked over the slopes of Maidenhope. She untied the ribbon and held the pendant in the palm of her hand. Lovingly, laboriously, Rob had carved Freya's initial and his own, entwining them in an embrace which they themselves had never known.

Rob was anxiously observing the scene from a little way down the burn. He was uneasy at the subterfuge, for usually he was careful to respect Freya's privacy. Several times in the course of the summer he had seen her slip up the burn into the place of tumbling waterfalls, but he had never followed her there nor thought to spy on her. Instead, he had sought a vantage point between the track and the rocky defile from which he could watch the approaches to the place and thus be certain that she would remain undisturbed in her sanctuary. But today was different. He needed to know that Fine had succeeded in bringing her to the place and that she had found his present.

Thinking about how to make it had filled Rob's daytime thoughts as he strode the hills. He remembered how as a small boy he had run his fingers over the loops and curves of intricate knotwork that were carved on the font in the little church near his home. This ancient stone had become his inspiration for the carving, a labour that had filled the lonely hours between sunset and sleep.

Martha, a pedlar woman from Yetholm, had provided the ribbon onto which he had threaded the finished work. She had passed through Glittering Shiel some two weeks before Christmas selling her wares: linen pillow cases, embroidered tray cloths, ribbons, buttons and thread.

Rob had hung about the farmyard until he saw her leave. He waited a quarter of an hour, then followed her across Skirlmoor, catching up with her at Dumb Crag where she had stopped to rest and smoke her black cuttie pipe.

Her eyes twinkled with delight when he asked if she had a ribbon in her basket because she guessed he wanted it for his sweetheart.

"Aye laddie, I've ribbons a plenty! Sit yoursel doon and we'll take a look. Now then, what colour is it ye're after? And tell me, is it tae be broad or narrow?"

"Blue," he said, "and narrow."

Martha delved in her basket for a minute or two. "Will this do ye?" she said, teasing out a length of ribbon.

Rob nodded, smiling.

Martha chuckled. "I dare say this is as blue as the lassie's eyes what'll be wearing it!" she said as she coiled the ribbon.

Martha would not take his pennies. He tried to insist, but she would have none of it, saying, "Just think of it as a wee gift frae Martha!" So he thanked her kindly and left her sitting at the foot of the crag. She watched him go, thinking what a fine young fellow he was, and how lucky the lassie who had him for her sweetheart. It was not until later when she was trudging through the hills that she remembered where she had seen the lad before. He was Hob Hetherton's lad from Coverdale.

Standing beneath the trees, clasping the pendant in her hand, Freya longed for Rob. She looked about for Fine, thinking that if she could find the dog, she would find the master. A dipper caught her eye. She watched as it flew downstream and landed on a stone in the middle of the burn. Then, sensing a movement in the corner of her eye, she turned and saw Rob walking towards the stable.

"Rob!" she cried out.

He turned, instantly looking in the right direction. She waved and he ran to her. Then he took her in his arms and she felt his warmth and the pounding of his heart. After a time they drew apart.

225

"Thank you!" said Freya, her eyes shining with happiness. "It's beautiful!" Then a note of distress came into her voice. "But I ... I've nothing to give you!"

Again he drew her to him. "You're here, Freya!" he whispered. "That's present enough!" He closed his eyes and the image that had sustained him through the self-imposed solitude of autumn returned: Freya sitting in the window, the clover circlet on her head. How many times he had tried to imagine how it would be to hold her in his arms like this! And now that it had happened, it was like a dream and he was unbelieving.

Entranced with one another, encompassed within their own enchanted circle, they did not see Andro appear on the high scarp to the south of the burn.

Andro nodded his head wryly at the sight, feeling no more than the merest twist of jealousy. After all, it was only to be expected. A young lad and a pretty lassie ... There was nothing to it, not like between him and Freya. No, it was just puppy love, all empty sighs and vague yearnings.

But all the same, Andro moved a little closer. Freya was facing Rob, smiling at him, her face radiant with love. It was a revelation, for Andro had never seen her smile that way. Bitterly he registered for the first time how frugal she had always been with her smiles, which in any case were the palest imitation of what he now saw. And what was this? She was giving him a kiss, a tender kiss on the lips.

Andro's face darkened and he was filled with rancour that she should bestow so freely on the lad what she had always denied him.

The bad weather started on the eleventh of January.

"Aye, that's a feeding storm and no mistake," Billy remarked, by which he meant that it was the harbinger of worse to come. From early afternoon huge, snow clouds were driven inland on the east wind. The sheep sensed the impending change in the weather and began to move off the high ground, seeking shelter lower down. Then during the night the wind dropped and it began to snow steadily. By dawn the world was enveloped in a white shroud.

Freya woke to a palpable silence. Even the Eidon Burn had ceased its friendly chatter. Lying in bed, listening for some sound, she felt the fluttering movements of the child within her. It was not the first time that it had stirred, but it was the first time that she had noticed it. She lay very still and laid her hands flat on her stomach. It moved again, she pushed back the covers to look. One side of her stomach rose, then fell, as if a mysterious creature was slowly turning just below the surface.

She lay back on the pillow and closed her eyes. Now she understood why she had felt sick in the autumn, why her skirt would not fasten. She felt hot and then cold as the realisation dawned on her.

Soon she was in a panic-stricken turmoil. What could she do? Who could she turn to? To Lizzie? Lizzie was dying. Rose? That would mean telling her how it had happened and anyway what could Rose do? Andro? He would know soon, she could not hide it for long. What would he say? He called her his little wife and now he had proved himself a husband. And Rob? What of her dream of being with him one day? It was shattered, smashed to smithereens like the *Freya*.

Desperately her thoughts beat to and fro in her head. It was like a tight knot, a hard round knot inside her that she could not undo. The only thing to do with such knots was to take a knife to them, to cut the threads. Despairing, she shivered. It would have been better if she had never been born, if she had died when she was a baby, when the ship had been wrecked. Perhaps she could die now. If she pushed back the covers and lay very still, perhaps the cold would come and set her free. People said it was like going to sleep. The chill would enter her just as it entered the earth in winter, reaching deeper and deeper, turning her to stone. She would lie like the warrior, her head to the east, towards Lancelot's castle and the sea. And the thing inside her would also be turned to stone and never stir again.

Freya's agonising was interrupted by a bout of coughing. She heard Lizzie's feeble cry and realised that it was long past the time of her first visit of the day to the sickroom. Immediately she got out of bed. She could not abandon Lizzie, not now, not when she needed her so much.

The next few days Andro, Rob and Billy were out from daybreak till nightfall, seeing to the sheep, herding as many as possible into the stells. They got out the sledge and loaded it with hay for the hungry animals. Freya spent all her time preparing food and caring for Lizzie. Rose, with young Billy to help her, was left to do the milking and feed the pigs and hens, while Rob carried peat in from the stack by the back door before he left for the hill.

Since Christmas Andro had been taciturn and morose. There was no pleasing him and he was at odds with everyone. In the evening, he would sit by the fire and brood. He glowered at Rob, found fault with Freya, with Lizzie, the food, the weather, everything.

Again Freya tried to talk to him about Lizzie, but he would not listen. He did not so much as put his head round Lizzie's door to ask her how she was. The truth was that he could not bear the sight of her, could not bring himself to breath the air in her room.

A week later the wind went round to the west and the temperature rose a few degrees. They risked letting the sheep go higher again, feeding them from the stacks of bent on the open fell, but it was only a temporary respite.

The full fury of winter was unleashed a few days later, at the end of January. It began with a steady fall of snow. Then the blizzard began in earnest; fine powdery snow whipped up by the savage east wind filled every dip and hollow. The track down the valley was blocked with drifts.

They woke one morning to snow so deep that the windows on the ground floor of the house were buried. They had to make a tunnel from the back door and dig the windows free of snow to let in the light. The simplest tasks took four times as long as usual.

Coats, plaids and footwear were permanently sodden and put to steam in front of the fire the minute they were taken off. The men wore snow logs, woollen leg warmers knitted out of coarse, oily wool, which they pulled over their socks, binding them tight around their calves with a piece of rope.

The house shouldered the blast. There were no windows on the east side, but still the cold wind found a way in through every crack and crevice. Freya put on layer upon layer of clothes, crossing her shawl over her chest and tying it behind her back. Lizzie, on the other hand, began to give out heat, to burn with a slow fever which sapped her remaining strength. She would no longer eat. In desperation, Freya gave her warm milk laced with whisky. Then one day she began to cough up blood and the coughing itself got worse with every passing day, the struggle for air more desperate.

The seeds of Lizzie's illness had been sown in early infancy, in the cold damp winter of her birth. Life in the hills had kept it at bay, but the grief of losing two of the people most dear to her, added to the difficulties and drudgery of recent years, had weakened her body and her spirit so that eventually she lost the will to live.

One night Freya sat with her until after midnight. When she fell asleep, Freya crept off to her own bed, leaving the doors open so that she would hear if Lizzie called out.

Freya was woken by the sound of violent coughing. In seconds she was by Lizzie's side. Lizzie stared at her terrified, her hands grasping the edge of the white sheet, pulling it towards her as if she would sink beneath it. The sheet was soaked and spattered with bright red blood.

"There! There!" said Freya. "Don't fret! I'll see to it!"

There was water in the bowl on the washstand and fresh linen in the press. Freya fetched the water and a cloth so she could wash Lizzie's face. She took away the blood-stained sheet and replaced it with a clean one. Lizzie's eyes followed Freya's every movement as if she were spinning a gossamer thread by which she might attach herself to life for a little longer. Freya lit a new candle, wrapped herself in one of Lizzie's shawls, took Lizzie's hand in hers and settled down to wait for dawn.

Just before Lizzie drifted into a light sleep, she turned to Freya. "I'm sorry, Freya!" she whispered. "I've not been much of a mother to you!"

Freya squeezed her hand and shook her head. "No, that's not true. You always did your best."

Lizzie was content with this and closed her eyes. She seemed peaceful, her breathing though light was even. After a time Freya too fell asleep and when she woke, Lizzie's hand was still in hers. Stone cold.

Freya was waiting for Andro when he opened his door just before dawn. "It's Lizzie," she said dully.

Andro nodded. He too had heard the coughing and suspected the crisis had come. "Come away downstairs!" he said.

They boiled the kettle and made some tea.

"We cannot bury her, you know that don't you?" said Andro. "We're cut off. A man might just get through to Herontop but never a horse and cart. And even supposing we got her down there, still she couldn't be buried, the ground's too hard!" His voice, which had been conciliatory, now became determined. "And she cannot bide in the house! I'll not have that! No, she'll have to go outside!"

He wrapped himself in his plaid and went off to see Billy and Rob. Rose came straight over to see what she could do to help. She found Freya sitting at the table with her head resting on her arms.

"Billy and Andro's in the cartshed looking for planks!" Rose informed her.

Freya looked up. "Planks?"

"Aye, lassie! Planks, for to make a box for her. She cannot go outside unless she's in a box, now can she?" Then seeing Freya's incomprehension, Rose added, "On account of the foxes and other vermin! Though I cannot for the life of me see why she cannot bide in the house! It'll be cold as the grave up there now the fire's out!"

Later Rose went upstairs with Freya and they prepared Lizzie for her coffin. Andro had given Rose strict instructions to put the bedding and the clothes Lizzie had been wearing into a bundle and give it to him.

Rose rolled up the blood-stained nightdress as she had been told, but when it came to the sheets and blankets, she hesitated. "What a terrible waste! Look at this sheet, it's not even been turned and there's years of wear in yon Otterburn blanket! I know, we'll just give him a couple of things. He'll never know the difference and I'll put the rest in the wash!" Then Rose, thinking that Freya might reproach her, added, "Your mam was always a careful housewife, it's no more than what she'd have done!"

Freya was paying little attention to what Rose said. She was in a state of shock, which increased as the day wore on.

In the afternoon, Billy and Rob came into the house with the makeshift coffin. They put it in the passageway by the back door, then carried Lizzie down and laid her in it. Andro was nowhere to be seen and Rob looked in vain for Freya. Then they nailed the lid on the coffin and carried it outside.

A stone wall ran up at right angles to the long north wall of the house, stable and byre. The snow had drifted against its east side and, following Andro's orders, they dug deep into the drift until they had made a space at the foot of the wall big enough to take the coffin. Then they put it in and packed the snow back around it. Snow began to fall as they were finishing and by the next morning there was no trace of what they had done.

That night Andro turned to the whisky bottle. Rob made the supper, bacon from the roll and cold cooked potatoes. While he was in the scullery, he listened for Freya. Rose had told him she had gone to her room above the scullery. Not having seen her all day, Rob was anxious. He was on the point of quietly calling her name, but then he decided not to. Andro might hear and she might be asleep.

Freya came downstairs at about seven o'clock. She looked like a wraith. Rob longed to take her in his arms and comfort her, but he did not dare. Andro turned to look as she came into

231

the kitchen. He scowled when he saw that she was wearing Lizzie's old, blue flannel skirt, which she had put on because it was bigger than any skirt she possessed.

An hour passed, with Andro refilling his glass several times and throwing peat after peat onto the fire. Although supper was over, Rob was loathe to leave Freya alone with Andro and so he waited.

Andro knew why Rob was hanging about. Several times he had caught the lad making sheep's eyes at her and it maddened him. The drink made him more and more truculent and possessive. Freya was his and it was high time he made that clear.

"Ah well, Freya," Andro began, speaking in a measured, philosophical tone. "I suppose there's nowt for it. We'll just have to make the best of it. Life must go on, eh? I might've lost my wife, but I've got the grandest lassie for to take her place! Come over here, Freya, I want to hold you in my arms!"

Freya looked at him, aghast.

"Come on lassie! Come here, I want you!"

Freya shot a look of horror at Rob.

"Just do as I say," growled Andro, "and never mind him."

She began to move slowly towards him.

"That's more like it, good lassie!" cooed Andro.

She stopped some three feet away from him, but quick as a flash, he caught her in his arms and swept her onto his lap, locking his fingers around her waist lest she had any thought of escape.

Andro turned to Rob, his lips twisted into a smile of satisfaction. "Now see here, my lad! There's something you must understand. Freya here belongs to me! Except that that's not your real name, is it my beauty?"

Freya stiffened, dreading what he would say next.

"But then, that's just one of our little secrets, isn't it, Issabel?" said Andro with mock tenderness. Then he moved his hand down over her breast, looking to see Rob's reaction as he did so. "You see laddie," he went on righteously, "I've a perfect right to her!

232

Did I not take her in when she was but a baby, give her a roof over her head, feed and clothe her all these years?"

Andro's words were a torment. What did he mean? Take her in! A perfect right to her! Rob couldn't think straight. All he knew was that if he stayed in the room a minute longer he and Andro would come to blows, so quickly he stood up, violently pushing back his chair which made a raw, rasping noise on the flagstones before it tumbled over. Then he made for the door, fighting his way out of the room like a drowning man.

24

Lizzie's continuing presence, the fact that she was dead but not buried, provided a counterpoint to the rhythm of life at Glittering Shiel. Whenever anyone crossed the yard, bent on some task intended to ensure survival, their own or that of the animals, they remembered Lizzie, lying only a few paces away on the other side of the wall.

The winter storms held their lives in abeyance; they were prisoners of the snow. Freya sometimes dreamt of escape, of running away down the valley to seek refuge with Grace Murray. Grace had not forgotten her. There had been a card at Christmas, begging Freya to write. But even if Freya could have got away from Glittering Shiel, she would not have done so. As long as Rob was there, she would remain there too.

Freya's fears for Rob's safety increased greatly after Andro's outburst the night after Lizzie died. She could not understand why Andro had tormented Rob. He had shown such bitterness towards Rob that Freya became even more convinced that there was truth in what Lizzie had told her. She decided that she must warn Rob that his life was in danger, but she was beset by problems. It was impossible to have more than a minute or two alone with Rob. Andro watched them both like a hawk, never allowing them to be alone together.

And supposing she did manage to talk to Rob, what would she say? How could she begin to explain her fears? Lizzie's belief that Andro had killed Sam and that he would do the same thing to Rob, Freya's dreamworld of Elfhame where Andro was doomed unless he found some other man to die in his place, and her ritual baptism with the seven year pact had merged in her mind like the tributaries of a stream. The ideas ebbed and flowed, intermixing without logic. Now that she was faced with making a story out of them, she sensed the impossibility of the task. The story would either dissolve into meaninglessness or sound impossibly far-fetched.

And there was another difficulty. Would she be able to speak of the threat to Rob without mentioning what Andro did to her? After the way Andro had behaved that night, stroking her breasts, Rob must be suspicious. Perhaps he had even guessed. One thing was certain, he would want to know all about it, how it had come about. And how could she explain to Rob what she did not herself understand?

When Andro had held Freya on his knee the night he taunted Rob, he felt the firm rise of her belly. His suspicions were confirmed three nights later when he ordered her to come to him in the big bedroom above the parlour.

Despite the cold, he told her to take off her clothes. He was lying stretched out on the bed, his hands cupped behind his head, watching her. His voice was playful. "Well now! What have we here? If I'm not very much mistaken, my Issabel's proved she's a woman! Aye, and more to the point, Andro's been man enough!" Then he laughed and made her come and lie down. "Give me a kiss, Issabel!" he said in a coaxing voice. "Give Andro Man one of those sweet kisses of yours!"

Freya turned her head away, wishing that she could be like the Queen of Elfhame and turn herself into the vilest hag so that Andro would shrink from her.

Andro pretended surprise, mixed with mild reproof. "What's this? Will you refuse your master when he bids you? Remember now, you made a pact with me!" Then he became angry and forced her head around to face him. "So you'll not give me what you've been giving to yon scallywag out in the stable?"

She caught her breath.

"Aha! You thought I didn't know what's been going on, did you? Well, my fine miss, just you wait and see what happens when folk get to know what yon young tup's been up to with my fine ewe lamb! No! No! No! It's no good looking like that! Make no mistake! It'll be my word against his! And he's been

235

here plenty long enough to be responsible for this!" Then he ran his hand over her belly and his voice changed again. "But never fear, Issabel. I'm a generous man, a forgiving man. I'll not throw you out, though plenty would. You can still have a home here, aye and the baby as well when it comes!"

February brought day after day of snow and grey skies. The daily routine was always the same. First, Billy and Rob carried hay downstream to the ewes in the lower fields while Andro saw to the animals in the farm buildings. Then after breakfast Andro would help them load the sledge with hay, which they would haul through the in-bye fields, so they could feed the sheep there. After that, they went to the stell above the Maidens, where Andro's sheep were gathered. Finally, Rob and Billy loaded hay onto their backs and went their separate ways, trudging on farther to feed their sheep. Rob had the furthest to walk and he was always the last home.

One evening Andro had a quiet word in Billy's ear.

Billy was surprised at what Andro told him. Of course he knew that Rob was fond of Freya - that was plain to see. She was a beautiful lassie, if a bit pale and skinny for Billy's taste. He was amazed that they had lain together. Freya was so shy and he could not believe it of Rob. He was a straight, honest lad. If he had wanted Freya, why then surely he would have courted her and in due course he would have asked if he could marry her.

That night in the snug privacy of their box bed Billy whispered the news to Rose.

Rose chuckled. "Oh Billy, I know perfectly well that the lassie's expecting! Sometimes it's my opinion you men are blind as bats!"

They lay quietly for a while, then Billy rolled onto his back. "It's no good, I can't get over it."

"Get over what?"

"Why Freya and Rob, being that speedy! When d'you reckon it's due?"

"It's hard to tell, especially as it's the first and she's all happed up with clothes. About lambing time maybe."

"Well there you are then! It must've happened in July time. No, it's never Rob. I don't believe it!"

"Well I can't see who else it can be."

"Can you not?" said Billy, mysteriously.

"Billy! You're not saying it's ...?"

"I'm not saying nowt!" Billy interrupted sharply. "And you'd best do the same!"

Rob too began to have his suspicions about Freya's condition and with the passing days they were confirmed. He was sick at the thought. Freya, his Freya, expecting Andro's baby. His hatred of Andro reached a new intensity and in his wildest moments in the depths of the night he thought of killing him. But at other more lucid moments he thought of his father. When he had been at home briefly before the start of winter Hob had given him strict instructions. He was to watch but do nothing. If he felt himself in danger, he was to leave and come back to Coverdale if conditions allowed or else go over to Bart Dunne in Herondale.

Rob too dreamt of escape, of taking Freya away from Andro, away from Glittering Shiel. Night after night he lay in the stable listening to the wind moaning in the wych elms, tortured at the thought of what was happening in the house. He cursed Andro Man and after that the weather, for he knew that in her present state Freya could not survive a long walk through the snow.

A week later at nightfall Billy and Rob were standing talking in the yard. Freya came out of the back door, carrying a pail.

Billy nodded in her direction. "You'll have to be getting a shift on!"

"What do you mean?" asked Rob.

"Why man, to tie the knot! To get yourselves away down to see the minister before it's too late!" Billy paused for a few moments before commenting wryly, "One to bury and one to baptise, eh!"

Rob was stunned. "What are you on about, Billy? Tie the knot?"

"Why yourself and Freya of course! Geez, lad, you were quick off the mark there!"

"Who's been telling you that?" stammered Rob.

"Why the boss! Who else? It wouldn't be Freya now, would it? She's a close one, that! Not so much as a word in Rose's ear, woman to woman like! Not that Rose didn't figure it out for herself! But all the same, I don't mind telling you, you could've knocked me down with a feather!"

"But, but, that's not right! It's not right what he said!" said Rob angrily.

"What d'you mean?"

"It's not mine! Though I wish it was. Oh, I love her right enough! But the baby's not mine!" Then without giving Billy time to respond, Rob turned and walked away tight-lipped with rage.

The calendar, which hung on a nail by the dresser, indicated that it was the last day of February. At the end of each day Andro, like a ship-wrecked sailor cutting a notch in a piece of wood, put a thick black pencil line through the day that was ending. The lambing was due to start in six weeks. Scores of ewes had perished and those that survived were pitifully weak. Just when they needed extra feeding to build up their strength, they had to make do with less. Food for both humans and animals was running short and had to be rationed. The paraffin had run out in the middle of January and by the end of February they had almost reached the bottom of the meal chest.

That night, there was a particularly severe frost and in the morning, the wind began to strengthen from the northeast. The sense that another blizzard was on the way made man and beast edgy and restive. The sheep, particularly those on the high ground, became restless and began to move off to the south. This they were able to do because there was a thick, icy crust on the top of the snow which was now so deep that neither stone walls nor the Eidon Burn were a barrier to their progress.

In the course of the morning Rob decided that the next few hours would probably be his last chance for some time of getting away from Glittering Shiel. The fact that Andro intended to accuse him of being the father of Freya's child clinched his decision. The situation had become unbearable and he could no longer answer for his actions. He was distraught at the idea of leaving Freya alone with Andro, but he could think of no other way. His father would know what to do. His only hope was that whatever it was, it could be done quickly and he would soon be back at Freya's side.

At dinnertime Rob tried to have a few words with Freya, but Andro never gave him the chance. Rob could not contemplate going away without leaving a message for her, so after dinner when Freya and Andro were in the kitchen, he slipped upstairs to her room after he had carried some dishes to the scullery. He took his lucky silver coin from his pocket and put it in her bed. He told himself that she would find it when she went to bed and would guess that it was a sign that his disappearance was planned.

As soon as he returned to the kitchen Andro got up. "We'd best be making a move or else those sheep'll be off."

The second the door was closed behind them, Freya felt an overwhelming conviction. She must act, she must warn Rob and since she had been prevented from talking to him, she decided to write him a letter. She went up to her room to fetch some paper and a pencil. Rob's pendant was lying on the the shelf. She picked it up and slipped it over her head. She would take it off before they came back so that Andro would not see it. Then she went and sat on the window ledge.

She saw the three men leaving. They were trudging along in Indian file with both arms covering their faces, each man accompanied by his collie. The collies moved along on the top of the snow, cowering in the lee of their masters. Every ten paces or so, Andro, who was in the lead, would stop and turn his back to the blast, squinting through the crook of his arm to decide which way to go. Rob, who was at the rear, turned once and looked back towards the house before his blurred form vanished in the driving snow.

Freya made several attempts to write the letter. Many pieces of paper were thrown in the fire before it was done. She sat and read the final version out loud.

> *Dearest Rob,*
>
> *Please, I beg you, go away from here. I fear for your life. It is not just me, Lizzie was afraid as well. She said Andro might do the same to you as he did to Sam. Andro is a bad man and I have been bad as well. Go before it is too late.*
> *I love you Rob Atherton.*
>
> *Freya*

She folded the letter into a tiny package, then she went out to the stable. Rob's possessions were neatly folded in the manger. She considered slipping the letter in the front of his book of marks but she rejected that idea. He might not look in it for weeks. He would be soaked to the skin when he came back and was sure to change his shirt, so she fetched a dry shirt from the kitchen and slipped the letter inside.

As usual Andro was first back, his face swollen and sore from exposure to the icy wind, his fingers white and bloodless from the cold.

The time dragged. Darkness fell. The clock struck six. Freya laid the table while Andro warmed himself by the fire and had a nip of whisky. She was on tenterhooks, waiting for Rob. The broth was bubbling in the yetling, the bread lay ready on the board and still she waited.

Eventually she could contain her anxiety no longer. "Surely, he should be back by now?" she said to Andro.

"Don't fret! He'll be back before long. But we'll not wait supper. I'm starving!"

Freya ladled the broth into a dish and set it in front of him. She could not eat, neither could she sit quietly and wait. She went up to her room and looked out of the window. The sky was pitch black. After a few minutes she went back downstairs.

"I'm going across the yard to see if Billy's back. He might have seen him," she said.

"Aye, all right. You might as well, for all the good it'll do!"

Fear made her bold and she rounded on him. "What d'you mean, for all the good it'll do? What have you done to him?"

"Me? Nowt! All I'm saying is that there's no sense in going looking for him in this. It's death out there. Anyway d'you not think we've got corpses enough round here?"

Freya wrapped her shawl around her head and opened the back door. She crossed the yard and knocked at Billy and Rose's door, but they could not hear above the noise of the wind. She made her way along to the window and rapped on the glass. Soon Rose's face appeared and she let Freya in.

"What's wrong?" asked Rose.

"It's Rob! He's not back yet!"

Billy was sitting warming himself in front of the fire. "But he should've been back long since!" he said.

"I know! I'm worried! What can we do?"

Rose put her arms round Freya. "Whisht, lassie! There's nowt to be done tonight! He's a sensible lad. He knows every cleugh and gulley in the hills. They'll have taken shelter, him and Fine. They'll be waiting till the wind blows itself out and then he'll be back, you'll see."

Rose closed the door. Freya rested her back against it for a moment, wondering what to do next. She did not want to go back into the house. She would not sleep there. She went instead to the stable where she lit a stump of candle. She unfolded Rob's blankets and wrapped herself up in them, layer upon layer. As she picked up his clean shirt, thinking to use it as a pillow, the letter she had written that afternoon fell on the ground. She shivered as she picked it up and put it in her pocket. Then she curled up on the bed of bracken, her cheek resting on the rough flannel shirt and for a long time she lay, listening for the sound of his finger on the latch.

The next morning when Andro came downstairs, the fire was out and the supper dishes lay unwashed in the scullery. He went back upstairs to wake Freya and found the bed made. Had she got up already and gone out to search for the lad? He went over and slipped his hand between the sheets to see if they were warm. They were not, but his fingers touched on something. He pulled out Rob's silver coin and examined it. It was neither Scottish nor English and there was neither king nor queen on it, only an ordinary looking fellow with some sort of bonnet on his head. Mystified, Andro shook his head. What could the lassie be doing with such a thing in her bed? He shook his head again, slipped the coin into his waistcoat pocket and thought no more about it.

The storm had abated in the small hours and the day was clear and bright. It was Billy who found Freya curled up in the stable and went to tell Andro.

"I fear Freya's taking it very hard," he told Andro.

"No wonder, with her expecting his bairn!"

"Aye, right enough!" Billy agreed, after a moment.

"I wouldn't give much for his chances."

"So you think he'll have perished then?" Billy asked.

"Well, what's your opinion?"

"I cannot say. But we must go and search for him now the weather's eased."

"There's no sense in both of us going. There's too much to be done. You go and I'll see to the sheep."

Billy fought his way through drifts, working his way back and forth over Rob's beat, plunging his stick into every gulley he could think of, but he could find no trace of man or dog. At nightfall he returned home exhausted and told Rose to go and tell Freya that his search had been fruitless.

Rose found Andro alone in the house. He told her that he had not been able to get a word out of Freya, though he knew she had been in the house because some food had gone.

"Will you let her bide in the stable then?" Rose asked.

Andro shrugged. "If that's what she's minded to do, I'll not stop her. Best to leave her till she comes to her senses!"

Rose went to the stable where she found Freya buried beneath a pile of blankets. Only the white oval of her face and a hand folded tight around a baby's rattle were visible. Her eyes were wide open in a blank stare and she did not stir when Rose came in.

Rose knelt down beside her. Freya was little more than a child, and a motherless child at that. As if she had not had enough to bear nursing Lizzie, and now her young man was gone, and her with a little one on the way. Billy must have been wrong. It must be Rob's baby. Why else would the lassie be so grief-stricken?

Rose stroked Freya's forehead and spoke to her softly. "Billy's been out all day searching for him." Then Rose broke the Lord's commandment and told a lie. "Billy says to tell you that if he and Fine had perished, he'd surely have found them. They'd have been together, him and Fine, so you mustn't give up hope Freya, not yet!"

Rose's words seemed to fall on deaf ears. She waited patiently for some response, but there was none. Deciding that there was nothing more she could do, she tucked the blankets around Freya as if she was one of her own children. "That's it," she whispered, "you get some rest. Try and get some sleep."

25

Freya did not sleep in the house again, neither did she say a single word to Andro. She took refuge in the stable, though hunger drove her into the house to seek food. At first she waited until Andro had gone out, but after a few days, when it became clear that he was not going to interfere, she became less reclusive. He tried to talk to her, but she seemed not to hear him, moving about with the serene, untouchable dignity of a queen. He spoke sharply to her, reminding her of her vow, her pact with him, but it was to no avail. Finally he tried kindness, but nothing could penetrate the protective aura with which she was surrounded.

With the exception of Rob's pendant and Jock's rattle, which she kept with her at all times, Freya abandoned everything in the house: her room, her books, her other few possessions. She moved the centre of her universe to the few square feet of stable floor where Rob had slept. It had been his place and now she made it hers. She gave up all housewifely duties and established new habits in their place.

Soon there was a well-trodden path through the snow from the stable to the alder grove. Twice or thrice a day she would visit the pigsty, taking with her some fresh bracken for the sow to rootle through. The sow, like the ewes on the hill, was undernourished and her piglets would be weak. Freya would scratch her in the middle of her back and was rewarded with grunts of pleasure. Sometimes Freya crept into the dark inner part of the sty and sat on her haunches in the corner. She liked the warmth and the sweetish smell because they reminded her of when she used to bottle-feed the unfortunate piglet that did not have a teat.

The morning after Rob's disappearance Andro had redistributed the tasks. He said that he would see to Polly and feed the pig. Thus, Rose and Billy had no occasion to go into the stable or the pigsty, though occasionally on their way in or out of the byre they would catch a glimpse of Freya's skirt vanishing around the corner, but neither of them ever came face to face with her.

The only normality at Glittering Shiel was to be found within the walls of the Lillicos' bothy, though the children, confined like baby rabbits to their earthy warren, had become quarrelsome and fractious. Outside, a dull madness hung in the air. It was the quiet, crazed desperation that comes at the end of an arduous journey, when the weary traveller believes the destination to be close and yet when every bend reveals a further stretch of road.

Rose often found herself gazing out of the small window of the bothy. Her eyes would move down the stone wall, pausing at the place where Lizzie lay. Then she would stare at the long, blank wall of the stable, byre and pigsty and wonder what was happening behind the wall of stones.

Life went on much as before except that, with Rob gone, there was more work to be done. However, with the passing days Andro seemed to become distracted as if his mind was engaged upon some weighty matter. Billy had to repeat almost everything he said to him, and even then he would receive either an absent-minded reply or none at all.

Progressively it was left to Billy to take responsibility for the farm, to worry about the animals and the weather. Morning and night he looked at the sky, praying for a change in the weather. Before long, it was Billy who was regulating the dwindling resources and deciding what was to be done. Andro continued to turn out each morning, but he looked haggard and unkempt. He worked mechanically, without thought and often he would stop what he was doing and stare into space.

Billy came into the bothy late one afternoon and shook his head. "I don't know what's going on," he said wearily to Rose.

"What d'you mean?"

"I don't know. I can't put my finger on it. It's like the boss's lost interest in everything, like the heart's gone out of him!"

"If you ask me, he's touched!" said Rose. "Maybe it's on account of Lizzie and he'll be all right as soon as she's buried."

"I hope so."

When Rob disappeared Andro had felt a bitter satisfaction, but as the days went by he began to feel cheated, because Rob's fate had been taken out of his hands. And then there was Freya. Somehow she too had escaped, had slipped beyond his control. He began to dread the hours of darkness because it was then that he was beset by a sense of hopelessness and guilt. He would stay in the kitchen, drinking whisky till after midnight, loath to go upstairs to bed for he knew the nightmare that awaited him the moment he closed his eyes.

He would be trapped in a powerful vortex of wind that wrenched and twisted his arms and legs. Naked as Adam, he was whipped and lashed until his flesh bled. Then he was sucked down into a bloody, brawling torrent. A sinewy tree root would hold his neck in a stranglehold. He put his hand up to try to break free and felt not a tree root but the gnarled hand of a hag. No sooner had he escaped her toils than he was caught in the ghastly, suffocating embrace of a bloated corpse. Its monstrous lips brushed his cheek and as he recoiled he saw the face of Will Hetherton. Aghast, he raised his hand to hide his face and found his fingers had plunged deep into a bloody gash. Terrified, he struggled to escape the surging tide. At last he felt an iron grip around his wrist and he was brought up onto the bank. He looked around to see who had saved him, but there was no one. All was desolation and a spreading darkness. The grip on his wrist was like a vice. It tightened until the pain made him cry out. It was the pain that woke him and he would lie on his bed, sweating with terror and confusion until he realised that it was his own left hand locked around his wrist.

The last storm came on the third of April, a date engraved for ever on the memory of the shepherds and their families because it marked the end of the worst winter in the Cheviots for more than thirty years.

The following day the wind moved into the west. When Billy heard the burn sing, he knew that the thaw had begun and immediately he thought of Lizzie. They would have to move quickly if they were to get her down to Herontop church before the Eidon Burn rose and made them prisoners once more.

Billy went straight to see Andro. "How about we try to get Lizzie away down to Herontop this forenoon?" he suggested.

Andro looked at him with a dazed expression.

"If we don't take the chance now it might be a week or more before we can get across the ford!" Billy urged.

Andro nodded. "Aye, I suppose so," he said dully. "You see to it." Then he turned and walked away.

"But you'll be coming, won't you?" said Billy, afraid that Andro expected him to take Lizzie down to Herontop on his own. "I might need help to get through the drifts and anyhow you'll be needing to speak to the minister, see about a proper box and all that sort of thing."

Andro turned and threw him a world-weary look, but made no reply.

Half an hour later Billy and young Billy had dug Lizzie's coffin out of the snow. They lifted it onto the sledge and secured it with stout cords.

Soon they were ready to leave. Rose with the children clustered around her was standing in front of her door ready to pay her last respects. They waited five minutes, then ten. At last the back door of the farmhouse opened and Andro emerged. He had shaved for the first time in weeks and Rose was shocked to see how hollow his cheeks were and how sallow his skin. Billy looked at Rose as if to ask whether he ought to wait to see if Freya would make an appearance. Rose shook her head. Lizzie had waited long enough.

"Right then! Let's be off!" said Billy, sliding a shovel alongside the coffin.

Andro nodded and the little cortege moved off into the mist. Rose stepped out into the middle of the track to watch them go; the two men, one on either side of Polly's head, and behind them the coffin, gliding above the ground like an apparition. Rose shivered. "Come away in!" she said to the children. "It's cold out here."

Later Rose went to find Freya. She walked round to the front of the farmhouse and, seeing the track that led down to the alder grove, she followed it. Freya was sitting on the bough of a tree. Huge drops of water were falling from the trees onto her shoulders but she did not seem to notice, so intent was she on watching a wren which was hopping about in the branches in search of something to eat.

"That's them away down to Herontop," said Rose as she approached. "You can rest easy now, Freya. The minister'll take care of her, say some prayers, do everything right."

Freya nodded.

"I thought I might do a bit of baking," said Rose cheerily. "There's enough flour left for a few scones. It doesn't matter if I use it up because Billy'll be bringing a fresh sack back with him. Will I bring you a few scones over later on?"

Freya smiled a vague faraway smile accompanied by another small nod. Rose chatted about this and that. Freya's head was bent forward and Rose assumed that she was listening, but soon Rose ran out of things to say. "Right then!" she said in a busy, bustling way. "This won't get the scones made! I'd better go and get on!"

Later as she was putting the scones on the griddle, Rose realised that she had done all the talking and that Freya had not uttered a single word.

The lambing began two weeks later. It was a miserable business. As the snow melted the sodden carcases of sheep appeared all over the hills. Throughout its history the borderland had been a battleground. Scots and English had fought over the desolate wastes of Otterburn, Flodden and Chevy Chase, but that winter, the winter of 1885, the battle had been against the elements and it had ended in a terrible rout. The flock at Glittering Shiel, like every other for miles around, had been decimated.

On the last day of April Billy came out of his bothy at first light and walked to the west end of the farmhouse to look at the sky. Though the summit of Cheviot was in cloud, Maidenhope's snow-covered slopes were sharp and clear, and, black against the white, there was a lone figure. Billy stood and watched until the person had vanished over the shoulder of Maidenhope.

Andro did not appear that morning, so Billy and young Billy had to do all the work. Young Billy and Violet carried frozen lambs to Rose's bright fireside where Hazel tried to coax them back to life. After dinner Billy went and knocked at the door of the farmhouse. No one came. Then Rose tried. She could get no response either, so she opened the door and went in. The fire was out in the kitchen and the curtains closed. There was not a sound, even the clock was silent, its glass door hanging open. She went upstairs. Lizzie's room was untouched. Freya's was orderly but uninhabited. Andro's door was ajar. She pushed it open and gasped. The room was chaotic, with clothes and pillows strewn across the floor, the bedding twisted and tangled. She took a step forward and knocked over a glass. She bent to retrieve it and saw an empty whisky bottle by the skirting-board.

She went back downstairs and through the kitchen towards the parlour. The bolts on the front door had been drawn back and the door was ajar. Then she heard a noise in the parlour.

Freya was standing by the window, holding a piece of paper in her hand.

"It does look like him, doesn't it?" she said, conversationally, as soon as she saw Rose. "I couldn't see it before, but now I do."

"Freya! Where's the boss?" said Rose, ignoring Freya's remarks. "Billy's not seen hide nor hair of him all morning!"

Freya's face showed no concern. Then, registering Rose's mounting exasperation, she raised her eyebrows in mild surprise.

"Freya!   You must tell me what's going on!" said Rose urgently. "Where is he?"

"Oh yes. Where *is* he?" echoed Freya meditatively.

"You *do* know who I'm talking about, don't you? I'm talking about Andro! Do you know where he is?"

"Oh him," said Freya, suddenly losing interest. "He went. It was time, so he had to go."

"What d'you mean - it was time so he had to go?"

"That's what he said when he saw the bird."

"Bird! What bird?"

"My bird. A raven with a broken wing."

Rose could make nothing of Freya's nonsense, so she tried a different line of enquiry. "Has anybody called here at the house?"

A furrow of concentration appeared on Freya's brow and for a moment Rose was hopeful, but then Freya shook her head.

Rose left. It was hopeless, there was no getting through to the lassie. Besides, if somebody had come to the house it was unlikely that Freya would know about it, given that she was sleeping in the stable. Andro must have taken off. After all, he had done it many a time before. Still, it was strange. Freya was near her time. How could he leave her?

Freya's pains had begun soon after she had got up that morning. She knew what they meant and was not afraid. She welcomed them because they were a sign that her long wait was coming to an end.

For some time after Rose left, Freya stayed in the parlour. She gazed at the photograph of Will Hetherton, went and ran her fingers over the glass dome with the peregrine falcon inside, took a book down from the shelf, but found she had no desire to read and put it back. Then, like a chance visitor to a dusty bric-a-brac shop whose owner has gone away, she moved about the house, opening doors, peering into drawers and cupboards. Upstairs, in Lizzie's room, the bed was stripped and bare. A wooden box with a shell motif on the lid lay on the bedside table. She picked it up and opened it. A black brooch and a few hairpins with strands of hair around them lay inside. She took the brooch and fastened it to her blouse. Then she went to her bedroom. Nothing had changed, yet everything was unfamiliar. She looked around the room, at the washstand, the cornflower jug and basin, the little window with a jar of withered flowers on the ledge. She did not linger, but withdrew quietly, closing the door behind her.

Down in the kitchen she came across a few pieces of dry kindling, so she lit a fire. There was water in the kettle, so she moved it onto the heat and made some tea. Was this what Goldilocks did? She thought of making herself a little porridge. There was a handful of oatmeal left in the bottom of the crock. She held her hand over the pan and let the grains trickle through her fingers the way Lizzie had taught her. They were like the grains of sand which flowed down through the neck of Mr Dogberry's hourglass on Tuesdays and Thursdays. She used to watch them mass into a little hillock which by the end of the lesson had become a perfect miniature mountain.

As darkness fell Freya left the house and went to the stable. Nobody came to disturb her. Violet had brought a plate of scones over before dark and Rose, having seen the smoke from the fire, had assumed that all was well and that Freya had moved back into the house.

The pains were more frequent now, but Freya was calm. She went and curled up for a while under Rob's blankets. She must have slept a little, for when she woke the sky was clear and bright with stars. The pains became more intense. She became restless. She lit the candle and paced up and down the stall until they eased. She remembered the adder stone hanging on its red string. She wanted to hold it but it was too high. As the muscles of her womb tightened, making her stomach iron-hard, she gripped the rounded lip of the manger. Over the years horses had worn it away, leaving semi-circles like the lower part of a pair of stocks. She did not notice the tiny splinters of wood that pierced the palms of her hands.

When the time to give birth was near she left the stable and went outside. A slender new moon was hanging above the warrior. She stood and looked at it for a few moments and then with a blanket in her arms she sought out the dark warmth of the pigsty. She crept under the low stone lintel and into the furthest recess.

At that moment in the small hours when time, like the turning tide, is momentarily suspended, the baby slipped from her. It cried only once and then was silent. As soon as she was able, she wrapped the tiny creature in her shawl. Then she moved so that her back was resting against the wall and she could cradle the baby in her arms. Murmuring quietly, she moistened her fingers and wiped its eyes and mouth. She could not see its face and she did not think to wonder whether it was a boy or a girl. All she knew was that it was hers and that she would care for it. For a time she sat in the darkness. The only sound came from the sow shifting on her bed of bracken a few feet away and soon she fell asleep with the baby in her arms.

She woke just before dawn and heard the fluty song of a missel thrush. She knew then that it was time to leave. Somehow she found the strength to move and, clutching the baby, she emerged into the open air.

The warrior, Maidenhope and Cheviot were cloaked in darkness, but away to the east there was the palest glimmer of light, the promise of dawn. The sound of the Eidon Burn reached her and like someone lost in the hills she knew that she must follow it downstream. Many times she had to stop and rest, but always she gathered her strength and went on.

The sun was high when Tom Pagon stopped off at the ruined still to check on a ewe and pair of twin lambs he had left there the night before. To his delight he found the lambs on their knees, tails twitching as they fed hungrily from their mother. Then Tom noticed Meg, investigating something at the far end of the building.

"Well, if it's not young Freya Man!" he exclaimed. "Dead to the world!"

He decided to sit and smoke a pipe until she woke. What could the lassie be doing there? Was it perhaps something to do with her mother? It was less than a month since Andro and Billy Lillico had taken the poor woman down to Herontop to be buried. Could the lassie be on her way to visit the grave now that the weather had improved? Or maybe she was running away? Tom had heard a whisper that she was expecting and that the father, Rob Atherton, had perished in the storms.

Just as he was thinking that he would have to wake her up, Tom saw someone approaching from the direction of Herontop. Soon he recognised Grace Murray on her cuddy.

Grace was on her way to Glittering Shiel. She had heard about Lizzie's death and had decided that she would ride up to Glittering Shiel and see Freya as soon as the road was open.

Tom allowed time for the donkey to pick its way across the ford, then he got up and walked down the slope ready to catch Miss Murray as she passed.

"Good day to you, Miss Murray," he said as she approached.

"And to you, Tom!" Grace replied. Then she caught a glimpse of the twin lambs in the still. "That's a fine pair of lambs you've got there, all things considered!"

"Aye Miss, that's right To have twin lambs alive is just about a miracle!"

Grace was about to urge her donkey on up the track.

"Er, would you be so kind as to step up here for a minute, Miss Murray?"

"What is it, Tom?"

"Well Miss, it's young Freya Man. I came on her not an hour since. She's lying in there!"

Tom helped Grace to dismount and lent her his stick. Glad to be relieved of responsibility for Freya, he stayed with the donkey while Grace made her way to where Freya was lying. He did not hear what was said, but after ten minutes or so Grace came back to him.

"I need your help, Tom," she said anxiously.

"Aye, miss. What can I do?"

"Freya is poorly, very poorly. She cannot ride and I cannot walk, so I would be very much obliged if you would go down to the Home Farm and ask Mr Matheson to send the pony and trap. I'm going to take Freya back."

"To Glittering Shiel?"

"No. I shall take her home with me."

26

Three weeks later Luke Hobbs, a young shepherd from the valley of Bolbent on the Scottish side, was searching for lost sheep on the northern flanks of Cheviot. He was picking his way up the side of the tumbling waterfalls of Henhole ravine when he came upon the body of a man with a broken neck, lying at the foot of a towering grey crag, one of a pair which rose up on either side of the chasm. A broken shepherd's crook was lying a few feet away near the remains of a black sheep.

Luke guessed what had happened. The man had doubtless lost his way in the dark and had strayed too close to edge of the chasm and tumbled over, breaking his neck in the fall. Luke picked up the top half of the stick and hooked the curved ram's horn into his belt, thinking that it might help identify the man. As for the black sheep, Luke assumed that it was just another casualty of winter and did not give it a second glance.

Luke hoisted the body across his shoulders. As he threaded his way out of the ravine, he did not hear the sound of a silver coin as it fell out of the man's waistcoat pocket and onto the stony ground.

Once Luke was on open ground and could move at an even pace, he began to reflect that this was the second victim of the winter he had found, though this poor man had not been as fortunate as the first.

Luke tried to remember exactly how long it was since he had rescued Rob. It must must have been a good ten weeks before, when the winter was at its most ferocious. Luke had found him in a cave, except that it was hardly a cave, more like a deep cleft in the rock. He had a broken leg and had had nothing to eat for two days. It was his collie that saved his life. Late one afternoon the dog had spotted Luke far away in the distance and attracted his attention. Luke had carried Rob back home just like he was doing now. And Rob had stayed with them for about four weeks. Of course he'd been another mouth to feed, not that he ate much, not at first. He was in a fever for two weeks and as soon as he got over that he was like a caged animal desperate to get away, but he couldn't on account of his leg. And he'd been hellbent on getting word out to his family, but there was nothing anybody could do. They were blocked in and hadn't seen a soul since the end of January. So Rob had had to bide his time and hadn't got away until after the lambing started.

The Lillicos kept Glittering Shiel going as best they could. Billy said that the farmhouse put him in mind of a story he had once heard about a ship that had been found adrift on the sea without a soul on board.

Two days after Freya disappeared, Billy saw Tom Pagon who told him that Grace Murray had taken Freya to the schoolhouse. Billy hadn't liked to mention Freya's condition and Tom had said nothing about it. News of the baby came two weeks later from Will Matheson who said that the baby had been stillborn and that Grace Murray had arranged with Mr Dogberry for it to be buried in the graveyard beside Lizzie.

Andro's body was taken to Willove where it was not formally identified for some time; the death of one man being but a small part of the aftermath of winter and not a matter of urgency. It was Jenny Robson who finally identified him from the deformity of his foot. The news came swiftly to Glittering Shiel and a few days later Hob Hetherton fulfilled the promise he had made to his mother. He and Rob came over from Coverdale and reclaimed the wild acres of Glittering Shiel.

Freya was walking slowly across the field towards Herontop school. It was a sunny Saturday afternoon and she was on her way back from the churchyard where she had put a posy of primroses on the grave, a pauper's grave without a lettered stone.

She climbed over the stile and into the triangular field where she and Jenny had spent so many hours together. The air was soft and warm and she was reluctant to go indoors just yet, so she made her way around the edge of the field just as she had done the day the Herontop girls had taunted her about her clothes. Finally she came to the chestnut trees by the bend in the road. The branches were bare, though brown buds, shiny and sticky as if they had been dipped in toffee, held the promise of summer shade.

She rested her back against a trunk and closed her eyes. She felt again Lizzie's arms around her the morning she had left for Seamouth and then she saw Lizzie again, dressed in black and struggling for breath as she climbed the hill. Instinctively Freya put her hand to her breast to touch Lizzie's jet brooch, but instead her fingers closed around Rob's pendant. As if she was praying, Freya held the piece of bone between the heels of her hands and pressed so hard that the intertwined letters became imprinted on her skin. It was an act of faith that she was in the habit of performing from time to time. She sighed and opened her eyes. It was time to go in. Miss Murray would be waiting and they would have tea together. As she was walking slowly along the path towards the schoolhouse, she thought she heard someone call her name, but she did not stop because her imagination had deceived her too often. Her finger was on the latch of the gate when she sensed a movement behind her. She turned. It was Fine, who thrust his muzzle into her hand in urgent greeting. She gave a little cry and then with beating heart, she turned and ran back. She looked up the hill. He was there in the distance. With arms outspread, he was running down the hill towards her so fast that she thought he would take wing and fly.